M

TRANSYLVANIA

part one

THE DRACULIAN REBELLION

an original novel

By

TONY BURTON

Ponytailpoet Publications

MMXVI

PONYTAILPOET PUBLICATIONS 2016 Preview edition

AUTHORS INTRODUCTION

There are a great many Transylvanias, possibly you have already explored some of them. This is my offering to that somewhat crowded collection. No doubt the experienced reader will note some ideas here that have their genesis in the works of established authors, this I cannot deny, but the temptation to develop and extend is just too great, especially Terry Pratchett's socially responsible revenants! I hope I am adding something original and entertaining to the genre nonetheless and invite you to come and play in my own idiosyncratic version of Transylvania! This is the 'pre-view' edition, and an experiment in writing, please see the end papers for more details.

As usual normal rules apply, all characters are imaginary and any resemblance to any individual alive, dead or in between, is entirely coincidental. Comments, criticisms and suggestions (positive ones) gratefully accepted!

The Ponytail Poet Spring 2016

CHAPTER ONE

Her Excellency Their Britannic Majesties Ambassador to Transylvania stood regarding the rich, varied and assorted collection of delegates. It really was so much easier in the old days when there was just the main party and the opposition, plus a few civil service 'experts'. Now, what with the Constructivists, the Beliefers, and the Human League and the 'minor parties', it was getting a bit too, too, crowded, and their Majesties (or rather Mr Plenderleith the Prime Minister) had seen fit to give the Armaments Industry the same status as a political party, so they now had a full complement of delegates as well! Not of course that that was all bad. The salesmen for the big companies probably did far more these days to keep the peace than any of the political parties.

'A weapon is for having, not using.' somebody had said to her at an Arms Fair, and it made sense in an oddly convoluted sort of way. All sides across Europe mistrusted each other, but they trusted the salesman! *They* never reneged on their promises, and they kept confidences. You got exactly what you asked for, and they never held back on what was coming up next in the endless struggle for a new angle on offense or defence!

'If we didn't invent these devices someone else would! Isn't it far better that *we* do all the research and development, *not* a government, and then sell the system to everyone?'

Well, now they were all waiting on her words. She comforted herself that she would begin with the standard Transylvanian Briefing, something that made the old hands fall asleep, and the new boys (and girls) sit on their seat-edges with terror!

"Ladies and Gentlemen, you are now east of the Rhine, you are not in Germany, you are not in France, and, most emphatically, you are not in England!

Your job for the forthcoming ten days is to represent our national interests and to avoid being *damaged* by the experience! The Transylvanian diplomatic corps is renowned for its hospitality and its generosity, but not always for its capacity for accommodating the foolish or the unwary! First and foremost, you will, each and every one of you, wear your Forster rings at all times, you will sleep with them on, you will bathe with them on, and you will *not* remove them until you step ashore at Dover when the mission is complete! Do I make myself clear? Please all raise your hands now and let me, and your colleagues know, that you are safe guarded, and that so by extension, they are also safe!

I know that most of the Transylvanians can be trusted, and that many of you have been here before and have good friends 'on the other side', but for your own sake, and for any friends you may have among the revenants, wear your protection, then there can be no unfortunate accidents, no incidents that may lead our two countries to war! There are those on *both* sides whose plans would profit from an incident! Our task is to show how our two cultures can work together, to pave the way for harmony, to *avoid* conflict. You have been chosen for your wide range of outlook and commitment to political ideals, please make certain to 'sell' what we have to offer. Our way of solving problems, of arranging matters to mutual satisfaction of all parties, above all our *liberalism!*" she paused, and scanned the audience. The Constructivists and Beliefers were nodding sagely, but the Human League delegates were tight lipped and far from engaged. The commercial delegates, all old hands at travelling and working in Transylvania, just looked bored.

In the front row, one leg crooked across the other in a lazy manner, his hands now and then cradling his ankle, sat Sandy McLomond, negotiator and salesman for Essex Armaments. At this moment his left hand hung down languidly, it was encased in a slim white satin glove beneath which a ring could be clearly seem, bulging through the fabric. The other hand was un-gloved and currently occupied in holding a folded sheet of paper outlining the forthcoming weeks programme.

The glove was a little piece of politeness that most of the politicians present were unaware of. It covered up the Forster ring and also advertised its presence, the fabric would be sufficient to prevent any harm coming to a revenant who accidentally brushed against it, and so said very clearly that the wearer was 'open for business '.

Her Excellency was now placing very large photographic images on an easel and taking the audience through each one in turn.

"I trust that you have all seen these before, but in case you have not, or if your memories are faulty this is intended to prevent embarrassing situations. This," she banged the card board with her pointer, "This is a member of the Kravitzen. They are *not* revenant, they are human, *but* they are 'in charge', the rulers of Transylvania. Do not attempt to shake hands or try any kind of physical contact. They are a very haughty race who believe that to touch anyone other than another Kravitz is to be defiled.... they are also toxic! The precise details are still unknown, but they are in fact poisonous to vampires, werewolves and any non-Kravitz humans. This is why they are the leaders. You will *not need to communicate with them*. Is that quite clear? All communication will be through the Vampire contingent, but when the Kravitzen enter the room please be silent and await developments, try to avoid eye contact, and for the sake of both etiquette and your own health stay well out of their way, if they drop a glove or knock over a glass or have a minor mishap, do not approach, look away. Is that understood?"

It *was* clearly understood, because all the politicos made a note on their writing tablets, and even the Human League delegates seemed absorbed.

The next photograph went up onto the easel.

"Vampires are far easier by comparison! Please make sure that you use the correct forms of address though. A Grand Duke is Your Serenity, a Duke is 'Your Grace', Counts and Countesses are addressed by their titles, everyone else is Sir or Madame, or Lord or Lady if you want to be more formal, much the same as at home. Fortunately they now have standardised regalia and badges of rank, as shown here."

She tapped the picture again indicating a nine pointed star for a Grand Duke, a seven pointed star for a Duke, five pointed for a Count and the general Lunar jewel worn by all Transylvanian diplomats.

"The Transylvanian Vampire contingent have invested a great deal of time, money and effort in making this conference work. They are the main modernisers, and closest to ourselves in terms of outlook." There was some sarcastic coughing from a couple of Human League delegates, but this was ignored by everyone else.

"If you want more information beyond the official manual, Mr McLomond from Essex Armaments, sitting in the front row looking bored will be more than happy to oblige.

Now, moving on, this picture is of a Werewolf Baron. Note the badge of rank, *black* enamel over pure *gold,* symbolising a great treasure hidden in darkness. Werewolves do not concern themselves with politics, and so there are no ranks below or above

Baron, but each Werewolf delegate will be wearing a clan or a pack badge. It is polite to ask them which group it denotes, you will in fact be expected to ask each and every werewolf about their badge, even if you have just had it explained by another clan or pack member, it may seem tiresome….but it's just the way they are."

The briefing continued and Sandy looked down the programme list. Lots of familiar names, but with new titles and job descriptions. Transylvania really was pulling out all the stops! The military personnel seemed to have been given new roles as cultural advisors and commerce development experts. Unusually non-Kravitzen humans were there as well. They made a lot of things happen in Transylvania, but mostly they weren't acknowledged. Today they had been organised into some kind of civil service with English titles that made you think of Whitehall.

The remains of that day's programme were taken up with a 'getting to know you' event. Concluding with an evening at Der Rosenburg no less! He'd only ever been there twice, not even as the shadowy man who made sure the Emperor's bodyguard were proof against modern assassination techniques did he merit regular invitations to that splendid place! More than just a restaurant, more than a ballroom, an experience! Attached to the programme was a gold edged envelope with the words *INVITATION* written in more gold on the rich creamy paper.

"Tonight you are all invited to a reception at Der Rosenburg. The object of the exercise is to allow each of you to meet and talk with your Transylvanian 'opposite numbers'. The meetings planned for the coming week are all about how we can work together, resolve differences and profit from partnership. England and Transylvania are both ancient countries, rich in tradition and history, but we are both beset with external enemies, threats, difficulties. If we can *both* resolve our differences, then we will in turn be the catalyst for other European powers to join our partnership and the result will be a union of power that can stand up to the military and commercial threats posed by China and America. I'm sure you have heard this time and time again, *ad nauseum* in fact! But now you are all living in the reality of the first steps towards such a union. I beg you, each and every one, to bury your party differences and come to the aid of England if not that of our neighbours. Now, please, open the invitations you have attached to your programmes, they detail your companion or companions for this evening!"

Generally speaking the newcomers to Transylvania had been partnered with old hands, and most were to attend in small parties, but some of the more experienced delegates had drawn individual Transylvanian diplomats for one-to-one discussions.

Sandy looked at the gold edged card with interest

> The Lady Carlotta Esteban
>
> Requests the pleasure of
>
> Alexander McLomond
>
> Table 3
>
> Der Rosenburg 19.00 June 23rd

There followed, on the reverse, written in black ink, a signature and a thumb print (which was, for those accustomed to Transylvania, a guarantee of safe conduct, *no matter what*!)

The briefing was largely over now, a small group were standing around Her Excellency asking questions, other groups were growing as delegates found out who they would be attending with and who their Transylvanian hosts would be. Sandy moved through the press to find the representative from United Weapons.

“Sholto! Who have they put you with?”

“Oh! It’s you! Got to look after a bunch of Beliefers, too friendly for their own good! I’ve already had to read the Riot Act to them about not smiling at the Kravitzen when they go past, and if we get through this without one of them being bitten it’ll be a miracle! What about you?”

“Carlotta!”

“Some people get all the luck! And Der Rosenburg too!”

“Yes, makes it all a lot more attractive! Hundmann’s here you know? The ‘weredog’? He’d give your Beliefers a good time!”

“What a good idea! I’ll look him up, where’s he billeted?”

“Right here! Hotel staff! I’m sure they’ve got him working as a lobby boy, his Baron is the manager by the look of it, taken over for the duration of the conference I guess!”

....

Carlotta was *suddenly* there! ‘The old vampire trick’, thought Sandy, ‘she just can’t resist it!’ And that was it, vampires had style, class…and they knew it, and were controlled by it, but Carlotta was different, and right now she was about to show it. She swept up to him and purposely took his left hand, the one with the white satin glove.

‘Darling! That’s sensible! You are wearing your ring!’ She actually took his hand and raised it to her lips, lightly pressing the fabric covered metal against her lips and almost, but not quite, convulsing as the Forsterite alloy sucked at her essence.

Sandy was visibly upset, despite that fact that this was a regular greeting from Carlotta, worried that she'd gone too far this time with her flirtation and would be physically harmed by the ring.

'Please, Carlotta! Be careful!' he was very attached to Carlotta. Even though it was his job to negotiate, to arrange deals, to work with the 'undead', still Carlotta was special. He'd taken himself in hand and assured himself that she wasn't viewing him as a victim, but that they had a real friendship.

Everyone said 'Don't trust them! All they want is another conquest, they'll bleed you dry!' …but, Carlotta *was* different.

He'd had to work with the Countess at Budapest, and the Grand Duchess of Splitz herself, but although you could see that they would not suffer fools gladly, and would be more than happy to 'assimilate' an unwary negotiant, Carlotta was *different.* However, in deference to company policy he always, always…. kept a barrier, thin at times maybe, but a barrier still, between them both. But it was difficult. Carlotta was the only one who 'kissed' his ring, the only one who shared details of her personal life with him. He had hopes…but he was always, so, so, sensible!

Carlotta was starting out in classic form, but as ever, when they were together she started to lose her Transylvanian accent and go back to standard English. Once, and she'd had quite a lot to drink that time, she'd confided that Carlotta Estaban was in fact Carole Stevens from Croydon, but for a vampire that was the human equivalent of admitting to a tattoo below the bikini line, and he'd not pushed it further!

"So," he said to Carlotta, "Where have you been lately?"

"Survey visit. To the hole!"

"Mphh! Risky! Anything new?"

“No, it’s still a hole! But the spiders are getting bigger, I wouldn’t like to have to fight it out with one of them!”

“Nasty! But, the field is still stable?”

“Oh, no changes there, still just the same as it was two hundred and fifty three years ago.”

“I like your precision!”

“A vampire is always…*precise!”*

Yes. And of course you were there at the time?”

“Very nearly….very nearly.”

It is usually considered impolite to talk about a vampires personal origins, and this was verging on intrusive, so he changed the subject.

“Sholto’s been put in charge of a party of Beliefers, I suggested he get Hundmann to spend some time with them. That *is* him working as the Lobby boy?”

“Absolutely!”

‘Why have we been given a table in the ‘Rose Petal’ room?’

‘Ah! Now you have me! I am assuming that you and I, as consistent and long term players in the game of collaboration are far, far too dangerous people to expose to the newcomers and so are better kept apart…but visible!’

‘So…we are a show piece! Just see how nice it can be for a Vampire and a Human to get along together…Except you are really a human too, and ‘my people’ are far, far more violent and scheming than any Vampire!’

'Oh! My poor dear Sandy! (I do like that name so much better than Alexi!) You are being too liberal again! Just relax and let it all work! Concentrate upon the menu and the wine list! Tonight the big bosses are paying for everything! No need to consider your expense account (I know how you manage to treat me!) Sit back in your chair 'und vatch der rose petals fall', this place costs more than anybody thinks, I've only ever been here four times, and never with such charming company!'

The table was screened off from its three neighbours and set in the very base of the great soaring light well that dominated the core of Der Rosenburg, Transylvania's premier restaurant. Above the tiny courtyard the balconies stacked up, one above another, each wreathed in great trailing vines of red and pink roses that grew out in enormous thick thorny stems criss-crossing the space between the balconies. Thousands of rose plants, their blossoms swelling and spilling over, eternally showering petals down upon the diners below.

Above the courtyard the tiered balconies were filled with tables populated by the rest of the delegates, candles glittered their light upon cut glass and highly polished copper bowls and ewers. No silverware, *ever*, in Transylvania, in deference to the Werewolves, and likewise flavourings lacked the garlicky tang of cooking elsewhere in Europe, but for all that opulence and richness ruled. The country had definitely 'come of age', and multicultural dining was now a fact (though to be fair the revenants had largely had to adjust to the 'human' dietary.) Werewolves were quite happy with steak tartare, day in, day out, and Vampires had learned to get along with a wide range of pasta dishes and sauces where the 'secret' ingredient was a dull, red, powdery material politely referred to, mostly, as 'donated substance'. Everyone could, with care, get along together.

“So, you can see we’ve got the Human League along to the conference, what about your side’s dissenters?”

“Ah! The Draculians! They are not happy. I see in them the same blank looks and sneers that I know your Leaguers have. Perhaps we should lock them all up together and let them wipe each other out?”

“I’ve very rarely had dealings with Draculians. Just how bad is it? Are there that many of them?”

“Not so many as your Leaguers, but the problem is their influence. Of course they get fewer and fewer each year. You can’t just ‘become’ a Draculian, you have to have been ‘made’ before the Great Accident, and even then there are petty rules and exceptions. New World vampires are *never* admitted for instance…..No, they get fewer and fewer, *but* they have the ear of the Kravitzen, and they in turn have their supporters. No Draculian would admit to it, but without human assistance they’d get nowhere.”

“Unfortunately the Leaguers grow in number daily, and they don’t need any assistance, *but* they don’t have many connections with the great and the good. However, if it comes to an election, things could go badly. If we can just show ordinary everyday people that there’s nothing to be afraid of any more….well…. they’d start to lose followers.”

Sandy paused and tasted the starter they’d just been served.

Four large pieces of ravioli with a little slash of sauce and a sprinkle of freshly chopped herbs. His with a white sauce and spinach flavoured pasta, and hers with what looked like tomato flavoured pasta and a tomato sauce. However, if you knew your Transylvanian conventions the colour was from ‘*substance*’, not tomato.

A photographer stepped around the side of the screen and magnesium flared up to illuminate the scene. “Sorry! Just a picture for the papers! How we can all get along together, and the ravioli is just sooo, so photogenic!” and then he was gone.

Sandy extended his right hand to Carlotta.

“Are you alright? The flash I mean? You weren’t prepared for that, neither of us was!”

“It’s alright. I’m quite good with things like that now, it’s just strong sunlight that’s still dangerous these days. They could have warned us though!”

Somewhere in the background a violinist was beginning to play and there were sounds of glasses clinking and the subdued rattle of cutlery on china.

“Is it good?” Sandy asked as Carlotta finished the first mouthful.

“Yes! I’ve rather a taste now for the new dishes. Of course it’s quite novel having to chew, and swallowing solids took some getting used to. Odd…. it sort of woke up memories so distant that they seemed like dreams….or perhaps they were just dreams…” she sat very still and silent, then roused herself and shook her head. “Sorry, I was miles away there! How’s yours?”

“Very good indeed! The wine is good too!”

“It should be! Europe had 4 million hectares of vines before the accident, and now all that is still cultivated is the very best of that amount. It follows therefore that….” And Carlotta, quite unconsciously started to deliver a lecture on why wine today *had* to be the best in the world. Sandy stopped eating, and slowly sipping the velvety soft vintage he watched Carlotta, as he had done so many times before at their meetings. It wasn’t (he knew) the Vampiric fascination. He just was very, very fond of her (but he wasn't going to do anything foolish, because that would hurt her more than it would hurt him.)

Carlotta suddenly became aware of what she was doing, paused and grinned, a fang slightly caught up on the edge of her lip. "Sorry, but you know how it is!"

Fortunately the waiter arrived with a tray and began clearing away the first course and opening the wine to go with the next one. He placed the bottle on a small stand next to the table, unobtrusively swept away the rose petals from the table cloth and withdrew.

There was no choosing, no menu, at Der Rosenburg you accepted what was put in front of you, and it was always good. An experienced Vampire *Maître de* could always find out what a guests foibles, intolerances and favourites were without asking, and the kitchens, without exception, were able to deliver.

"Who usually eats here?" he asked.

"Kravitzen, Dukes, Barons, Diplomats. Plus it's a popular venue for welcoming the 'newly made'. The Americans have the money, so they all eat here at least three times before its time to go home. And, of course they never get a chance to come back, so it's worth it."

She was referring to the fact that anyone from outside Europe, anyone born and bred outside the perimeter of the great accident, could only reasonably spend a total of two years on the inside during their natural lifetime.

"What about the Chinese?"

"Ha! They spend the whole time they are here in rubber suits breathing filtered air and feeding on chemical sludge through a straw. Not only that, they reek of Forsterite, gives you a headache just being in the same room. No! They most certainly don't dine at Der Rosenburg!"

Sandy recalled that China had not had the advantage of an ocean between it and Europe when the Great Accident occurred, and that they'd had to cope with an extensive land border heavily polluted with Revenantic Fall-Out. Since it had fallen outside the perimeter it didn't produce good honest Werewolves and Vampires, but Zombiesque monsters. No wonder they weren't keen on going home with a body burden of RFO that could easily tip over the edge if you ate a badly sourced noodle! Still, Transylvania saw the prophylactic suit as a veiled insult and only just tolerated the Chinese embassy. The Americans by contrast lived life to the full during their two year tour and occasionally left behind a compatriot who had elected to 'donate substance' and so become a permanent resident.

By now the table had been arranged to the satisfaction of the two waiters laying out the next course, the wine had been poured, and after making a minor adjustment to the floral decorations they withdrew and Sandy and Carlotta continued their conversation.

"So, I gather then that the single biggest threat to peace negotiations , that is to a permanent treaty, would be the Human League? Even though they have sent delegates?"

"Yes, but as I said, they lack influence. Plenderleith has Their Majesties to consider, but with four of them that's all about consensus views, and he can easily play them off against each other. The voters are another matter. If the Human League got elected as a significant party, and not the fifteen percent of seats they hold at present, they might influence policy. Which is why, what I'd like to see is a watertight treaty, agreed now, that any future administration can't wriggle out of."

"Much my own feelings, a good solid treaty that links our two countries together and gives an honest trustworthy basis for France and The Germanies to join in with."

"I hear that they both have observers here?"

"Yes, along with China, America, Italy and Spain…even the Portuguese have come along!"

"The world is watching!"

"I know, and you and I will be in the newspapers tomorrow morning as an example of how discipline, respect and sensibleness bring harmony and progress! It is nice to know that the papers are on our side!"

"Back home in England it might not be that *all* the papers will echo that view. We do have a more *varied* range of journals."

"Ah! The problems of a Free Press! Still, mostly it will be a favourable report?"

"Oh yes, even the papers backing the Human League give lip service to a treaty, but they'd leap at the chance to say 'I told you so!' if something went wrong. But, what about your Draculians?"

"They are not *my* Draculians! Sorry….I don't like them one little bit! They want a return to absolute rule by the Dukes, all moving to one step, all ruthless unpitying domination of humanity. Werewolves knowing their place. You just don't know what it used to be like! I was so glad when the reforms began."

"But they couldn't really *do* anything could they? Not with there being so few of them!"

They continued with the meal. Carlotta with her eyes a little downcast, Sandy observing a polite silence since Carlotta was clearly troubled.

At last the waiters re-appeared and removed the tiny bones of the quail that had formed the main course; his with a white wine sauce, and hers with a richly red compote of 'berries'. And, since this *was* Der Rosenburg, they whisked away the very table and all its contents and re-equipped the diners with a much smaller, more intimate table that they set for dessert. A genuine Rosenburg mountain of candied rose petals, crystallised blossoms, tiny glazed fruits, minute crisp pastries, strands of saffron, frozen globes of sorbet and strange, dark, dried vine fruits soaked in ancient brandy. On top was a single fondant rose, its petals so deeply red that they seemed black. Sandy knew exactly what the item was, and that etiquette demanded that Carlotta offer it to him, and he accept it. Above them the rose blossoms continued to let loose their red and pink snowfall, and the diners on both the balconies and in the little courtyard were showered with soft petals. They settled on hair and shoulders and fell into wineglasses and onto the crisp white table cloths.

He took the sugary morsel from her fingers with his tongue and allowed its sweet, but oddly salty taste to spread throughout his mouth, his saliva dissolving the delicately sculpted petals. Then he swallowed, and smiled.

"Go on! Have a good mouthful of wine to clear the taste! You're the only person I know who does it all so well!"

Sandy accepted the proffered glass of sweet strong Tokay and took a small sip, just enough to wash down the sugary 'treat', not enough to suggest that eating it had been anything less than delightful.

"You know those things cost a great deal to make!"

"I know, and I am aware of the problems in manufacture. Don't forget, it was my firm that found out how to process 'substance', and we did that in order to make a reliable field ration for Transylvanian troops! But that's a secret, as I'm sure you know! Imagine the row if the Human League realised just how Essex Armaments had contributed to the last Balkan campaign!" He brushed some rose petals off of his sleeve, and hooked two specimens out from his wineglass. They didn't in actual fact add that much to the flavour, and these ones seemed to have imparted a queer chemically taste, which was a pity!

"But you did. Plenderleith knows all about it, and so does your Queen, and I mean *your* one, not the Scottish *scurmvurm*....sorry!"

"Oh don't worry about that! She's only really popular in her own land. They call her far worse than that at Westminster."

Carlotta moved her chair slightly closer to Sandy and reassuringly lightly touched his gloved left hand.

"Please, things are not quite as stable in Transylvania as they seem. In America, where they still have electricity that works they would be saying 'the place has been bugged', but here there are lots and lots of *other ways* of listening in. Above us people may, just possibly, be using telescopes to lip-read what we are saying. Beneath this table there might, just possibly, be certain little creatures that, while they are in no way sapient, are sentient enough to listen, remember, and report! Keep your left hand on the table, and let me put my hand next to it. It is a guarantee! I know that *you* trust me, but *I* don't trust me! Especially when I can tell you that they say somebody has found the Archduke."

Sandy did an excellent job of not showing alarm, but instead came a little closer, as he had always longed to do, and let his lips brush against Carlotta's sable black hair.

"Are you quite, quite sure of that? I thought…"

"Thought that we had made sure his remains were lost forever after the last incarnation? Yes, a lot of us *thought* that that was so. I *longed* for it *to be so*, I had to live through those times, to do….things that I still regret, Vampire that I am!"

"Has he been….er…resurrected?"

"Not yet! We'd all know about that! I would have walked out into the mid-day sun before I'd ever be under that terrible dominion ever again…I really would!"

"Yes, yes….I can see that." He raised his right hand and gently stroked back her hair which had fallen across her ivory white cheeks. "But….you've all grown so much since then! The Dukes are still as potent as they ever were, and the Counts, but you don't all obey them unthinkingly anymore!"

"That, of course, is true. But, if my Duke or one of his Counts insists that I do something, it is at a very great personal cost that I rebel! And I am seen as one of the difficult ones!"

A tear (and a Vampire tear is a rare and precious thing), oozed out and trickled down her face. Her eyes themselves burned dark, suggestively like iron beginning to gain colour in the blacksmiths fire.

"I am afraid! Afraid for good people like you. People who have befriended us! Who have made sure that there is always reliable counsel, good advice and wise words to help us avoid conflict. If some fool of a Draculian opens his veins and spills his blood on that dreadful dust! Where *will* we be?"

Outside the privacy of the screened-off table the noise of Der Rosenburg's diners and revellers continued. Carlotta took another and yet another mouthful of the wine. The fire in her eyes seemed to grow more and more intense. Sandy also gulped at the wine, and Carlotta seemed to become the centre of the universe. Something was wrong, but he was intent upon two very significant things. Firstly that The Archduke, the Fountainhead, Dracula himself, was about to return. A matter for his company to be aware of, for people at home to understand, for so, so, many friends, colleagues, contacts, ordinary everyday people to know so that they could take precautions! Secondly, and oh, it was a supreme sense of duty that made him see it as *secondly*, that he was madly and irrevocably in love with Carlotta!

CHAPTER 2

Sandy struggled to rouse himself from the all-pervading stupor, the paralysis that seemed to be possessing him. Somebody was hitting him, slapping his face.

"Wake up traitor! Wake up and get ready for your vile, undead, girlfriends kiss!"

Sandy managed a degree of focus. It was Heyward, the leader of the Human League delegation. The screens seemed to have been drawn even closer around the table, and Heyward was standing there, gloating, obscenely glorying in something, but what?

"Poetic justice! This is the foul brew your people wanted to sell the undead filth! What was it? One drop and your warriors become invincible berserkers? Except it was a disaster! But not for us! Oh no! Very, very strangely exactly what we wanted! E17!"

Sandy's brain ran through its catalogues and recalled ' E17, experimental drug....battlefield performance enhancing substance....we discontinued research...just as well....it does give vampires an uncontrollable feeding frenzy, but it induces temporary paralysis of the legs...we got further work banned because we thought it wasn't nice...! Then he thought... side effects! The researcher said he'd experienced powerful aphrodisiac effects....plus an initial loss of consciousness...no good on the battle field...although consciousness would all cut in again you'd be unable to move from a to b!'

"Isn't this nice!" Heyward continued " The little vampire lover will just sit there unable to move! His *girlfriend* will wake up, oh so hungry! So hungry in fact that she will drain him dry! And, and!

He will actually offer himself to her, let her send him into oblivion! And! The papers! Oh yes! You my friend are personally going to destroy any chance of a peace treaty forever, and ever, amen! It's all working! Nothing you can do about it, despite the fact that it was you and people like you who made it all possible!"

Sandy felt the horror, the emptiness, the spite that Heyward emanated. How, on Earth or out of it, could he fight back! And then Heyward did something that completely altered the universe. He hit Carlotta. He smashed her across her face with the back on his hand, and turned contemptuously and strode away through the gap in the screens.

Sandy's blood boiled! His own safety was no longer worth a wilted rose petal , Carlotta was to be protected, to be saved, to be prevented from becoming the pawn by which the peace was lost. The plans began to form, to progress, to alter, to regenerate.

Carlotta opened her eyes, a look of anguish moved across her face. Her mouth fought with her consciousness, and very, *very,* slowly she started to speak.

"Sandy…I have always loved you…please…take off your ring and give it to me…before it is too late…I can still….still…control myself…I will swallow it…the end will be sudden, swift…I know that…and you will be safe…and Europe will be safe…the world will be safe…do it…let me die before…" then her words died away and her eyes became burning red pits of fire.

"No….there will be another way…you will not die…I promise it…Carlotta!"

Their seats were almost touching, and despite being unable to move from the waist down they did indeed begin to move closer and closer together. Carlotta seemed to be fighting with herself, her hands even moving up to her throat and seeming to essay self-strangulation. With a gasp she cried out "Sandy, Sandy, don't listen to me, it's *not me*, it's not me! Sandy! Sandy! IF YOU LOVE ME!!! TAKE OFF YOUR RING!!!!"

If there had been a close observer, instead of the photographer leaning out from the balcony above, they might have seen a look of calm, satisfied delight upon Sandy McLomonds face!

The Forsterite ring and the white glove were thrown together across the table.

Carlotta fixed her fiery gaze upon Sandy, who unavoidably, became frozen stiff awaiting the strike of her canines!

BUT! For those who *know* there is a fraction of a second when a Vampire throws back its head and prepares to bite when contact is lost and the intended victim is free of all influence. It was in this fraction of a second that Sandy put into play a private and personal theory he had been nurturing for a great many years. He also drew back, opened his mouth wide and as Carlotta swept her fangs downwards he bit deeply and firmly into her throat!

Teeth gripped, twisted, disobeyed their sockets, one even snapped and became for a very short while a razor sharp edge of enamel. Carlotta's skin broke, it's capillaries tore, and her blood leaked, in minute amounts, out of her body and mingled with Sandy's saliva, and was sucked down into his body, her substance joining with his and making their entities one!

On the balconies above little was noted, a kiss exchanged, as expected, between the two people most expected to symbolise the new Europe!

……………………………………………

Miss Freeman stood surveying the class. They had all done very well indeed this term. A term devoted to Geography. The walls of the little class room were plastered in drawings, maps, lists of products and cut out paper shapes of people carefully coloured in with crayon.

Outside it was getting gloomy, the late September sky clouding over and threatening rain. In the street the lamplighter was lighting and turning up the oil lights, there was the very distant whistle of a train, and much closer the crunching sound of carriage wheels on the gravel road surface.

"Now children, tomorrow we have a visitor! The Inspector is coming to see just how well we have all done this term! We *want* to do well, *don't we children?"*

And, of course they all really and truly did want to do well, and wasn't it so good as well that they were such a varied class?

"Now, the Inspector will ask us all sorts of questions to see just how clever we all are! So I think we should have a little practice? Don't you?"

A great chorus of "YES MISS!", very gratifying!

"Timmy! What is the date today?"

"Wednesday the thirtieth of September Two hundred and fifty three P A. Which means *post accident.."* he was about to continue, determined to recite every last item on the remembered list, but Miss Freeman pointed instead to another child.

"The Great Accident happened 253 years ago and changed the world which is why we count the years from that time. The world is divided up into four big parts, Europe, America, China and Australia…" and the next child continued…

"Europe is made up of Spain (which is the biggest country) Transylvania (which is next biggest) Italy, France, The Germanies and…ummm…errr…"

"Come on everybody…remind him!"

"…England, Ireland, Wales and Scotia!"

"Well done! The Inspector will like that! Now, what do we know about the borders of Europe? James?"

"Europe, Miss, is bordered to the North by the Polar Ice Cap, to the South by the Great African Desert, to the West by the Atlantic," then he paused for dramatic effect, and finished "and to the East by China, andthetoxicwastewherethezombiesare! Please Miss what exactly is a Zombie?"

Miss Freeman looked a little worried. 'Do not, ever, ever, even for a moment allow children to be frightened by people from other lands', she had been told, repeatedly!

But, how could you do that *and* tell the truth, the other essential of being a teacher.

Miss Freeman held up a hand to hush the excited whispering.

"Yes James, some people do call the poor creatures who have to live in the wastelands , err.. *'zombies',* it isn't a nice word, and you should never use it, never! They are just, *unwell,* and they very kindly have decided to stay in their own land so that other people don't…err…become unwell too. Now! Who can tell me about 'The Hole'!"

This was a master (or mistress) stroke. The 'Hole' was another no-go area for detailed discussion, but at least it was easier to deal with than the awful fascination the children had about zombies.

"It's what was left after the big experiment in…Swisserlant… went wrong. The Transylvanians look after it and we all have nothing at all to bother about, and it is a good thing really, so that is all right." He finished breathlessly

"Ummm!" thought Miss Freeman, "let's hope they've not heard about the spiders!"

She decided to divert attention now away from the more gory aspects of Geography to political issues.

"Now, who is going to be first to tell me about the nice people who live in Transylvania?"

Rolf shot up his hand. His newly awarded Clan badge was still bright and shiny and pinned ostentatiously to his cardigan.

"Please Miss! My family is from Transylvania, and so I'd like to answer this question! In Transylvania there are many types of people. It is an ancient land and was once a mighty Empire. Humans, Werewolves (I'm a werewolf you know!) Vampires and other races live in harmony. England is a special friend of Transylvania and we are going to Prague next summer for our holiday and I hope to meet my great, great, grandfather who is a Baron!" Rolf seemed to run out of steam at this point, and wondered if he'd perhaps done *too* much. Kate, whose parents were Human League was looking at him sourly, but Gretchen whose mum was a Beliefer was positively beaming at him, so on balance he decided it was probably all alright.

"Excellent! Excellent! Now, before you all go home, all together, as a class, slowly, carefully and in your own time. What is a Revenant?"

And the whole class, with due gravity and clear diction recited "A Revenant is a human being, just like myself, to be cared for and cherished as a friend and neighbour. The word revenant means 'one who has returned' and refers to the fact that some people when they die find that things are not ready for them and so they come back to live another life until they are ready to move on. They are normal people and nothing to be frightened of!"

The class carefully put their books and writing materials into their desks, filed quietly and responsibly into the cloakroom to collect hats and coats, and formed an orderly queue at the classroom door, two lines, boys and girls. Gretchen managed to be alongside Rolf and gave his hand a squeeze!

……………………………………..

On the topmost tier of the balconies, seated at the least prestigious of the tables, the American pressman squinted into the viewfinder of his camera. Dammit! It was so much easier back home! The computer just sorted it out, the image intensifier clicked in, the pictures just came up. But here! God damn Europe! Not even a spark of static let alone real genuine electrics! And all that damn fuss about no firearms, what was it the ambassador had told them?

"If you've brought a shooter hand it over now! Pull the trigger and nine times out of ten nothing will happen, the explosive don't work properly over here, and one in ten the whole damn thing will explode and take off your arm"

This was just *not* the good old US of A, but it was a short assignment, and he'd most certainly not be coming back! So, get on with the job!

This was the very, very best in lenses that the Germans could grind, and they still were the world leaders when it came to mechanical stuff. Trouble was you just had to hope what you'd seen was what you were going to get after all the god damn fuss with the chemicals! Looked like a let-down anyway. That damn

English politico had assured him this was *the* news picture of the conference, the one that would blow it all apart! And what just *had* happened! The two best bets for integration had had…a…what was it the Brits called it?….A snog! He turned away from the balcony's edge, put the camera and its oversized lens down on the ground and focused instead upon the food!

Far below in the apparent privacy of the screened off table Sandy brought both hands up to cradle Carlotta's cheeks, relaxed his jaw and with the greatest trepidation raised his face to look directly into hers. His whole body tensed, expecting the fabled Vampire strength to assert itself and for Carlotta to continue her assault. However, Carlotta remained as his hands positioned her, and her eyes, though still an intense fiery red, seemed no longer dangerously threatening, but majestic and controlled.

"Carlotta!"

"Yes Master!"

That really was a shock! The E17 was still having a very powerful effect upon him, and to possess Carlotta's love was still greatly to be desired, but even more powerful was a sense of right and wrong.

"Carlotta! We are equals , I am not your Master!"

"You have drunk my blood, you have overcome me, you have a passion for me," it was all coming out in a level, measured voice, as though planned and delivered from a long way away, "Even without the trick they played upon us, you have feelings, and I….still….have some…elements of…self-control….you *are* the Master, whether you like it or not, and we must move forwards. *They* must not win!"

Mindful of possible watchers, and also very, very much wishing just this once to do what he had always wanted to, Sandy leaned forwards and gently, tenderly, kissed Carlotta on the lips.

"Carlotta, listen very carefully. In a while the drug will wear off, and we must both live with the consequences of our actions. While it is strong I will say that I love you, and that I am thinking about the very best way to help you, also I trust you absolutely….so now here goes!

'Carlotta Esteban since I am your Master I am going to give you two orders which I know you have the capacity to obey forever. The first order is that you will, by force of your self will, easily and without pain or discomfort overcome the peril of daylight and all other difficulties experienced by Vampires. Secondly you will in future only obey instructions and commands of your own free will and shall never have to call anybody, any creature, or entity Master or Mistress.'" And with that Sandy planted another light kiss upon Carlotta's lips and upon her brow and then sat back.

Around them the background noise continued. Carlotta was very still and silent, then after gathering her thoughts she spoke.

"You could have asked me to love you forever, to have been your protector, to have fought against the things we both hate, but….you have given me to myself. I have not been that for many lifetimes, even as Carole Stevens I was not so free as you have now made me….and you have not told me not to be a Vampire, infact….in your love for me you have made me more powerful than any other Vampire in Transylvania….But….you are a clever fellow, you know me so well, and I don't really think that the drug has led you to this, not quite. Well, now you must see just what you have let loose upon the world!"

Carlotta sat up straight in her chair, swept back her raven black hair and smiled in a way that just let the tips of her fangs show, pressed against her blood red lips.

"Sandy McLomond, you have overcome me, drunk my substance and fallen in love with me, so in keeping with Transylvania tradition you are now my Lord! You are now the 'Lord of the Masterless Lady', and I will be looking to you for guidance! Goodness only knows what you have done, but the bloody Draculians had better look out!"

………………………………………………..

The photographer returned, and once again expended a considerable amount of magnesium (which since it had to be imported from America was far from cheap!)

Carlotta smiled and remarked *sotto voce* that it certainly didn't make her eyes water anymore! Sandy, when pressed made a few comments about nations coming closer together, and the photographer (who seemed very bemused) retired from the scene.

Carlotta suddenly became intensely interested in Sandy's sharp and sudden attention to the opening in the screen to their right. Without shifting his gaze, somehow or the other his whole being was focused on the gap.

"Heyward, please don't linger the otherside of the screen. Come in, come in. And don't be so nervous, your heart is all a pitter-patter!"

'Oh dear!' Carlotta thought, 'What is happening to him! Only a vampire would have been able to know that!'

Heyward reluctantly emerged from around the corner, almost dragged against his will, or so it seemed, but with perhaps a morbid fascination to see just how Sandy had fared from the effects of the E17?

As he came around the corner Heyward's hand began to stray to his breast pocket. Despite his eyes still being fixed upon Carlotta's face Sandy's hand shot out with lightning speed, grasped Heyward's wrist, and gripped with such ferocity that Heyward's fingers spread in a sudden spasm. The object he had taken from his pocket fell, and was immediately caught in Sandy's other hand.

"Hmm! Forsterite Air Powered Dart Gun! Totally illegal both here and at home! An offence to own, to deal in, and to handle! Where did you get it?!"

Heyward's face paled and grimaced with the pain of Sandy's grip. Sandy turned and focused his gaze on the man and his eyes seemed to bore into him.

"Tell me! Those things are *terrible!* Do you understand? *TELL ME!* ***N O W!"***

Carlotta's face paled, and she tentatively extended a hand towards Sandy.

"What do you care?" said Heyward, "It's a weapon, it's for killing peo….things!"

"It doesn't just kill them you bastard! It ends their existence! Do you understand? DO YOU!"

There was a pause, then Carlotta's voice.

"Please Sandy, *My Lord*, please! He doesn't understand! He hasn't bothered to find out how things are, please! Let him go!"

Sandy relaxed his grip, and Heyward's wrist responded by taking on a twisted, distorted appearance, its bones crushed and compacted. Sandy took a deep breath and composed his features.

"Heyward, you have betrayed the trust placed in you by our country. You have attempted to bring about both the death and dishonour of two people who wanted to create peace and harmony…. and then you skulk around to see *if it has worked!* I do not know just what I was going to do to you….BUT….I strongly feel that your life has just been saved by the plea of a very senior Vampire! Stay just where you are, don't try to run away. You will tell now how you came by this weapon and the E17 you put into our drinks. Currently you have diplomatic immunity, but that won't stop me taking action because I'm not a Transylvanian!"

Heyward had by now sunk to his knees and was hugging his crushed wrist close to his body. The space behind him was suddenly filled with two dark suited figures, blocking any escape route, and reaching down to haul him back onto his feet. Sandy recognised them from the hotel, Werewolf security guards, quiet, restrained, but full of hidden menace.

"Milord? Milady? What has happened here?"

All Transylvanians prided themselves upon an excellent standard of English, however Sandy replied in their own tongue, assuring them that the situation was under control, that the miscreant was unfortunately under diplomatic protection, had no understanding of Transylvanian, but would need to be questioned immediately by the Britannic Ambassador, and could a senior Duke be in attendance?

Heyward cringed between his two guards, and remained unaware of the content of the conversation. By now they had been joined by various Transylvanian officials who had politely but firmly assured the other guests that nothing was the matter, and had instructed the musicians to continue to play and the waiters to bring out the champagne that was to provide the conclusion to the meal and to herald the opening of the ballroom.

Above on his balcony the press photographer peered down again and saw some activity around the table he had been watching earlier, but since waiters seemed to be clearing the small courtyard of its tables, and that people were starting to move through to the ballroom he assumed he had not missed any significant activity. “Hey buddy!” he called out to one of the other pressmen. “Hey! How do we get these stories out, there ain’t no damn telegraphs!”

“The people here are very good!” replied a French journalist seated beside him. “At first light there’s a heliograph service that will get your material to the agency in Portugal, they’ll forward it on! Now, put that ridiculous camera away and come and enjoy this champagne!” and so he did, thus missing the chance to see the transfer of Heyward, under close guard to the manager’s office.

Her Excellency, a Grand Duke, the local Werewolf Baron and several security guards filled up most of the space. Heyward was placed in a chair. Sandy spoke.

“As Essex Armaments senior representative at this conference, and the subject of this unprovoked attack by Mr Heyward I have very direct concerns with this incident. I hope that you, Ma’am, and Your Serenity will pardon me for ‘taking over’. I will at this stage introduce The Lady Carlotta Esteban, who as chief armaments purchasing negotiator for Transylvania’s Defence Force is also critically involved. Mr Heyward has, by some means or other acquired research materials from Essex Armaments, I recognise the dart gun as one of a very small number licenced by both our countries for research into anti-forsterite body armour. The E17 drug must have been independently produced from the formula that we hold, since all stocks were destroyed and further development of the drug stopped by joint agreement between our two countries. This outlines the situation as far as my professional brief runs, so Ma’am, Your Serenity, do I have your permission to conduct my own investigation?”

The Grand Duke looked inquiringly at the Ambassador, then began in Transylvanian.

"I am given to believe that the prisoner knows nothing of our language? Yes, I see from his thoughts that this is true! I understand that this Lady and Gentleman were the subject of an attempted plot to disrupt the conference and push our two countries to war! This is a matter that requires formal investigation by both Their Britannic Majesties Embassy in Transylvania and our own authorities. There is in addition Mr Heyward's apparent attempted assassination of The Lady Carlotta. We must assume that she was the target since the weapon would not have had any serious effect upon a, er, 'human'. However I am content that Essex Armaments conduct their own investigation simultaneously with any activity we are planning. We do recognise and respect the diplomatic immunity pertaining to Mr Heyward, and in many ways Essex Armaments taking custody of Mr Heyward would be a convenient situation.

Sandy sat watching the Grand Duke and sorting out several conundrums in his own head. He knew that Carlotta, seated beside him, was also puzzled.

It was quite clear that the speed with which he had moved to prevent Heyward's attack, the prescience that led him to know that Heyward was behind the screen, added to the immense power of his grip that had broken Heyward's radius bone and rammed it into his ulnar suggested that some of the powers of a vampire had passed into him. Clearly he had acquired mastery over another vampire, but if this had made him 'one of the undead' he did not know. He was beginning to gather thoughts, unspoken utterances and emotions from the people present, which was supposed to be a speciality of vampires, though not really exclusive to them. He'd picked up the Forsterite ring from the table without any problems, and it was currently in his waistcoat pocket. The dart gun he'd at once taken to pieces, tipping the little magazine of Forsterite needles into his card-case and wrapping that in a handkerchief for safety. Hit a vampire with a Forsterite ring and they'd be painfully inconvenienced, rapidly stunned, but….just let one of those slender notched needles break the skin and lodge in vampire flesh and it was all over! A minute or two of total paralysis, then permanent dissolution, no easy way back, at least no one had seen anyone come back from that sort of 'accident', which was why they were banned, and the anti-forsterite armour project was incredibly secret. How on earth, or off of it, had that gun got out of the armoury?

Her Excellency was speaking now, and also keeping to Transylvanian.

"The peace conference is vital. We've been very lucky that these two people were able to deal with the problem, and I *would like to know just how they did it!* But not just right now. I am prepared to sanction whatever action Essex Armaments and Your Serenity recommend. As I see it there is a precedent for Mr Heyward's diplomatic immunity to be null and void, although that could create even more problems when the news gets home."

"We will make available to Essex Armaments secure premises and trained personnel to imprison and guard this miscreant." Sandy listened to the Grand Duke's words, and also heard his thoughts, since they clearly directly involved Sandy. "My friend, I don't know just what you really are, but I sense you are 'on our side' whatever that may be!"

Sandy spoke "Your Serenity. Ma'am. I think that Transylvanian custody of the miscreant and Britannic questioning *via* the informed agency of Essex Armaments summarises what we have just discussed, however I insist that any questioning be undertaken by myself accompanied by a Transylvanian representative at all times. The existence of Essex Armaments equipment along with the apparent ease that Heyward has operated here suggests that both of our nations have issues to investigate."

There was agreement. Werewolf officers and Vampire representatives came forwards, and Sandy spoke to Heyward, in English, outlining how he would be confined, cared for, and counselled. He stressed that the more Heyward could tell them the greater his chance of being returned to England. He could feel the terror in the man's head, the horror of….somehow….being assimilated into Transylvania! It was tempting to scare the man senseless with the fear of being made subject to a vampire so that he would be obliged to tell all that he knew….but it wasn't the way you did things….even if you did have the power. The thought comforted him, and let him feel that whatever had happened, he personally had not become a vampire! And yet, he thought, I am in love with a vampire, how can I feel relief that I am not one?

Heyward was led away, handcuffed to his guards. Her Excellency smiled, gave a brief nod to everyone, and withdrew.

The Grand Duke remained, and approached Carlotta and Sandy.

"Well my children! Somehow or the other you two are now the oddities of our age! I don't know what has happened, what you have done…. but it is far beyond anything that I have experience of. You, Sir, seem to have all the powers of a Vampire, but you are most certainly not one! You Madam! Ohh! I just don't know. I am frightened, and I am pleased. I am terrified, and I am delighted!

You both have the potential power to be far beyond any authority that I have.

We so often talk about the ancientness of Transylvania, and parts of it do indeed go back to the dawn of time, but, in reality we are very, very modern. We have had more change, more modernisation, than outsiders see or our own people will admit to.

So! I am the Grand Duke, well one of several actually! It is part of my job to nurture the future, but to safe guard the past. You two are most certainly the future, and I have a gift for you! Don't look so mystified. I know a pair of lovers when I see them! Here are the keys to the Imperial Suite. I have already *taken steps* to inform my staff. Your things are even now being transported to the suite. There is nothing to be done until the morning, for the conference at least, but for now take yourselves off to the suite and do your best to make a future for both our nations!"

Sandy and Carlotta, mindful of conventions, both gave a little bow, and the Grand Duke lightly touched their heads in blessing.

CHAPTER 3

The Imperial Suite was all and everything you could wish for, and there is always the advantage that with a vampire run establishment your every wish has already been catered for. The dear old Grand Duke had clearly started sending his thoughts to the staff throughout the meeting, for things had been cleared, his own bags packed up, and the bed linen replaced. Fresh vases of cut flowers, a bottle of chilled champagne, a tray of delicacies, both vampire and human, and in the atrium before the suite proper a small string quartet softly played romantic Viennese waltzes, and looked settled to do so until told to desist. Sandy let them carry on, knowing Carlotta's attraction to such things.

Servants had indeed already visited Sandy and Carlotta's separate apartments and brought their belongings to the suite. Everything had been distributed just as they would have wanted, and there was very little in the way of possible displacement activity available as they both drifted closer and closer together and clung to each other, enjoying for the first time that evening some true privacy.

The quartet played on, drowning out the distant sounds of the much larger ensemble providing music for the dancers in the great ball-room. The air was as warm and subtly scented as only a Transylvania atmosphere can be. Great waxy snow-white lilies produced an almost tangible perfume, while the warmth from the candles and the oil lamps added to the early autumn night's heat.

Sandy put his arms around Carlotta and drew her closer to him, settling them both into a standing embrace which gently and naturally became a waltz that slowly and softly moved them both in unison around the great lounge and so at last into the bedroom.

'Just relax.' Sandy told himself. 'Whatever is happening keep on going, ride the tide!'

Carlotta was thinking about different matters.

A long forgotten evening in Mitcham, before the 'accident', a teenager who was about to lose her virginity. A shabby nightclub, too much vodka, far, far too much vodka! A desire for something special, doing something to make yourself different from the rest, move up to the next stage of growing up! And it had been a disaster!

Then the years of trying so hard to make life more exciting. Until that day Angela had given her the paperback, all about Vampires.

She was the one who introduced her to the holidays! And the clothes, and the films, and....then she had taken the strange job Angela had found for her in Austria.

After that the evacuation of Europe.

She knew what was likely to happen next! So she decided to stay put! *And it happened! It all happened just as Angela had said it would.*

And so there was in fact a *second* chance to lose her virginity! And wasn't *that* wonderful! That transformation, that movement across the great divide!

Rebirth!

The power she had always longed for!

That *really was* growing up!

And the Count was, just so....wonderful! All her dreams realised! But....they did things differently in Transylvania, fledgling state as it was! She was a new, vibrant, enthusiastic member of the community! And it was the enthusiasm that carried her along. She was sent to 'carry out assignments', to eliminate opposition, to establish the Empire! But it wasn't all so good, not once she started to dig beneath the surface, once she had found out just what the 'Archduke' was after. But….she'd held on, and the six Grand Dukes had finally had their way….

Now? Well, an unexpected new beginning, like the virginity thing all over again. The way his bite had so remarkably changed everything, and the way he had given her liberty! Not told her what to be, but told her to be herself. *Le grande introspectif vampirique,* however was threatening to take over and spoil the moment, so she disengaged from her reverie and turned to Sandy.

'Darling, can you unbutton me please?'

Of course she could always have just managed a vampire shrug and the clothes would all have fallen away by themselves, but this was different.

Sandy was still in his evening dress suit, only his tie and collar undone. He deftly undid the line of buttons at the back of her stiffened black and violet silk bodice, and the loosened the ties around her waist.

'Yes,' she thought, 'he knows what to do, he has had lovers before….as have I, too many and so many….but never before has he made love to a vampire….and never before have I been subject to a human….well….not in this life…'

Now he was carefully easing the bodice downwards, and further loosening the skirt so that they both slid gracefully down and landed with a rustle of crushed silk onto the thick blood red carpet. She turned to face him and he began unlatching the front of her basque, pushing each tiny silken loop off of it's mother of pearl clasp, until the whole structure fell away revealing her perfect milk white breasts. She let his hands slide downwards and the finger tips inserted themselves into the waist band of her undergarments so that they too fell to the join the rest of her clothes on the carpet, then she knelt before Sandy, enfolding him in her arms.

'My Lord! I am your bride!'

'And I' said Sandy, raising her up from the floor, 'am your groom, if you will have me.' He in turn knelt in front of her, pausing as he did so to kiss her on the brow, the lips, her nipples and finally her sex.

Carlotta stooped to return him to a standing position and began to unbutton, unstrap and generally disrobe him with what she hoped was not unseemly haste.

'Oh…yes….I would indeed have you….as my husband….as my lord….but….do you trust me?'

The removal of male apparel is far less romantic than the removal of feminine clothing, but as each item was shed Carlotta's amorous frenzy began to rise, to mount, to flow towards high tide.

'My Lady….I trust you….do you forgive me?'

'Why…should you ….need…*.forgiveness?'*

'I have changed you.'

'For which I thank you….you have given me my freedom, I thank you for that and your trust!'

The final thread of clothing fell, and with no barriers now between them they entwined their naked bodies together, delighting in the ever closening union.

………………………..

By the slow sedately ticking wall clock and by the soft, distant, muffled chimes of the grand ormolu-mounted time piece in the atrium Sandy became aware that it was now three o'clock in the morning. Beside him Carlotta was deeply asleep, her features beautiful but impassive. Of the bite on her neck there was now no trace, not even a reddened mark. Sandy felt his incisor tooth with his finger. All smooth enamel once again, no evidence of the harsh broken edge that had resulted from his gripping Carlotta so tightly with it.

'So,' he thought, 'obviously I can repair myself now. Useful!'

In the warm darkness of the room he felt relaxed, calm and safe. With a little effort he could sense the presence of people other than themselves. A werewolf guard somewhere in the outer part of the atrium. Vampire servants in the kitchens at the rear of the suite, gently dozing but still strangely aware of his probing thoughts and ready to respond if needed. All of Carlotta's thoughts were open to him, but he felt it was not right to intrude, and found he could easily draw a curtain across them. As the distance increased what sensation of other minds were there became faint and confused, so that, he guessed, the ability to make any useful advantage of this acquired power would be limited by distance and numbers of people.

He turned and raised himself upon one elbow and gazed once more upon Carlotta, her raven dark hair, snow white skin and intense ruby red lips. Her long lashed eyelids fluttered and she looked at him sleepily, then she reached out and took his arm, gently pulling him towards her and turning at the same time to ease her body curve against his in the time honoured way of lovers, so that she was sheltered within his body's embrace. She took his hand and wrapped it around her own, burying them both deep in her breast.

"Darling…" she sighed, "Thank you, thank you…."

"What for?"

"Loving me, trusting me, setting me free….everything!"

Sandy replied with a gentle kiss and hugged Carlotta even closer to himself.

"Thank you for accepting me." Then he paused... "I suppose tomorrow we must plan for what happens next, but for now…"

"Yes," Carlotta said, "I'm afraid that worrying thoughts about the future are there in the wee small hours even for Vampires, but generally the morning is the better time to deal with them. Kiss me again *My Lord!"* and Sandy did.

……………………………………………

It was a strange dream, one that became steadily more and more crowded with people and full of noise and confusion. Sandy awoke with a start, as did Carlotta, who gripped his arm, her face full of startled alarm and fear!

Almost at once there was a rapping on the bedroom door, and worried raised voices outside.

Sandy grabbed breeches and a shirt, amazed at the way buttons seemed to be almost fastening themselves! Carlotta was already enrobed, and the door was opening to admit one of the Werewolf guards.

"MiLord, there is something very wrong, I think you and your Lady are at serious risk of harm. Please get ready to leave!"

"Stop! Just what is happening!"

"Somebody has set the prisoner free, and the Human League delegates are running amok. I'm afraid they seem to be armed with those dart guns! Oh! And the Draculians are involved as well. The

Baron says to get everybody out. He and the Grand Duke are trying to organise some sort of defence."

At this moment a second guard appeared supporting an unconscious colleague.

"They've taken the atrium. I locked the doors and dropped the bar, but the atrium's over-run. And I think Ernst is done for, they had crossbows with silver heads!"

He dropped the lifeless figure onto a couch. Sandy stooped over it and deftly pulled out a crossbow bolt that protruded from the werewolves shoulder. The tip was still intact. A little more colour seemed to come back into the werewolves face, but he still did not breathe or stir in any way.

"Right! Thank you. You see that black leather case over there with the silver locks? Handle it carefully! Hold it by the leather grips and get it through onto the dining table, call in as many of your people and the Duke's as you can find. Lock the doors to the atrium and put up the shutters on all the windows."

The werewolf moved quickly into the other room, cautiously carrying the huge black leather case with both hands, and trying not to allow the locks and clasps to come anywhere near his skin.

"What are you going to do?" asked Carlotta

"Keep us safe, and try to look after our people. That case is my confidential samples bag. Purely defensive items, but all still largely unknown. You've seen some of the devices, but no one else has….I'm afraid it looks like the Peace Conference has had it for now, but at least we can show the critics in both our countries that there are people still willing to work together!"

The heavy wooden shutters swung into place on the windows, but not before a few random missiles smashed through the ornate glass lattices. Crude lumps of limestone with tiny fragments of Forsterite gummed to their surfaces, they hit walls and furniture and shattered, scattering lethal particles of the alloy across the rooms. Sandy strode from one spot to another, scooping up contaminated material and throwing it into fireplaces or room corners. Carlotta, after a moment's pause did likewise, and soon thc suite was secure. The guard had thrown together a scratch defence team of four werewolves, three vampires and two humans.

They assembled in the dining room where Sandy was still ministering to the fallen werewolf, swabbing the wound with something from a bottle in his samples case. He looked up and then turned back to Ernst and tried to find a pulse, he seemed to be satisfied with whatever he had been doing and turned to the new comers, somehow already knowing their names, their strengths and weaknesses.

"Right! Hans and Adie, you are our attackers, Forsterite is painful if it gets under human skin, but it won't kill you. Franz and Heinz, you look after Hans and Adie, be ready to use your cross bows to shoot down anyone that threatens them, you'll be far faster than any non-vampire so work as a team and you'll safeguard each other. Werewolves! These are Forsterite shields, they also stop Silver, not very big, so you've got to be quick. Any of you play squash?" Three of the four raised their hands, "OK, treat it like a racquet, swipe the bolt or the dart out off the air, if you think you can't do that then use the shield to block the missile. That leaves Jacob." A rather small inoffensive Vampire cautiously raised his hand, "First Aid. Put these gloves on and you can handle a Forsterite dart safely, this solution slows down the effects of Forsterite, make the patient drink at least four mouthfuls, pour the rest over the wound and use the scalpel to open up the skin and dig out the metal, take a fair amount of flesh with it, because it contaminates its surroundings. Same thing applies to silver! Got it? Everybody ready? Good, now let's see who our callers are!"

....

There was a spy-hole in the double doors to the atrium, but somebody on the outside had covered it with tape so that the defenders would have no idea of what was going on. However high above the lintel ornamental stained glass panels depicting the Transylvanian Coat of Arms allowed a reasonable view of the atrium, and Sandy standing on a chair perched upon a table soon had a clear indication of who the attackers were. Surprisingly a mixed group, of humans *and* vampires. There were nine in all, and they had drawn up the heavy carved wood chairs and sofas to form a barricade, and then taken up firing positions behind it. The humans appeared to have dart guns, while the vampires were armed with small crossbows, presumably with silver points. They also appeared to be waiting for something to happen, and kept looking over their shoulders at the wide atrium entrance.

Inside the suite Hans and Adie stood ready and waiting, both armed with impromptu wooden clubs. Jacob was fussing over the bottles of Anti-forsterite, Franz and Heinz had still impassive faces, their minds trying to penetrate the thoughts of the people outside in the atrium. Carlotta was also trying to intercept thoughts, to silently assess the situation. Sandy stepped lightly down from his look-out post and carefully turned the key in the lock of the door and drew back the great oaken bar.

"Nine of them, and they've got five dart guns, which I think are all they have in that line. There never were any more than the set of six in the armoury, and I know they are our ones because I recognised the serial number on Heyward's one. If we can deal with them first then we only have to keep the werewolves safe from harm and the vampires can have a free rein. Do you think they have back-up? They seem to be waiting for something or someone."

"Something big has happened, this is just part of it. I was beginning to tell you earlier , but we got interrupted. There may be a plot among the Draculians to revive the Archduke, if that happens then we're all back to square one with peace in Europe. Let's just hope this is only an attempt to break up the conference and not the start of an uprising."

"Well, I'm pretty certain that whoever they are we are their prime target, why else would they use all their fire power against us rather than spread the dart guns around a bit more!"

"True," replied Carlotta, "however perhaps they think that the Grand Duke is still in here? He's been the most outspoken and most influential person in the peace process, and he really hates the Draculians and all they stand for. Many Draculians would be quite happy to accept irreversible dissolution if they could shoot him with a Forsterite dart first."

"So this is an assassination squad? The Human League and the Draculians in an alliance to restore the Dark Years?"

"More than likely. Everyone's mind is in such an uproar at the moment that they can't sense if the Grand Duke is in here or not, but this is where they think he ought to be, so here they are. Are we going to attack them? Or wait for help?"

"If we sit tight then that lot can't do much to hurt us, *but* if they are waiting for back-up, which seems likely from what preparations they've made, then we don't stand much chance at all. Five dart guns and four of us who can't be hurt by them. The werewolves will move fast enough to dodge the darts or block them, but they are vulnerable to the four vampires with the crossbows. A tricky situation, but we need to do something right now so that if they *are* joined by their friends at least the dart guns are removed. Hang on! I've just remembered the samples case has an anti-Forsterite lining, so that gives us another large shield."

....

The heavy wooden double doors burst open and the Human League assassins had barely time to level their weapons and loose off a couple of darts before blows rained down upon them and swift hands snatched the weapons from their grasp. In less than a few seconds it was all over. Jacob was crouched over one of the werewolves, pulling out a crossbow bolt and administering medication. Franz had turned one of the captured dart guns upon the four Draculians and was shepherding them into a large closet. Sandy and Carlotta were interrogating the one Human League assassin who had survived the foray, and the three remaining werewolves were securing the atrium entrance.

"Someone coming!" yelled Ulf, who seemed to be the werewolf senior pack-member.

The sofas and chairs were hastily returned to their function as a barricade, this time a little further away from the doors to the Imperial suite. The crossbows and dart guns were checked, and everything readied for whatever circumstances would bring.

Suddenly the wide entrance of the atrium filled with figures. The Baron's own bodyguard and a score or more of ordinary pack members who fanned out checking the corners of the room, looking behind chairs and curtains. Securing the area, a few humans in the Baron's livery seemed to be making a closer examination of the room, searching with fingertips along the edges of picture frames and so on.

"I am very pleased to see you are all still alive!" the Baron barked. "Very pleased! And you have a prisoner? Jah!"

Beaming all over what could be seen of his heavily bearded face he marched up to Sandy and Carlotta and laid a heavy hand on the terrified captive.

Sandy was about to "Sorry, but he's *my* prisoner sir!", however at this moment the Grand Duke arrived with his attendants, and the Ambassador.

In the resultant chaos and general confusion no one was quick enough to spot the prisoner put his hand to his mouth and swallow a small white capsule. By the time his guards realised that he was losing consciousness it was too late for any action to be taken. His final slurred words were "You are all too late. Tomorrow the Archduke awakes!"

Today, however, it seemed to be that the Grand Duke was in charge.

"The Government of Transylvania unfortunately regrets that it can no longer guarantee the safety of its visitors. There is a large well organised body of insurgents carrying out an attack not just on this building, but upon the entire city. The Baron and myself have made plans to ensure the safe evacuation of all delegates and diplomatic staff to the border of The United Germanies. I would be very grateful if you two, *both of you*, would prepare yourselves to join this group. I have an inkling of what may happen next, and know that it may be necessary for there to be a Transylvanian Government in exile in London. Your Ambassador agrees, though we as yet have no idea how it can be managed!" and with that he and the Ambassador withdrew.

A small group of werewolf guards took charge of the captured Draculians and very shortly the suite was empty except for Sandy, Carlotta and the little group that had helped then defend the atrium.

"Er, Sandy," whispered Carlotta, "You will need to give them orders of what to do next, for the moment you are their *lord*, you need to return them to their usual allegiances."

"Sorry, what do you mean?"

"Somehow or the other you have acquired the powers one usually associates with a Grand Duke. That's what it's like for everyday folk in Transylvania, they just latch on and do as they're told."

"Goodness! I'd never have urged them on to the attack if I'd known that, I thought they'd just agreed to follow me!"

It was a somewhat unusual phenomenon for a Transylvanian, being asked just what they would *like* to do, and Carlotta was quite sure that the 'love potion' effects of the E17 were no longer affecting either her or Sandy when they both almost (but not quite) lost patience with each other in sorting out what Sandy thought was an equitable solution.

The werewolves would be part of the escort to the border and expressed a desire to see Sandy and Carlotta safely there. Hans and Adie, fearful about what life in Transylvania would be like in a civil war suggested that they could be enrolled as servants, and Franz and Heinz regretfully decided to return to their Counts service, but hoped to be meeting the couple again!

CHAPTER 4

The wind howled and shrieked around the windows, several of which had finally sprung from their frames, ancient as they were, and now let the cold blast into the board room.

Plenderleith hugged his cloak tighter around him, and wondered just why this company still insisted upon using the ancient tower for their meetings. The view was, to be honest, stunning, possibly the very best in Europe, and the heliograph station positioned above it communicated directly with Antwerp (well at sunrise on a clear day, any way!) You could also glimpse the ice to the north, and see the channel, etched in the marshland of the North Sea, and the steamers struggling along its narrow reed crowded waterway.

"Prime Minister! We are ready for you now!"

Plenderleith followed the secretary into the Board Room. Goodness knows why he'd agreed to give them the same status as a 'foreign power', but it had been done now. Probably a good thing as far business abroad went, well, you couldn't do with too many voices could you? But, at home! They were just a bit too sharp really, much more focused and critical than the representatives at Westminster!

He took his seat at the great wooden table and acknowledged that his exalted position was equal to that of three commercial companies and two overseas representatives. His two assistants sat down either side of him, and he felt reassured by their ability to interpret for him. That fact that one was a werewolf, and the other a vampire hybrid were less worrying to him than the fact that a Chinese diplomat seemed to be chairing the meeting.

…………………………………………

Prague has seen many transformations over the millennia, and Prague as it might have been known *pre accident* bears few resemblances to how it is now, as the new Capital city of The Transylvanian Empire. In the big main square, walled off from the lower town and separated from the river with its special revenant friendly bridges (designed and built by Britannia) there is plenty of space to organise a caravan (such a better word than 'convoy'!)

Carts, wagons, pack-horses even, and string after string of saddle horses. Transylvania had long ago decided against railways, and although all the infrastructure had been there, the original 'pre-accident' steel tracks were now ancient relics buried beneath wind-blown loam and invading grasses.

The great caravan was to reach the railhead just beyond the border where the refugees would transfer to regular steam powered transport up to Wilhelmshaven and along the Wesser and then the channel that would lead to London River.

Closed carriages with darkened windows contained the Chinese contingent. The Americans were still loading more and more rolls of film into mechanical German cameras and snapping away happily. The American Ambassador was busy talking to a group of three Grand Dukes about the care of, and consideration for, American ex-patriots in Transylvania. Embassy security staff had the entire Human League contingent, in hand-cuffs and under guard. The great gates in the northern city wall were signalled as open, and more werewolf guards than you would have thought possible patrolled the roof tops, the side streets and the outer ramparts.

"So, what happens next?" Sandy asked the werewolf Baron.

He nervously fingered his black enamelled badge, "Oh, once we've got you all safely across the border we come back. If *he* has truly come back then the general order is for all urban packs to leave the cities and return to their traditional territories (ours is just a day's run away) there we will wait until we know what is happening. There are plans, plans you do not need to know about just yet. It all depends upon which way the Kravitzen turn, and also there are the *electifs,* the humans who would like to join the revenant community. If they come in with the Draculians then there will be many, a great many, that will support an uprising. They can all handle silver, and they will have craft skills that the vampires do not have, weapons will be made, the persecution will return.

We need to be safe in the woods.

Safe, but I am ashamed to say we will be uncomfortable. Modern werewolves have come to expect a lot more out of life than cold wet woods where there are no rugby pitches, or squash courts and no steak tartare!"

He paused for a moment gloomily staring into his own great black beard.

"And of course no big soft sofas and blazing log fires! But we will do it, once the Grand Dukes start their strategy we will be ready to support them, and if we can do anything in the meantime, you will only have to ask us. England has many fine, modern thinking werewolves, when you get back you will find ways to contact us! Good luck!" and he walked away to give further instructions to the escort.

A vampire Count whom Sandy had not met before came over to them.

"Thank you for the return of Franz and Heinz! They have been most impressed. I think that I shall have to be taking lessons in leadership now!"

"They were a credit to you." said Sandy making a short bow. "How will you cope with what happens next?"

"I would very much like to be leaving the city, going away to some remote place and hoping for better times, but my Duke is made of sterner stuff. We are to fight against the Draculians. Unfortunately for us *death before dishonour* isn't an option, but many will, let us say, not be loath to let ourselves be sent away for a long rest perhaps? Stay out of it until people like yourselves have settled the Archduke. It sounds like cowardice, and no doubt it is, but to think of yourself being forced to act under the command of that *monster*, to have to kill, not assimilate which is sometimes not so bad, but kill just for the pleasure of your master!" (he spat out the word master like mouthful of poison) "Well, I would rather spend all eternity in the caves of waiting before I do that again! You do not know what a great gift you have given the Lady Carlotta in freeing her from that shadow!"

He turned, as if embarrassed, and was lost in the growing crowd.

"Before we leave Sandy. Before we leave! There is one place I must show you. We may not pass this way again for many years. Please?"

And despite the rising urgency as each section of the caravan rolled, ground or trotted forwards towards the Great Gate, Carlotta led Sandy off down a side turning and up a winding stair onto the ramparts of one of the little forts that sat, each, in a corner of the great square.

"This is special, the secret that a vampire never shares! But I want to share it with you before we leave Prague. Please stand just there, and hold me in your arms. This is....this is...where I was 'made'! And please now, kiss me, just as you did last night in that wonderful bed. You have re-made me! I begin again! And I have freedom!"

Carlotta hugged Sandy to her, and almost wept with joy. Far below them the wagons and carts and horses moved in a strangely fluid fashion out and through the portal, but the couple remained for a while savouring all that was good of the buildings, the panorama of roof tops, the glint of the great river and the smells and perfumes of the city.

“I will like London,” Carlotta murmured in Sandy’s ear, “but Prague is where I have been born, twice now, we will return someday. We *will* return!”

There was the sound of hurried footsteps on the uneven stone stairs, a panting that was half human and a bit more than half canine.

Hundmann, (the ‘weredog’ to his friends) came stumbling around the corner.

“You’ve got to help!” he gasped,” They’ve got the Grand Duke!”

……………………………………

“Which one?” asked Carlotta as they hurried down the stone steps, “Which one?”

“Yours, Orlov! He was supposed to be addressing a meeting…. and he got there early…. and they were waiting….we lost ten pack members who were his guard….can’t help them….notched arrow heads….no way to get them out!”

“Who were they?” gasped Sandy, trying hard to keep up (because when a werewolf is really in a hurry literally *nothing* on heaven or earth can equal the pace!)

“Draculians and humans…. *Electifs* perhaps? ….Who knows, but they grabbed him and now we’ve….got them cornered…the Baron….seems to think….that you….can help!”

A few hundred metres outside the south gate of the great square, and hard up against the wall that in the past had traditionally separated the human quarter from the vampire domain was a Bier Kellar. It had been built in high Gothic style and looked like a medieval fortress, not just looked but in point of fact closely resembled.

Outside its great oaken doors and portcullis entrance there was a double ring of werewolf and human security guards. One or two vampire officials, holding up immensely heavy metal shields were also engaged in maintaining the cordon.

Sandy noted that the human guards were actually protecting their werewolf companions. A few had wooden shields that already bore embedded crossbow bolts, they also had a very small number of Forsterite daggers, but only a few.

Transylvania had actively avoided investing in them, maintaining that they would never be needed, and anyway were too dangerous.

'Now' he pondered 'they might be really useful. I wonder how we all got stuck on that line of thought?'

He heard Carlotta respond to his thoughts. "We did what we thought was right. We all did. We never thought that we might become our own enemies!"

There was a rough barrier of tables across the door way, and behind it several vampire bowmen, each looking very uneasy, and backed up by humans, pointed their bows across the barricade at the werewolves.

The Baron was sheltering behind a large bronze statue of Kravitz the Third, (on horse-back), and beckoned Sandy and Carlotta over to him. As they scurried across the open space a small flurry of crossbow bolts zipped and whined around them, but were easily dodged.

"They tunnelled through from the *Quartier Human.* Don't worry they won't get back that way, we've been dropping masonry blocks off the walls and onto their point of entry. This was to have been Orlov's farewell speech. All the Grand Dukes, the Dukes and most of the Counts had planned to put themselves beyond the Archduke power. I don't know if it can be done now!"

"How do you mean, 'beyond his power'?"

"It was a secret plan, well as secret as anything can be in this country. Without the structure of the aristocracy you can't easily control vampires. This is what we planned. A trusted non-vampire friend for each vampire lord would be here at the meeting. As the last of the caravan left the gates, everyone would say goodbye, stakes would be, err…delivered! And the dust of every single vampire would be kept safe, secure, secret, until the Archduke was once again disembodied!"

Sandy and Carlotta, still crouched behind the bronze equestrian statute were silent for a while, taking in the self-sacrifice, the absolute trust, the sincerity of the vampire lords (and ladies)

"Why weren't we told about this?" asked Carlotta

The Baron looked embarrassed, and werewolves have all of a dog's head-hanging, shamefaced look, when they are embarrassed.

"I must apologise. Apologise for everyone! You should have been told after last night's events. You, Carlotta, have always been the most independent among your people, and you Sandy…well you have always had our trust. We did not expect events to happen so fast….in time you would both, separately, have been taken into our confidence. Now. Well, I am Baron of one of the most ancient packs of *loup garou* in Europe, and I have not seen anything like you two….ever! Keep yourselves safe, for all our sakes! And now, what do you suggest we do next? They have Orlov, my ancient friend, the Grand Duke who I am supposed to be keeping safe until the dangers are past, holed up in some dark dank beer cellar. I would never be happy again if they….they…put him beyond return!"

"Well…" began Sandy, but he didn't get a chance to finish. A new group had come onto the scene. Four embassy guards, in full Essex Armaments body armour and with strange complicated looking weapons in their hands, in front of then Her Excellency Their Britannic Majesties Ambassador to Transylvania!

"Ye gods!" though Sandy, "Those outfits are not meant for anything short of outright full scale war! Even I don't know just how those suits will behave in combat!" then he recomposed his mind and added "Perhaps now's the right time to use them!"

Her Excellency swept past the two circles of guards and stood before the barricade. She was not wearing any conceivable form of protection, and even her Forsterite ring was conspicuous by its absence!

"Who's in charge here? Come on, don't muck about who's bloody well running this show?"

Crossbow bows wavered, were redirected, humans and vampires rapidly conferred, and then reluctantly a Draculian Count appeared from the shadows beyond the door way.

The brutal direct approach of Her Excellency had had its desired effect! The Count was temporarily over awed by her presence.

"Err, myself Your Excellency!"

“Jolly good! Now prove to me that you are really in charge and not some minor timewasting underling!”

Sandy and Carlotta could feel the resentment, the anger, the vicious hatred building in the Count.

“I am at your service, *milady!”*

“Right! Good! Simple hostage situation, chance for me to do the right thing. Bring out Orlov and I’ll take his place. Simple! Bet you haven’t got the guts to do it though?”

Sandy could feel the sadistic thoughts of the Counts mind. ‘Yes, just let her make the swop, we’ll get Orlov later, but *you* milady, *you* will join us, whether you want to or not! A great and powerful weapon in the coming war!”

“Bloody fool,” Sandy whispered to Carlotta, “she can’t trust him!”

“Keep your thoughts secret!” Carlotta answered. “This is a lady who knows what she is doing.”

With indecent haste Orlov was hurried out, and thrust, almost hurled, into the arms of the werewolf guard.

Her Excellency stepped forwards and took the hand of the Count, his eyes, his mind, his every thought was now focused upon taking Her Excellency as his next victim, assimilating her, making her into one of his helpless, unwilling followers, plundering her store of diplomatic and military information. His attention was in fact so supremely committed upon this act that he did not see the embassy guard toss a Forsterite ring in to Her Excellency’s hand. The punch into his midriff took him entirely by surprise and he collapsed, falling across her out-stretched left arm, leaning back and exposing his throat, out of which the human Ambassador of Their Britannic Majesties took a small but significant bite!

Sandy's mind caught the full blast of her thoughts. "Thought that was how you did it!"

……………………………………

The Count d'Earpingham (formerly a Draculian Count, along with his two thousand followers, all answerable to his every whim joined the rear-guard of the caravan as personal body guard to the Ambassador. The Count was very unhappy indeed, but complied. A significant number of his followers however were privately rejoicing. They were going to England!

……………………………………

The ordinary everyday people of Transylvania (one cannot, and should not, call them peasants in this day and age) looked thoughtfully at the very, very large quantity of wolves, trotting peaceably and carefully along the main roads, a great number of them seemed to be wearing little panniers, almost saddlebags, and some (usually with what looked like an escort of extra wolves around them,) had carefully protected glass flasks filled with a grey powdery substance .

"Father" asked Eva, a young girl of perhaps ten or so, "Father, can I be a werewolf when I grow up?"

Her father looked thoughtful for a little while and then replied.

"You'll need to think about it a good deal, a very good deal. But….I don't see why not. After all your Grandmother was one."

……………………………………

Prague was emptying. There were very few werewolves left, and apart from the few volunteers in the staunchly held Grand Square there were no Non-Draculian vampires left. The north gate and the road out of the city were still held by a rag-tag army of every conceivable species, including a few ethereal shape-shifters who weren't even supposed to officially exist. A strong body of Germanic 'freedom fighters' were helping to hold it all together, but it was obvious it would fall soon.

In the greater part of the city people awaited the outcome. The Kravitzen were locked away in their fortress, sure of a negotiated settlement with whoever won. There were no more 'outlanders' visible, and the American ex-pats had definitely gone underground, into crypt and cavern. The old Embassy buildings in all their glory had been over run and converted into Draculian offices.

"Sandy!" said Carlotta, " we must make plans to leave soon, we both have to be in London. We should have done as we were told and left days ago! There is nothing that can be done here!"

"Another day, just another day so that we can get the last of the people out and away to safety, then we leave the city!"

"Right, another day! Don't forget you gave me free will. I will insist that we leave, you *and* me, I am not allowing my lord to endanger himself!"

And so they began another tour of the walls, ducking, dodging, visiting the minor gateways through which from time to time (but now much less often) a little huddled group came asking for a chance to leave by the north road, the road to the Germanies, where they might, just might, be safe.

At one of the tiny corner forts they climbed a narrow spiral stair up to the turret room that Grand Duke Orlov was using as his command centre

"He still hasn't openly revealed Himself yet, which I guess is just as well!" said the Grand Duke. "I suppose he's waiting to see who truly is really loyal before he takes over"

"What happens when he does?" asked Sandy.

"Well, that's when we all find out just how strong we really are. I managed last time, but it was difficult, many, in fact most, didn't. They just acknowledged the 'fountainhead' and followed orders. Things were very bad indeed. Nowadays? Who can tell, we've all been used to far more independence, even the lowliest 'newly made' has far greater freedom now than anybody in the Dark Days. I think he knows that, and that's why he's biding his time to see who he can really trust, but his thoughts are there, I can feel him! Probing, listening, a nagging presence at the back of my mind. A feeling of having left some important thing undone, of having neglected a duty! Do you not feel it at all?"

"No, I can feel your thoughts, feel the whole ocean of minds around me, not very clearly or that usefully most of the time, but I can't feel what you are describing."

"Neither can I!" remarked Carlotta.

"That is good." The Grand Duke sighed, "Perhaps you two will make a difference, but who can tell?"

A werewolf guard came into the little turret room where they were talking.

"Your Serenity! There are strange reports from the South Fort. Cracks are appearing in the outer bridge, and there looks like an attack building up."

Sandy suddenly looked very concerned. "Sounds like they've undermined the gateway. They've certainly had enough time to do it. It's a very dangerous thing to try, but I suppose the *electifs* will do just about anything to get on board before the Archduke returns. Get all the defenders out of the gatehouse, drop the portcullis, bar the doors and start building a barricade on the inside of the square.

I'll be there shortly to activate the final defence mechanism, after all it is my company that designed built and installed it. We'll need to abandon the south wall, so get everyone from there on to the north side. I think we need to make final preparations to leave!"

Carlotta breathed a sigh of relief, "A sensible decision!"

……………………………………..

The road north from the gateway stretched away through stately avenues and groves where once, long ago, the suburbs of ancient Prague had stood. Now the beautiful sweep of parkland and the deep flowing majestic river provided the refugees a far better chance of escape than would have been possible formerly.

Sandy, The Grand Duke and the Werewolf Baron stood looking back at the gate.

"You are sure it will hold them?"

"Absolutely! Those walls and the gateway are all Essex Armaments best! Once you pull out the access pins, the shutters, the gates and the portcullis lock into place, a simple mechanical device that once operated cannot ever be undone without destroying the whole structure. They'll have to break down the walls themselves to follow us….or get some ladders…if they can find any long enough to reach. No we've got a good hour or more before they can even start the pursuit, plus we can collapse the river bridge, we'll be long gone before they get started."

Inside the great square, flooding in through the ruins of the undermined south gate the Draculian forces took possession. Pressed gangs of human workers toiled to clear the masonry from the gateway and establish a thoroughfare, and up from the street beyond came carts bearing various devices. Flying vampires, not seen for generations of Post-Dark humans, made brief and often perilous forays above the battlemented walls to try and assess the situation. Werewolves were conspicuous by their absence. Humans were divided between the overly enthusiastic *electifs*, the openly mutinous, and a much larger body of those who were 'waiting to see which way it went'. And still the Archduke had not revealed Himself.

....

"Will you *please, please,* come away now!" Carlotta begged Sandy.

"Just a second or two more. Once the main gates *and* portcullis are challenged there should be an extensive retaliatory device, I'd just like to know if it works!"

The device did work! As the noise of the first thunderous blows of battering rams echoed upwards from the square a vast cloud of masonry dust arose showing that the whole inner lining of the gatehouse was now collapsing and burying the Draculian attackers within the outer shell of the bastion, and raining down debris from the inner edge of the curtain wall.

Unfortunately it was also the very moment that the forces within the Great Square had set up a siege catapult that had been in preparation for several days, it was guided by instructions from the newly airborne Draculian vampires and projected a huge net of fist sized rocks over the gateway. The net burst in mid-flight, and a destroying cloud of stones scythed down directly upon Sandy and Carlotta.

CHAPTER 6

Sandy's mind swam back out of the darkness and depths of shadow where it had been thrust. He recalled the scream from Carlotta, the Grand Duke and Baron starting backwards, and Carlotta rushing forwards to protect him. He didn't recall any pain….just an overwhelming sense of anger that he'd not be able to complete the task he was committed to. Intense annoyance at being interrupted in what he was doing. "Dead?" he thought, "Can't be having with that, I've got things to do!"

He seemed to be surrounded by a clammy white mist, and lying upon damp, or rather wringing wet, moss. Some stones protruded here and there from the vegetation. Following his annoyance his next thought was 'Carlotta!'. She must have also been hit by the stones….how stupid!.....He should have known, should have been more ready to get out of the way!...But….find Carlotta…help her…and then find a way of carrying on!....There *had* to be a way!

He started to think logically, 'Mist….rarely ever extends right down to the ground…but is this place normal…you're dead now….Am I?...very likely…well if there is mist, and moss, and stones…then clearly its similar to home.'

Sandy pressed his left cheek down into the moss and took a sighting across the narrow gap that did in actual fact exist between the surface of the sopping wet moss and the first tendrils of the mist.

A short distance away he could see, dimly but with certainty, feet, and hands clasped around them, as of somebody sitting hugging their knees to themselves, and that somebody was Carlotta!

He struggled across the moss, sinking in quite deeply at times, and threw his arms around her shoulders. She was shaking, shivering and gently rocking herself to and fro.

"Dearest! I'm here! It's going to be alright!"

"Sandy! Thank goodness! They told me you were dead. That we would never meet again!"

"Who did?"

"The creatures who live here! You don't know….you've never been here before. We must get a place of safety, we must hide, before they return. *This place is terrible!"*

Sandy hugged Carlotta to him, drawing her into his arms.

"I think we must both be dead, but at least we are together, and whoever *they* are I'm sure they can be fought. Tell me where we are."

Carlotta continued to rock and sob, proving very difficult to console.

"Please darling, where are we, what do we do next. I've never been here before, but I suspect you have. Tell me!"

"Sweetheart! We are in the *in between*, lots of strange things live here, lots of very bad things, bad for us I mean! A vampire has to find a place of safety, one of the caves of resting, we are protected there, and when we are called we can return. Werewolves have no problems the….things…leave them alone. Humans just pass through and go into the golden mist. I do not know just what you are now, but I know if *they* find me they will throw me into the mists and….none of us knows what that means!"

"But you say the humans just pass into it?"

“Yes, for them it is natural, they seem happy with it, well the good ones do, but those with things on their conscience are less than happy….and a vampire has far more on its conscience than any human!”

“I’m not so sure, however we both still have unfinished business in Transylvania, so what are these ‘places of safety’ and how do we get to be ‘called back?’”

“Three times I have been here, each time I found a refuge, but others were less lucky. We are called back when somebody spills some of their essence upon our mortal remains, that part you know because of the work you have done with Forsterite…The refuge is usually a narrow crevice, a cave, you turn yourself into a bat and just wriggle in.”

“I don’t know that I *can* turn myself into a bat. When do you learn out about that?”

“I don’t really know. Werewolves just spend their time here as wolves, vampires spend it as very frightened bats, which is why they find a cave, hibernate and don’t wake up until it’s all over.”

“Hmmm! Doesn’t sound very safe to me! But, never mind, let’s start by looking for your cave. Is it all like this, marshy and mist clad?”

“No, there are forests, and fields and mountains, but the marsh is safe, *they* don’t come here!”

“Just who are *they?*”

“Nasty, vindictive souls. People, never animals, who are too frightened to go on and too scared to go back. They are stuck here, between things, and they pick upon the weak, the lonely and the lost. They knew I was here in the mist and called out all sorts of horrible things. I’ve seen them get hold of a lost soul and hurl it through the golden mist, or back into the world, or even into the darkness. *It is terrible!"*

Sandy spent a little longer consoling Carlotta, then,

"Where are the caves please? The nearest safest ones? If I can get you to them then I can start working out how to get us both back where we belong!"

"The mountains, through the woods and across the fields. But….where do we belong? One of the voices said that we 'belong dead'!"

"That is an archaic quote from before the Dark Years. You belong in the world of the living for as long as you wish to be there. Forget anything that has happened in the past, you are a creature of the present and of the future. Transylvania needs you, I need you and…and…*you* need you!"

…………………………

The mist had cleared, and the ground was now respectably dry and leaf covered, however the sky overhead remained at ten tenths dark grey clouds with a possible cloud base of five hundred feet (or so Sandy's mind assessed it)

Carlotta needed a lot of supporting, of holding up, and frequently stopped to stand clinging to Sandy and taking deep shuddering breaths. Sandy had been internally monitoring the situation, and making determined efforts to adjust the reality around him. It worked for a short period of time, and once he'd even been able to encourage a brief gleam of sunshine. Right now he was concentrating upon making Carlotta weigh only as much as a feather, however the advantages gained from this were outweighed by the mental exhaustion it produced, and at last he paused in a broad clearing and laid Carlotta down on the grass and sat beside her, metaphorically gasping for breath.

"Just a moment dearest. I must rest!"

....

"Wake up! Wake up!"

Sandy was being roughly shaken by somebody, or perhaps something. He didn't have time to find out which was the better description.

"Quick! They've got her! Be swift! I cannot help, but at least I can warn!"

Sandy sprang to his feet and saw at the furthest edge of the clearing a glistening golden curtain of mist. In front of it, and silhouetted against its golden glare were a small crowd of black, ragged skeletal figures, they were dragging Carlotta towards the curtain and from them a cackling, squarling, screaming chorus arose.

"Make her go! Ready or not into the mist with her!"

Sandy was already sprinting across the open space, scooping up a stone as a weapon and then smashing through the squat unseemly figures, using his stone to club and shatter and clear a path to his beloved. The figures, prompted to more swift action by his assault thrust her into the golden mist. He grasped at her wrist, the last part of her showing, and pulled hard. At the same time numerous dark leprous hands came up to thrust him into the mist along with Carlotta.

A brief, fleeting vision of intense white pure light, and then he felt himself pulling Carlotta, and himself back, back from the mist and into the forest clearing.

He saw Carlotta lying on the dead leaves and clumps of green, fresh, woodland grasses, and stood over her, lashing out at the circle of dark squat figures. As one attacked him from the front, so another leapt in from behind, but he shot out a fist to the front, kicked out to the side and then to the rear. Down fell two assailants, but many more were left. In desperation he attacked on all fronts. Fists, feet and even teeth served as weapons, and soon the circle of attackers dwindled, diminished and eventually became a mere remembrance of conflict.

Peace returned to the clearing, the forest glade, and walking stiffly from the shadows came the source of the warnings that had roused Sandy from his slumber.

He stood a full seven feet tall from his neat cloven hooves to his precisely curled and polished horns.

"I'm *so glad* you saved her!" said Pan.

……………………………………

Peterson sat in his chair, staring out at the inky black, velvet night sky.

'Nothing like a Vampire physician to let you know *just* where you are! The man was a decent sort, offered to give a 'no obligations' bite, Lucreztia had already suggested that. 'Jeffery, you are dying, let me just….just….keep you with me!'

But, somehow it didn't seem proper! He couldn't be beholden to either of them, especially Lucreztia, whom he loved so dearly. And with whom he had had done so much. Her restraint, her self-discipline, somehow it wasn't right. But, that was it. That's what you signed up for if you, err, what was the old fashioned term, 'went fantee', no, that just didn't respect the agreement, the bond, the special relationship. Still, if things went the way he was expecting, perhaps there were still a few scenes to play before the final curtain went down.

He let his eyes unfocus and dwell upon the night sky. As he had expected a point of definition began to appear. Suddenly, in fact, the dcfining point of the night was before him, on the carpet. A mocking, sarcastic voice.

"Milord! I come! You are ready to join us! No?"

"Cut with the phony accent Walter. I know you come from Yorkshire. What's the deal?"

"Oh, you know all about that! However, since you insist…. You are 'cured' of your little infirmity, I take back Lucreztia, and you become my assistant. Simple!"

"Ha! She hates you, always has! Have you nothing better to offer?"

"Better? Better? You are about to experience the ultimate decay of human flesh, the total separation from your loved one, and you ask for better terms than this? Madman! She will be happy, you will be happy, you won't even remember an unhappy time. How can you refuse?

"You'd be surprised Walter! Where's your back up? How many Vampire lords do I have to cut my way through?"

"Hah! Ever the joker! There! Outside! For the first time in many, many years they hover in the night sky, evidence of the return of the mighty one, the Archduke. You see them?

Peterson fingered the arm rests of his arm chair. "I see them. Do you see this?" he raised a small pistol cross bow, the tip of its bolt ominously dull, the Forsterite head only reflecting a small minority of the ambient candlelight.

"Hah! You think to shoot down my bodyguard? Yes, perhaps you will destroy one of them. Small loss! If they are stupid enough to be hit they deserve eternal dissolution. But you!.....You!...will serve in their place, my creature for all the ages that the world endures!"

Peterson nodded. "A small enough price, however, let us put it to the test. I am a reasonable man, have you wondered why you are not reading my mind? Is it because I have lived so many years with a Vampire, because I love and cherish your kind?" Peterson tugged at a small lever on the chairs armrest, it in turn operated a wire that released a switch, and a battery of small crossbows concealed in the window frames released their bolts. One alone of the five Vampire bodyguards failed to fall into the abyss, pierced by Forsterite crossbow bolts. The remaining guardian after a brief triumphal expression looked with increasing concern upon Peterson as he fired the tiny pistol bow and sent yet another Forsterite dart through the window and into the vampire's heart.

"So! You just give yourself more and more work to do once you are reborn! Foolish creature that you are!"

Peterson turned to the Count. "Ah Walter, or perhaps I should say 'Walters' John Walters, of Halifax! I raise my sword against you, as every gentleman should in the circumstances! How do you feel about that?"

Peterson had drawn a somewhat ornate Court sword from its scabbard, and with a certain amount of effort was bringing it to point. The tip wavered somewhat, but kept a reasonable insistence on pointing at the Counts chest.

"Even now you still persist! Can you not see that it is all over? The Archduke is restored, Transylvania is refulgent! Be sensible and join me willingly .It will be so much easier. I will even let you have Gretchen as your very own!"

Yes! But I don't want Gretchen, she has her own love. Are you still blind to what I am doing?"

"Fool! Do you think that that sword has any terrors for me? One bite and you too will see my point of view. Your last chance.... join us willingly, or be 'assimilated'!"

"*Your* last chance, Walter! Listen to your inner heart. All your people have it, despite what they think. Listen and respond. You *can* have the best of both worlds....if you try!"

"Idiot!" the Count surged forwards, actually impaling himself upon Peterson's sword.

Peterson leisurely extended a finger forwards into the complicated grip of the sword hilt and tugged at a small lever. Along the central axis of the blade small flaps opened and dull grey metal vanes extended. The Count seemed suddenly frozen, his arms rigid at his sides, his lips fixed in a sardonic grin.

"Essex Armament's best! This and the wiring throughout the room! Wonderful young fellow who sold it to me! He was a real gentleman. 'Don't leave the vanes up for more than thirty five seconds' he told me. 'That way they can recover after a week or two!' Rather nice I thought, really!"

Peterson leaned forwards from his arm chair and tweaked aside the lapel of the Counts evening suit jacket, exposing the point where the sword had plunged through waist coat and shirt and deep into the Counts heart. His questing fingers found the point where the wound, despite the blade blocking its point of entry, was oozing dark, black, sticky blood. He pushed his fingertip several times into the wound, and then slowly and deliberately withdrew his hand and inserted the bloodied fingertip into his mouth.

"You, Walter, are mine! Oh yes, I keep up-to-date! Lucreztia now has her mate for all the ages of the world, but you, *and your followers* are mine!"

....

It was a small, semi derelict inn, long since by-passed by the new road to the north. The band of *electifs (*lead by an unenthusiastic minor vampire) had briefly kicked down the door, rooted around in the cellar, and then got back on their way, eager to return to the main action on the highway.

Now, as the last of them vanished over the brow of the hill something stirred in the blackthorn thicket, and couple of low running wolf shapes, their tails brushing the ground, ears pulled back and down against their skulls insinuated themselves into the empty building. A similar shape made haste along the roadway and then remained seated inconspicuously, a sentry against the return of the *electifs.*

Shortly afterwards a distinctly human shape appeared at the doorway of the inn and signalled to somebody in the depths of the thicket.

The main room of the inn still had its large trestle table, and onto this the incomers gently placed their two burdens. Two great canvas wrapped bundles, secured with cords.

"Never have liked this bit!" said the Grand Duke. "I know that's a bit odd for a Vampire, but I just don't like bodies!"

"Come on old friend!" the Baron rested a friendly arm on the Grand Dukes shoulder. "You just stand over there, I'll let you know when we are ready to begin."

The cords were undone, the canvas sheets peeled back, and the two bodies exposed. No candlelight or dim lamp glimmer could have made their features seem more ominous. Everyone who a reason to be in the room could see perfectly well without artificial light, just the star gleam diffusing in through the windows was all they needed.

The Baron made some attempt to compose the limbs, brush hair away from brows and cheeks, gently reclose eyelids and bring some semblance of decency to the bruised and broken corpses. He sighed, shrugged his shoulders, and then turned to the Grand Duke, who seemed to be trying to lose himself within the winged collar of his great velvet cloak.

"We are ready, they are, I hope ready. Let us see if it will work!"

The Grand Duke turned around. He was wearing a very strange complicated head dress, almost a tiara, but with a red plush liner to it. His face was grey and little lines, like the creases that come to dwell on a visage untimely accustomed to great pain, crowded his features.

"My friend, once we have done this, be swift and let me rest!"

The Baron nodded, and twitched back his tunic to show a wooden stake stuck dagger-like in his belt.

The Grand Duke drew back his sleeve and took out a small knife from his pocket, stabbing it into his forearm. Dark blood spurted out and he caught it on his fingers and anointed first Sandy's and then Carlotta's brow with it. "Come back! Come back into the World! You are needed! Come back!"

The Baron reached out and with a strip of cloth bandaged the Grand Dukes arm, staunching the flow of black blood, and then hugging the frail figure to himself.

"There! It is done! Unfortunately such an act as that will have sent out ripples for all to read. You can do no more. Rest now!" and he plunged the stake home into the Grand Duke.

There was a moment of stillness, and the Grand Duke dissolved into a flurry of grey dust. Dutiful and careful hands began to transfer it into a strong glass flask, while others started to massage the hands of the bodies on the trestle table and to seek anxiously for signs of life returning.

CHAPTER 7

“Can you see who they are?”

“Not properly, looks like one vampire and six humans. Oh yes! I can see their banner now. Bloody *electifs,* they’re with Krackenheim if that device is anything to go by!”

“OK! That’s nothing we can’t handle. Wilhelm, get Franz and Heinrich up here with the crossbows, and check up on how Luther’s getting on!”

It wasn’t a proper gatehouse, it was in fact an old cottage with some holes knocked in the walls. The proper gatehouse stood a little further down the road and its windows and doors were now locked and barred. A decoy to attract the attention of any marauders.

Wilhelm beckoned Franz and Heinrich out from the backroom and pointed to the crossbows. No words, just gestures. If the other side were trying to mind read they’d not get very far if you didn’t use words. It was a very simple thing, don’t talk, don’t sub-vocalise, just point.

In a corner on an old mattress, half sitting half lying, was Luther, a very, very unwell vampire. He was wearing on his head a strange device of metal foil sheets, twisted wire and protective fabric pads.

“How is it doing Luther?”

“Not good, but I don’t think you will have to send me ‘across the way’ just yet. My Count seems to be having difficulties, perhaps that’s why he’s not trying quite so hard as he was to bring us all back to him. The helmet is working as well. What’s going on outside?”

"Scouting party. Six *electifs* and their vampire officer. We can take them!"

"Yes, but that only leaves one Forsterite arrow head. Make sure you let them get really close. I wouldn't mind their officer's field rations *if* you get the chance!"

"Will do! Anything else I can get you?"

"No, just send someone down as a messenger, in case I get through to anyone who can be of use to us."

Wilhelm left the backroom and returned to the loop-holes in the front wall. Outside shadowy figures were moving down the street, flitting from one patch of shadow to another, moving closer and closer to the town's gatehouse. Six crouching forms each ready to prove their worth to the vampire officer, each hoping to be accepted once the Arch Duke truly returned. The said officer was keeping well to the back of things, lead from the rear, *encourage les autres*, look after number one, all these maxims crowded into his mind. What matter if a vampire could move with the speed of thought, and feel a heartbeat in the darkness. The buggers had broken all the rules, they'd learned how to conceal their minds, how to fog the field of thoughts, and they had that bloody, bloody Forsterite didn't they? Get a bit of that in you and you'd be stuck in the 'other place' forever, until *they* got you and you went into the golden mist! Urgh! it didn't bear thinking about. Not what he'd got into vampirism for…. not at all! His thoughts were just a tiny bit disturbed by a little wispy tendril of warning creeping in…. and then the crossbow bolt struck him straight between the shoulder blades and he pitched forwards into the darkness.

The last of the *electifs* did have time for a vain cry about something to the effect that Dracula would return, but it wasn't that coherent, and no one who would be inspired by it was listening anymore.

Wilhelm slipped into the backroom, clutching the vampire officer's field ration pack. Luther was sitting upright with a happy expression on his face, the foil and wire device now laid aside on the bed.

"Wilhelm! Somebody must have taken out Count Walter. I think I am a free person once again!"

………………………………

Sandy cradled the tiny golden creature to his breast. A beautiful, exquisite golden furred bat. The tall figure before him said in kindly tones

"You are before the master of the beasts now! When we all of us find out what our inner form is, our 'totem' as some say, our 'sending'! I'm afraid that anyone who came into things through Carlotta's particular portal tends to end up with a flittermouse! But, is it not a beautiful one?"

Sandy pressed the tiny creature to his lips and gently kissed it

"She is safe, thanks to you! Let her be for a small while, look across the clearing, this is your moment of choosing, when you will find your creature. It is the price and the payment, the reward and the penalty for coming here!"

Sandy raised his head, still keeping the golden bat in his cupped hands. Pan slowly and gently raised his hand and the bat flew into its protective embrace. Sandy stood up and looked across the grassy clearing.

A great crescent crowd of animal figures began to appear, as if dislimning from the shadows beneath the trees, or becoming a solid part of the bright patches of daylight filtering down through the leafy canopy above.

Wolves, deer, bears, wild boar, even a unicorn, numerous small creatures, squirrels, otters, stoats, but, there in the centre of the great arc, starting to fill his vision a great white horse, and yet not always white, or so great, at times a foal with shaky legs, like the one he remembered from childhood on the farm, then the colt he had befriended as a toddler, and again the dun coloured mare who had been his first mount as an adult. It seemed to be at once young, new born, old, mature, young, fretful, confident, with a coat of every colour that it could be, and yet always one animal. He stepped forwards, putting out his hands to feel the warm soft gentleness of the muzzle, the hard strong whipcord strength of the neck muscles, letting his naked feet touch against the iron hard permanency of the hooves. He looked into deep liquid eyes that drowned you in a welcoming trust, and took one more step forwards into the body of the horse!"

Pan looked into the eyes of the tiny golden bat, "He has done well, your man! He has found his beast, now you can both be whole!"

There was so much that Sandy desired to do, so many questions he had to ask, and this place, so safe, so beautiful, so full of things to learn, but as he cantered forwards and softly and with the most wonderful harmony changed himself from the milk white horse back into his accustomed form and looked into Pan's face there was an urgent and powerful tug that grasped his very essence and drew it away from that paradise. He recalled afterwards that beautiful face, the sad eyes and the gracious curve of the horns and a parting message "We will meet again! You can always speak to me if you really wish, and meet others here, in the 'in between', not everyone shuns it! Do not be afraid, you and your lady have jobs to do! Go to them…. and be happy!"

……………………………………….

“Are you quite, quite, sure that you are alright Luther?” asked the leader of the squad

“Yes, quite sure! The Count is no longer my master.”

“Well then who is?”

“No one! Whoever sorted out Walter wasn’t interested in power. They let us all go!”

“Doesn’t that mean that someone else can come along and take you over?”

“No! That’s the whole thing about the....err....the Ambassador manoeuvre....you’re left to make up your own mind, still a vampire, but sort of....independent.”

“What about daylight, and garlic and all that sort of stuff?”

“I don’t know, I think that’s all a bit more complicated. All I know is that *I decide* what side I’m on now. I know the Arch Duke is out there, I can hear him calling, but it’s up to me to decide what I want to do. No more orders! Anarchy rules!”

“Well, if you say so, but please keep that helmet handy, just in case, eh?”

....

Sandy turned the ‘coronet’ over in his hands.

“Ye gods! A ‘kriegshelm’! He’d didn’t make it easy for himself!”

“No!” replied the Baron, “But of course he was one of the first 13, the inner circle, for years one of the Dark Apostles. Until he decided that it wasn’t right, and then he was the leader of the Great Revolt. The Arch Duke would be particularly eager to get his revenge, he would not make anything easy, and so poor old Orlov, of course he had to take all the precautions that he could!"

"And he is safe now? Really safe?"

"He will be! Once we get on the road! We cannot delay a moment longer, pulling you two back like that, it's made our position known across the Empire, be sure retaliation will follow, swift, sure, utter! We must disperse. I can spare you a scout, no more than that, we are so depleted in numbers that I cannot even be sure of getting ourselves to safety!"

"It is alright. Things have changed, we have….been away…we have learned things. It is vital we get back to England and start to organise resistance, but also that we stay in touch. Baron, I suspect that, at times you have people who every now and then…run in strange places? A meadow a long way away? Do you follow?" Sandy swept his hands up to his brow and mimed horns.

"Oh!" A moment of shock on the Barons face, and then a smile. "Ah! So you too have met *him?"*

"Indeed I have, and I think that his land is a place we can both meet when at need?"

"Perhaps….we shall see!"

……………………………………

It was a good thirty miles from the border between Transylvania and The Germanies. Far from becoming a secure border zone this was now a chequered land of tiny territories where each checkpoint handed a traveller carefully over to the next guard point.

Along the muddy track came a combination that did not, under any circumstances fit with what the guards had been warned about. "An Englishman and a Vampire Lady, detain at all costs!"

But, it couldn't be a Vampire Lady, she was riding a horse, and as everyone knows a Vampire can *never, ever,* ride a horse, no horse would ever permit *one of those creatures* to sit upon its back, it would rather die ! And, where was the Englishman, the man they said would never be far from her. The guard waved her through, noting her weariness and the drooping neck of the milk white horse, its saddlebags adding to its burden.

The guard turned back to scanning the road ahead leading down the hill into the more populous, refugee thronged, highway leading up from the direction of Prague. Behind him, un-noticed, the Lady somehow or the other was now wearing a very attractive pale grey riding habit rather than the deep purple one, and the horse had become a sympathetic dapple grey. No one noticed, which was exactly what the horse had hoped for!

....

The Innkeeper had been very kind. "Welcome Milady! There is stabling for your horse....oh....sorry...I have clearly mis-seen...you have no horse.....Milord, Milady, please do come in, I will have your bags taken up stairs. We are quite, quite safe here, the soldiers have already inspected the inn and made sure we are *safe.* Please, you have nothing to fear!

Sandy had carefully checked the approaches to the inn, there certainly was a 'safe' cordon around the inn, the local forces had declared the area 'Transylvanian', just what their criteria were was dubious, but for one night at least they seemed safe. Carlotta was still perturbed by the time on 'the otherside', she had 'appetites' he was sure, and needed sustenance. Well, having been a key player in the development of vampire field rations helped! Carlotta was going to need some very special dietary supplements, to put it mildly. Outside, beyond the bright red flags put up to denote a state recognised hostelry, were a mixed regiment! Human infantry under

Vampire officers! Just how long would they keep going? Once the Arch Duke declared himself the general view was that such units would be reorganised, but until that point everyone was carrying on and hoping for the best.

A good time for action.

Carlotta was comfortably settled down in the bed room, and he'd set a few simple traps to deter intruders. If any unwanted callers came Carlotta would awake, and he knew, absolutely knew, she would easily destroy any attackers.

"I'm just nipping out for a moment or two darling! There's a trip wire set across the door and I'll whistle when I'm ready to climb up the balcony"

"Right oh dear, Take care!"

And out Sandy went. It was, he felt afterwards a light hearted romp. He now had the ability to skip in front of vampire minds, to delude, to confuse, to confusticate! Each officer was persuaded to leave his post, to investigate, to deliver an opinion, and....then....once he had done his duty, somehow or the other his field rations pouch was missing. Odd, but there it was!

Sandy climbed carefully back over the stone balcony, bowed to Carlotta, and offered her four Vampire Officer field ration packs, each crammed with 'donated substance' pastilles.

Carlotta sat up in the four-poster bed, the counterpane drawn up around her neck and opened the first of the packages, to Sandy it looked for all the world like somebody being presented with an expensive box of chocolates!

After a while she closed the box of pastilles, placed them on the bedside table and beckoned Sandy to her side.

“Thank you! That must have been a lot more difficult than it seemed, I don’t suppose they gave up their field rations willingly!”

“Oh, not as hard as all that really, more sleight of hand than anything else. Anyway, none of them saw me, or even knows what happened, so it’s all alright. Do you feel a bit more comfortable now?”

“Yes! You know it’s not usually that much of a problem, you only need ‘substance’ once in a while….but after being ‘there’….ugh! Didn’t you feel anything unusual?”

“Very hungry, certainly, so I guess that’s the same sort of thing. You get some rest now, we need to push on as early as we can. They’re still very confused at the moment, but once they get sorted out it’ll be a lot harder than this to avoid being caught. Rest!”

Sandy seated himself in the chair next to the bed and leafed through a pocket atlas, he didn’t seem ready for bed yet, despite his advice to Carlotta.

“Aren’t you coming to bed as well?”

“In a moment! I want to fix tomorrow’s route in my mind first.”

Carlotta settled down to sleep, and Sandy soon stopped looking at the atlas and gazed fondly on Carlotta. There was something strange, strange even for a vampire, about her. He’d obviously only got Carlotta as an example of a ‘close up’ vampire, but she’d definitely undergone a subtle change since their joint outing to ‘the other side’. An odd aura, a glow almost, and there were times when he seemed to be seeing something like flakes of gold-leaf, microscopic fragments of purest gold in her eyes and at times in the warmth of her cheeks. The moment however passed, and he closed the book and slipped into the bed with Carlotta.

CHAPTER 8

"Last stage My Lady, last stage!" Sandy had paused, and was presently a very travel stained man staggering along under the weight of two large leather travelling cases, he also had a smaller shoulder bag with an inordinate number of buckles and clasps. (There are just so many times you can transform harness with baggage before things begin to get muddled.) The strain of staying in a transformed state for so long was beginning to tell.

"Even the best vampire never stays as a bat for more than a few hours, and as for doing it by daylight, well it's never been done. Goodness only knows what it's doing to you!"

Carlotta, in keeping with the characters they were using, was carrying nothing more than a parasol, she was however scanning the way ahead.

"There *is* a checkpoint before the border. I sense it just over the brow of the hill. All very confused though. Lots of people, people and horses. You *are* sure the Germans will let us in? I'd hate to make a run for it and be stuck with a raised bridge!"

"I have the password! It's one of the advantages of following the trade that I do, that there are all sorts of things you know."

"But, how do you know that they will know it's a password? Surely the thing gets changed regularly!"

"Ordinary passwords, yes. But if the captain of the guard puts *my password* into the decoder, then we are on a fast track to Reichenbach and Prince Ruprecht."

“How long does this take?”

“All Unsberg frontier fortresses use a generic ‘wake up’ word, that will alert the captain, then allow…say a minute or two for them to punch the password into the mechanism, another minute to turn the handles and read the instruction, a good two minutes of frantic shouting once they realise who’s outside, the gates open, and if we are really lucky they launch a sortie to bring us in!...Yes…we are going to need some time, just rushing the bridge-house and hoping to dash across *is* a little optimistic!”

“Oh well! Let’s push on a bit and see if there’s anything to be done.”

…………………………………………

The wind was blowing strong and fresh from the border. Carlotta thought it was being a bit over poetic, the smell of freedom and all that, but it was letting her account for the detailed make up of the checkpoint.

Horses and men, very sweaty men and very tired horses, lots and lots of them. No vampires however, which seemed a bit odd, but on the other hand the checkpoint was a only a little over a long bowshot from the border, and German border guards were notoriously trigger happy with their cross bows. It would make sense to only use human troops, expendable and quite unaffected by Forsterite. There was the distinct smell of the lily-of-the-valley perfume affected by the *electifs,* so no doubt that was where the leadership was coming from. She could of course try and find out if being a bat was still as perilous in daylight as it used to be, but it was quite enough managing to drag a normal body around without transforming as well, she really didn’t know how Sandy did it, but thank goodness he *was* doing it. She guessed it must be his different constitution, or his ‘sending’, after all Werewolves had no problems staying as wolves all day long if they wanted to,(though admittedly they took simple ages afterwards to stop suddenly sitting down dog-style and having a good scratch!)

Sandy returned, worming his way through the low bushes and staying well down. He outlined the disposition of the forces ahead of them.

"A complete squadron of Uhlan lancers with some very uncomfortable *electifs* on even more uncomfortable horses. Quite some picket line. We really *are* important! A hundred head of crack cavalry blocking our path! But, that's all that is there! No infantry, no police or border guards, in fact nobody at all that knows anything about the place, the Uhlans are from up away north, Krakow I guess. This might be to our advantage."

"I don't quite see how, they must have a picket line so wide that we'd never creep through. I would guess it would be a rider every ten metres, and they've probably got a troop deployed behind that to catch anyone who slips past. We need some other way, perhaps go along to the next crossing point?"

"You know that the last set of guards we got through (the ones at Stryberg?) they will be on our trail by now and they can't be very far behind. We can't double back, and anyway I'm just about done in, it's got to be now or never. I've got an idea, but we need to make preparations."

"What do you intend?"

"Not absolutely sure just yet, but first of all we need a well-built Uhlan, plus his saddle and lance. It needs to be done very, very carefully!"

Carlotta looked doubtful, "You have no idea just what you are asking, do you? It goes very much against all that I have striven for, but…a well built one you say?"

"Yes, but not a sergeant or a corporal, just an ordinary trooper. For choice one from the signals detachment at the end of the picket line. You see them?"

....

Trooper Hamstervich had no idea why he excused himself from the detachment, neither did his fellows, but somehow or the other it just wasn't their business, not their concern. Hamstervich blindly trotted off and vanished into the undergrowth by the little clump of trees along the south road.

"What am I doing here?" he asked himself, "Perhaps I need to dismount, tie up the horse in the shade just here, take off my uniform and rest?"

....

"You don't really need to do much!" said Carlotta, he won't struggle or anything like that, just tie him up and gag him, he'll come around soon enough once I stop staring at him. Why did we need such a well built one?"

"Because," said Sandy sorting through the man's uniform and turning sleeves and trouser legs the right way around again, " because you would never fit in the uniform of the average Uhlan trooper, lightweight men on lightweight horses, by Uhlan terms this fellows a monster!"

"Ah! I begin to see! You'll have to explain to me how the saddle works. You just transform your clothing into the gear when you change, I have no idea how it all works."

"Not so difficult, but you will need to get the girths right otherwise it could be excessively embarrassing! Right, start sorting through his saddle bags, if he's signals then there ought to be pennons, banners, flags, all that sort of thing."

Carlotta unbuckled small pockets and pulled out a mixture of multi-coloured silk flags and ribbons. Every now and then Sandy pounced upon one and attached it by its corner toggle to another flag already in his hand. At last he had a continuous run of eight brightly coloured flags, with a long pennant streamer at the start. Taking the troopers lance he treaded a strong cord through the ring just below the lance head and drew it downwards, attaching it to the string of flags.

"A signal? You think we can bluff our way through?"

"No, this is the password!"

"What?"

"Well, the secret about the 'special' passwords is that they aren't actually words. We ride up to the bridge-house and wave this at them, for choice you slam the lance down into the ground and leave it standing there to make sure they see it. Do you think you can do it?"

"What about you doing it?"

"I'm the horse, you are the rider!"

"Alright. I suppose I can handle a lance without falling off. How do the flags work?"

"You just hoist them up the lance and tie off the cord on the hand grip (it's got a special clip, just there), only don't do that bit until we're almost there, we don't want to give the game away to the Uhlans, they're not known for their sense of humour!"

"Very well, but it just leaves how we get through them!"

"I've been working on that. Plenty of time to think when you're being a horse. I know it's not 'politically correct' these days, but do you remember the 'children of the night' stuff.

Carlotta shuddered, "I don't care to, but it had its uses, however, there are no truc wolves anywhere near here, and even if you did have a pack or two I don't see….."

………………………………

Hamstervich seemed to be re-joining his detachment, no one was particularly surprised, though he did sit a little oddly, and seemed to be having problems with his hands. The horse seemed to be almost the one he usually rode, but no one really wanted to notice either that or the non-issue saddlebags he had acquired.

The signal detachment was stationed at the extreme west of the picket line, the *electifs,* still with very unruly mounts were stationed at the extreme east. A wave of uneasy began to flood along the line, and when one hundred plus very highly bred, pampered and over trained horses become uneasy it takes a great deal of skill, judgement and experience to restore calm. Normally a trooper and his mount are in a beautiful synergy, a symbiosis of action which some say comes far more from the psychic than the physical sphere. This may well be true. The Polish Uhlans were very practical men, not given to fanciful actions, they calmed and patted their mounts, they spoke soft words, but the fear and the terror began to overwhelm the horses, and perhaps it was true that man and horse had a far greater psychic bond that the Transylvanian manual of horsemanship would admit to, for the terrors began to grow also in the minds of the riders. As you might expect the squad of *electifs* broke first, stumbling from a canter into a full headed gallop as they fled eastwards over the sandy turf. The Uhlans, to do them credit did hold back just enough to laugh at the *electifs,* being thrown up and down in the saddle, franticly reaching out toes in a vain attempt to re-find stirrups, but then they too were overtaken by the equine tsunami. Oddly, very oddly no horse lost its rider, they seemed to take pains to make sure there were no empty saddles, but they covered the ground!

One rider remained, and its mount hurried it towards the Bridge-house, where the rider brandished a colourfully decorated lance, and then hurled it down so that its base spike embedded itself firmly in the timbers of the drawbridge. Then in the shadows of the bastion the rider dismounted, and after a slightly confused scene fell into the arms of a travel stained gentleman staggering under the weight of two large leather travelling bags.

Trumpets were being blown, gongs sounded. Gates swung open and from several postern gates armoured men equipped with crossbows tumbled out taking up defensive positions around the bridge head. More figures appeared, and assisted the two weary travellers across the bridge and through the gates. The sortie rapidly withdrew, and the drawbridge was raised.

When the guards from Stryberg finally caught up all they found was one standard issue Transylvanian cavalry saddle, which they kindly returned to its owner, once they had untied his bonds and removed his gag!

....

Reichenbach! If you have visited, and especially if you have been a guest of the principality of Unsberg, then you will not have forgotten the Grand Hotel, with its cliff top terrace, the endless cascade of the falls, the snowy peaks, so much more snowy nowadays than at any time in their past. The way the waiter places a sprig of Edelweiss on the table when he brings the Kirsch, the soft clonk of cowbells in the street as a sleigh goes past. And, over all the slate covered conical roof tops of the castle with its pennants and bannerettes and its gaily bedecked hoardings.

Unsberg has not the size, the complexity, or even for that matter the ancientry of the larger states, but it is special, and as the one of the Germanies most closely aligned to Transylvania it is very special (indeed Prince Ruprecht proudly shows a family portrait gallery that indicates both werewolf and vampire ancestry, but he is *of course* stoutly German and *human.* He also takes an active hand in running the country, particularly its defence!)

This is the throne room. It is in fact a suite in the Grand Hotel, far more convenient than the castle, which largely works as part of the lucrative tourist trade. Americans save for the best part of a lifetime to pay for a month here, and the Unsbergers are dedicated and generous hosts, but of course the guests can rarely return, which makes it so much more special!

Sandy and Carlotta have had a chance to freshen up after the train journey from the frontier. Not all a train journey, since in deference to Transylvanian sensitivities the railhead is fifteen miles from the frontier so that no polluting steam and coal smoke will taint Transylvanian air.

Carlotta has, of course travelled here before, but the reek of the steam train is always an exotic smell, and the luxurious cosiness of the carriages (the State Suit of Carriages has been put at their disposal) has been a welcome change after two weeks on the road, hiding and fighting their way out of difficult situations. A very polite and attentive junior officer has escorted them, and has listened avidly to Carlotta's account of the journey, backed up by Sandy's comments. Sandy seems to know the officer from somewhere in the past, and almost seems to be sharing a private joke with him, Carlotta is not put out by this, rather she is enjoying being the centre of attraction

But, anyway, now they are about to go into the throne room, they have to explain their presence in Unsberg, convince the authorities that they mean no harm to the principalities interests and institutions, and should then be allowed to move onwards to England. This should be straight forwards for Sandy, but it is not so simple for Carlotta, a Transylvanian national, whose country is now in the midst of what has clearly moved from an insurrection to a civil war, and could very soon be at war with its neighbours. What will the reaction be? Will the troubles spill over into Unsberg's somewhat mixed culture? Sandy is hopeful, but Carlotta is wondering if an 'official' marriage will be needed to confer English citizenship upon her.

The helpful young officer has vanished, and a pair of uniformed courtiers now beckon them forwards and pull open the great gilded ornate double doors.

Prince Ruprecht is clearly 'at home', people are queueing for an audience, officials sit at side desks and take down state decisions and issue passes, permits, documents etc. The business of state is going on at full bore. The prince is in fact seated on a simple gilt chair and dealing with difficult cases and making decisions that his civil service have lined up for his attention.

Carlotta is looking worried, Sandy still has a half grin on his face. On the walls portraits of past rulers are interspersed with oil paintings of wild rugged scenery and craggy hill tops beset with romantic ruins.

The figure on the gilt chair turns around and looks up to see them standing amid the crowd of supplicants.

"Carlotta, Sandy! Nice to see you!"

It is the nice junior officer from the train, but it is also *Prince Ruprecht!*

“Thank you for keeping the secret Sandy! Excuse me please Carlotta, a little foible of mine! I hope you’ve enjoyed the surprise! Seriously though, I prefer to hear people’s stories and get to know them *before* they know I’m a prince!”

“But how?” Carlotta began “Your thoughts….I never knew…”

“Ah!”, he was all beams and sparkles “Great-grandmother! You see, the painting over there! The lady with the black pearls and the gold filigree! She was ‘of the night’. I suppose I’ve got a few useful inherited traits from her, and keeping my thoughts private is one of them! But let’s get you sorted out. Gunther! Bring me the diplomatic bag, the London one!”

They were ushered into a small side room, its walls decorated in a red velvety paper, over which was laid a tracery of fine wires. Ruprecht pointed briefly to the wires. “Took your advice Sandy, thought screening, we use it for all confidential offices now!”

The diplomatic bag was placed on the table and once its triple lock was opened Ruprecht delved around inside and withdrew a bulky brown paper envelop. The flap was fastened down with red wax, and the great seal of England had been impressed upon it.

“Somebody expects you! These arrived from London last week. I suspect you are both now accredited agents of Their Britannic Majesties.”

Sandy cracked open the seal and pulled out a wad of official and other documents .Amongst them were fully attested English citizenship papers for Carlotta, diplomatic passports for them both and letters of clearance good for transport throughout the Germanies and every hotel between Reichenbach and Wilhelmshaven. There was also a purse of gold coins sufficient to meet every day travelling needs for quite some time. Tucked in between the various government papers was a small envelope with the Essex Armaments company coat of arms. It too was sealed down with wax, and Sandy made several minute examinations of the seal and the seams of the envelope before placing it, unopened, inside an inner pocket. His thoughts, Carlotta noted, remained veiled.

"So! A day or two of Unsberg hospitality, and then no doubt you will be on your way? I am thinking that a great deal of effort has been spent to get you both to London as soon as possible?"

"Effort has indeed been spent, but I'd welcome some news first of what has been happening. We have been adrift for quite some time. I estimate, what? Two weeks since the fall of Prague?"

"Three! Well, almost three. But, come into the 'Ministry for Foreign Affairs', it's just across the way, and you can read all the papers, and our own briefing reports."

The 'Ministry of Foreign Affairs' turned out to be yet another hotel suite, but this time set up as a very effective small library with atlases, newspaper cutting folders and a filing cabinet containing all the state briefings for the last eighteen months. Older briefings were archived in the hotels cellars. A speaking tube communicated with the kitchens, and food and drinks could be ordered directly and delivered through a dumb waiter. The fine metal filaments were again in evidence set into the wall covering. Sandy noticed that a much heavier metal matrix was stretched across the windows, and that the glass had recently been replaced with dense thick panes that seemed to be restricting the light. He looked quizzically at this arrangement. Ruprecht gave a wry grin. "Just a precaution!"

"Against what?"

"Assassination attempts! Our family has a complicated ancestry, and I actually have a small collection of Draculian cousins, I am making no accusations, but two of my relatives recently died in *unusual* circumstances. I very much doubt that the Privy Council would recognise my Great Grandmothers second husbands third wife's nephew, since he was adopted by assimilation rather than actually 'born', but there it is! Better safe than sorry! But, put away dull care as your poet says, for tonight we have a Grand Ball! It's about that time of month and we can't disappoint the Americans, the Royal Wardrobe is at your joint disposal, and given your new diplomatic status you will, of course, dine with me at the high table!"

CHAPTER 9

They were 'in' the Royal Wardrobe. Truly 'in'! Rows and rows of hangers supporting dresses, suits, individual garments, whole matching sets of items stretched into a dark, candle lit distance. Assistants equipped with lanterns hovered nearby, seamstresses awaited orders. A cane-work trolley on spindly iron wheels stood by to receive garments. Far away the pleasant scents of heated linen and cotton spoke of a pressing room where the best Parisian *blachiseures* kept irons ready to press, goffer and crimp.

Sandy had, so far been very conservative in his selections.

"Isn't there some sort of uniform? You would look so dashing with gold braid and a military jacket!"

"Well," he grudgingly responded "There is the company uniform…"

"No, that's not what I mean. Didn't you serve in one of the regiments once?"

"Yes, I was a full Captain in the Essex Hussars. Cherry pink pelisse with sky blue facings…I'd rather not!"

Carlotta dug, and dug, and unearthed in his thoughts something that was in fact rather special.

"Oh! Something's coming through!" Sandy looked embarrassed. "Good grief! The Unbothnian uprising? What on earth where you doing there?"

"Trying to stop people being stupid. It was my first big job. It went wrong!"

"No it didn't! I wrote up the paperwork! *You* were Sikander?"

"Just the way they tried to pronounce my name. Anyway it's a long time ago, and I wasn't in uniform, so that's that!"

"Oh no *my lord!* You rallied the defenders and led the cavalry charge!"

"Well, I did have the company's new body armour on, the stuff that only fits under a dress uniform, which is why I was wearing....what I was..."

"Yes, and that is why the mysterious Sikander was, *in absentia,* made a lifetime Colonel of the Hungarian Royal Guard!"

Sandy reluctantly submitted to the uniform being found among the great bank of outfits. "I suppose," he asked "I can't persuade you to wear an Uhlan's uniform, those jodhpurs, well, they were something rather special!"

It was not, at the end of the day, such a hardship, but the story would now have to come out about the cavalry charge outside Budapest, and that would mean lots of difficult explanations. Meanwhile Carlotta was trying to choose between a dress that was half of nothing and another that would, if broken down into sensible sized portions, cloth the population of a small village!

The seamstress was not in the least put out by Carlotta using the old vampire trick of willing the dress to fit, but she was gratified when Carlotta asked her to 'please sort out the button holes, I never *can* get them right!'

....

Alone in their suite they worked through the bundle of papers, an eclectic mixture passed on by the Foreign Office, but originating in many different quarters. After some half hour or so of reading through the mass of documents Carlotta spoke.

"Sandy! It looks like a government in exile is already being set up in London. Transylvania has, of course, declared that the set up is only a rebel group with no status, but England at least is recognising it, Ireland as well as far as I can see. They want me to contact them when we get there….Oh! The six Grand Dukes made a group communication before they…er… 'left', saying that as the legitimate leaders of Transylvania they do not recognise the Archduke, or the Draculian party….and that they will join with the exiles when 'the time is right'."

"Do they say who represents Transylvania until that time?"

"Erm…there's something here, it's from a letter to Their Majesties….. 'given the current difficulties, we advise that the werewolf Barons be considered the present spokesmen for the Empire and that all others (ourselves included) be treated with a kindly caution until the threat of the Archduke is neutralised'…well, that's straight talking, I can hear Orlov's words in there!"

"Anything else?"

"Yes, I, well both of us, have been requested to address the werewolf council in London, and the senior Baron leading the exiles, in consultation with Plenderleith, has stated that both you and I are now considered nationals of both England and Transylvania…Dual nationality! That's a first!"

"Umm! So now my loyalties are being divided between England, Transylvania *and* the Company. That's going to be fun!"

"How do you mean?"

“Well, as you know part of the armaments business rules are that we favour no single country, not even our own, they all get equal treatment so that war is less likely to happen. Now I’ve become a political figure….I’m not really complaining, but it will need careful handling.”

“Yes, but…you are committed to peace in Europe, to equality, to all the good things, won’t it just be easier now that you have a right to represent all the major players?”

“Possibly, but I just hope everyone else sees it that way. I know I’m going to do my best to make things work!...Anyway, since we now have no secrets, and to emphasise that we are a partnership, here’s some interesting news from EA! You’ll be aware of part of it already. You remember the Balkan Project? Yes? That little matter of a frontier defence barrier where the wastelands begin?”

“Obviously! The time we’ve both spent on it over the last three years of course I do!”

“Right. Now, did you know that the Essex Armaments construction battalion that was sent down there was engaged in a little light espionage? No? Well, neither did I, but it seems that Orlov and my Chief were up to something, and neither of us were told!”

“But what were they spying on? And what would they have to gain? Was it problems with the Draculians?”

“Seems that the local Kravitzen had made very clear orders about *not* carrying out any reconnaissance or border patrols, *and* that the Construction Battalion started to hear strange local rumours. It was kept quiet for diplomatic reasons, but the neutrality of the wastelands has been impugned!”

“By whom?”

"Possibly the Chinese, no one's too sure yet, but it looks likely."

"Where's the information coming from?"

"Well, you're aware of the 'Mission to the Wastelands?"

"..Yes…Greek humans and werewolves…they try to, er improve living conditions, that sort of thing. In fact I recall that your company made some sort of protective devices for them to use so that they could go on working with, er…difficult cases!"

"Yes, that's right. There's a common theme running through all revenants that a particular combination of metals will have a very unfortunate effect upon them , silver, forsterite, and so on….(goodness only knows what *my* nemesis is) Anyway, we found that a light metal wand made up of very, very pure bismuth sandwiched with platinum acts as a sort of cattle prod, if you use it carefully you can fend off a hungry Zombie, and after a while, condition it not to attack you. Very useful if you're trying to help them. But, to cut to the chase, according to this letter, some months ago the Chief received a report from the Battalion that they'd picked up a wounded werewolf, struggling back to the frontier with a human companion on his last legs who had in their possession a Zombie control wand marked with Chinese ideograms, it didn't look like an Essex Armaments wand. The werewolf only lasted a few hours, they tried to help him, but they missed a slender silver dart lodged in his neck, it had been coated with some sort of anti-corrosion varnish, so the effect was slowed down. The human survived a little longer, but he was only able to give a very incoherent account of a Zombie village being attacked, and people led off into slavery. The Chief spoke to Orlov, and together they authorised a covert surveillance project, the upshot of which is that we now know that Zombies are being rounded up as slave labour for some kind of mining enterprise located deep within what used to be Afghanistan. *We* need to look out for an agent apparently, and give him, or her assistance! Us! I'd at least hoped they would give me a contact to raise the local Companies agent to give *us* a helping hand!"

"Perhaps there's a reason. Consider, somebody at Essex Armaments was able to raid the armoury for those dart guns, and somebody stole the E17 formula. Who can you trust?"

"True! Alright! So, we have to look out for the company's agent and give *them* a helping hand."

"Fine! How do we recognise them?"

"That's all here, at least it is when I've figured out the code. The Chief was taking no chances, plain speak for the job, but we've got to check back for the password!"

"Can I have a look, *we're* very good at this sort of thing! Where do we start?"

"Well, the letter says to be prepared to help somebody passing the word 'houndstoothscheck', except that isn't the password. Houndstoothscheck is our clue to finding the real password, that way if anyone has intercepted.."

"Stop! It's not just us vampires that get too involved in having to explain all the details. I guess that since this is meant to be straight forwards ,we take each letter in houndstoothscheck as a number based upon position in the alphabet, and that checks backwards in the letter from the word houndstoothscheck and from that we then read out…gibberish! Um, oh, yes, take the alphabet backwards….yes, it's intervals between, not numerical value, and…ah…clever…."

Sandy watched bemused as Carlotta spoke faster and faster and ran her finger at lightning speed across the letter, finally stopping and saying in triumph

“The password is composed of two five letter words, ‘s’ being the indicator to change the sequencing, letter replication is not a clue to solution because the code refers to intervals between letters, not letter value, so ‘satin dress white’ is the answer!”

“Excellent! It worked!”

“What do you mean, ‘it worked’?”

“You found the password! The company’s code system is a little bit, er…naughty! We know that anything short of mechanical encryption isn’t going to foil a vampire mind. You’ve found the first half! The second part…..”

“Is a recombination of the two messages?”

“That’s what you’re supposed to assume, but in fact all cipher users commit to memory a simple phrase , which is currently ‘Pink Cotton Shirt’, basically colour/fabric/garment. The coded message tells you the order to use the three words in, there are 3x3x3 combinations, 27 different ways to use the three standard words. More than enough for safety, and the change to the code is simple to apply.”

“So the password will be Cotton Shirt Pink?”

“Exactly! Well, in fact those three words in sequence , maybe with spacers to make it look like a normal conversation. The standard reply to indicate that you know what’s going on is ‘chrysanthemum’.”

“That’s all really rather clever! Once you understand it, it’s very logical!”

“I’m glad you approve, you’re the first person outside the company to have it explained!”

"Thank you for your trust! Now, what are we going to do at this Ball!"

"Well, I thought we'd dance the night away and then make mad passionate love until sunrise!"

"Yes, that goes without saying, but we need to find your agent, and there's potential assassins to consider, not to mention the fact that we are now 'diplomatic personalities' and will need to be introduced to the company. Ruprecht will no doubt want to capitalise upon our presence for his paying guests!"

…………………………………

The great ballroom was slowly filling with guests, both paying and official. If you have never had the opportunity to visit Unsberg and its Capital Reichenbach, then you will not have seen the wonderful opulence, the 'luxury in depth' of the ball room. Where Transylvania excels in a dark, deep, romantic atmosphere so typified by Der Rosenburg, Unsberg has a golden, glittering jolliness about it that seems to boast how much it can afford to spend on its glamour. This is of course a deception, in many ways Unsberg is the least wealthy of the Germanies, but it depends upon its visitors believing otherwise, so gold leaf covers carved wood and mirrors reflect and double the size of rooms, and the number of chandeliers, and the quantity of candles being burnt. Satin masquerades as silk, and superbly cut glass gems do the service of diamonds, while an excellent and as yet undetected deception with the local white wine causes everyone to believe that only the best French champagne is being served!

In the minstrels gallery, overlooking the assembling guests are Sandy and Carlotta, Prince Ruprecht is pointing out the features of the room.

“All show, of course! The old ball room at the *schloss* is all made of the real thing! At least it was until we started to strip out the precious metals to pay for setting this up. There are advantages though about starting from scratch. All the walls are wired, ‘what happens in the great ball room stays in the great ball room’, well, more or less, but there are no prying minds trying to listen in. The huge number of mirrors and the reflections mean that it is easy for us to covertly observe the guests and prevent ‘unfortunate mishaps’, staff are trained to spot trouble and gently and diplomatically intervene, as a result we host most of the major diplomatic events throughout the Germanies, even the French come here if they want to feel really safe!”

“And yet you are concerned about assassins?”

“Yes, especially with current events. For generations it has been so predictable. An assassin would always be a vampire. Only they had the speed, the silence, the *aplomb* to succeed, so who would employ anyone else? But now? Well, you two are not the only ‘oddities’. Mostly it’s being done with very extreme devices. I guess your company knows about them, in theory at least, but…well last year I sent your ‘Chief’ a few artefacts we came across while dealing with a little problem. There had been an assassination attempt, oh, not on me! A relative, someone who was in somebody’s way, we don’t know who. Anyway, by good luck we had a mixed team on duty that day, and it was the human team member who spotted it. The vampire and the werewolf had no idea! Almost blind to what was going on! However the attempt was foiled, and they gave chase. Three assassins. They escaped on skis, it all happened up at one of the family chalets above the treeline. Kurt, that was the human, was on skis, and was having to talk the other two guards in. Even in open view they couldn’t seem to concentrate upon the enemy, as I said he was on skis, and the vampire and the werewolf were on foot, and going fast enough to have overtaken Kurt if they wanted to, but they couldn't, because they just had no way to *focus* on the assassins! The miscreants decided to cut across the glacier, that way they could have made their way up into the old mines and we'd have lost them, for sure. But they didn't. Kurt was certain they'd laid out their escape route already, he even found marker flags set up to take them across the crevasse, except somebody had moved the markers, and all three went straight down into the 'bone grinder'. It's a horrific chasm with a fast moving steam at the bottom, all boulders and grit from the melt water. Anything going into that place doesn't come out in one piece, or until the spring thaw. But, come out they did, or their bones at least, and that was the amazing part. We found a few pieces of long bones, and a large fragment of skull. That fragment was what I sent to Essex Armaments, it had a network of wires embedded in the bones! You could see the channels that had been made to let in the metal, and where the bone had grown over! I ask you? Who would let somebody do that to them? But, it explained a great deal, at least I think it did. A totally shielded brain that no revenant would be able to read or influence! Well, that's why we are no longer considering ourselves 'secure' any more. Out in that ball room may be all sorts of individuals, from goodness knows where, and working for….well I have my suspicions, but I'll say no more!"

The ball room was now a blaze of colour and glitter. Every paying guest seemed to have found some sort of uniform or decoration they were entitled to wear, and the richly restrained European military costumes gave an interesting background to American fraternity, army, navy and air-force costumes, including some dubious, but intensely colourful ones from the newer territories south of Panama.

"So," Carlotta asked "Just what security are you fielding tonight?"

"The waiting staff are a mixture of human and werewolf. We are lucky in Unsberg to have quite a few families that are true hybrids, they seem to be a lot more observant than most, they have been assigned to key points to observe. There are six vampires serving at table and trying to pick up anything odd, but with so many people it will be difficult. Together they will deal with the more everyday threats. Human watchers will be watching the revenant staff to see if they start to behave oddly, if they are being diverted or distracted in some way. There are marksmen in concealed positions of course, but that is only for use *in extremis,* it would be very bad for trade if we had to shoot anyone! *Ah!* It was so easy until the year before last, you just had to make sure nobody bit anybody (or at least didn't bite anyone unless they'd been invited to!)"

……………………………………

Sandy and Carlotta walked through the open doors into the ball room.

"You didn't let him know we were expecting to meet somebody?"

"No. I trust Ruprecht, but I don't always trust those people around him. Anyway, if there are assassins waiting to pounce then no doubt they will have identified most of Ruprecht's people by now, and if they see them looking out especially for us it could be counterproductive. No, we just work it between ourselves, the fewer people who know about it the better."

The footman waiting at the doors loudly announced their arrival, and they swept into the ball room.

The heat from the thousands of candles and the background of oil lamps was only partly taken up by the high vaulted golden ceiling, and both men and women alike fluttered fans to gain some temporary respite from the warmth. Liveried staff were unbolting the lofty glass-panelled doors that opened onto the terrace, and a welcome icy cold zephyr began to make the ball room a more conducive place for dancing.

The gallery was now filled with a string orchestra and traditional melodies from Vicnna and further south started to be heard. Just enough to awaken a gentle swaying of bodies and speculative trying out of dance steps.

Prince Ruprecht, escorting a very nervous paying guest, started the dancing, speedily handing his lady over to a gentleman-in-waiting after a generous circuit of the ball room.

He seemed to be very concerned indeed with the organisation of the waiting staff, which raised his estimation in the eyes of a party of elderly ladies from Nebraska quite considerably.

"A Prince, and he still finds time to make sure all the little things are done properly. Oh, isn't that just so Old World?"

……………………………………………

"Three of them, your Highness. Just like last time!"

"Are you sure Kurt?"

"Absolutely! Hans and Piotr have to try really hard to even be aware of them! It's just like last time. But I've got it sorted out! You can always find them just by having a human watcher team up with a vampire and count people together, it's easy that way. We've got them 'registered' now, and if they get lost we can pick them up at once. One of them keeps changing gloves, and button holes, all the little things we usually pass on to other watchers so they know who they are following, they know our techniques!"

"Very good! Who are they after?"

"That's the interesting thing Your Highness. They haven't found them yet. They just keep searching, searching and searching. Clearly it's not anyone using their normal identity. I think we have somebody here *incognito* that they are after!"

Hmm! Could be, or it could be a way to distract us from their real mission. Keep watching, and keep up the protection on all our *vulnerable* guests. Good work, too! That's a really useful way of finding them in future!"

……………………………………..

Sandy and Carlotta were a tiny self-supporting world twirling around amid a sparkling constellation of dancers, all moving in a cosmic swirling procession around the ball-room.

"Have you spotted anybody yet?"

"No, we just need to show ourselves to everyone, and then keep an eye open during the interval, perhaps we need to sit the next dance out together, on the terrace maybe? Give them plenty of time to and opportunity to come to us?"

"Seems logical! But what about our own safety?"

"Did you put that armoured sheet underneath your bodice?"

"Yes, it's not as heavy as the one I used to use. Are you sure it's good enough?"

"Quite, you don't have to worry about Forsterite splinters anymore! That will keep out daggers and crossbow bolts, and we know we can both 'come back' now. …So…. Nothing to worry about!"

"Ha! You may have had a good time 'in between', but it still makes me shudder. Something happened to me. I know you pulled me out of the mist, but…"

"I know, you've had a…a sort of…*golden* look ever since."

"Yes. Well, I don't want to go back for a second time just yet. Now, come on, concentrate on the dancing!"

CHAPTER 10

After the exertions of dancing and the still considerable heat of the ball room the terrace was pleasantly chilly! Waiters hovered about bringing glasses of chilled 'champagne' and trays of canapés designed to suit all palates and dietaries.

Several dancers had gravitated to the wide comfortable cane chairs, and every so often Sandy or Carlotta would stand up to greet another guest or to visit the small round table set with dainties.

Eventually the passage of guests became such that they both gave up trying to sit and remained standing with a small company of tourist guests asking about Sandy's uniform or about Carlotta's jewellery.

A rather dumpy American lady with all the soft drawl of the south was running her hands over the mock silver braid frogging of Sandy's tunic. Her fingers seemed intent on exploring all the twists and turns of the fastenings.

"Oh my dear! It's just so, so good to see such craftsmanship! My great grandfather had a jacket that came out of the old country that was so like this, but he just always wore simple things when he rode. A cotton shirt ! Pink breeches though. Always wore those!"

Sandy and Carlotta stiffened.

"Pink breeches you say! Yes, I had a pair once, with a chrysanthemum design on the seams."

The old lady's questing fingers hovered over the breast pocket of Sandy's tunic, and he felt a small, heavy object fall into it. Then she stood back a pace or two, and Sandy noticed that sticking out of her evening bag was the corner of a buff envelope, He looked questioningly at her, but suddenly the gentile seclusion of the terrace was shattered by three figures bursting in from the ball room and bearing down upon them. Sandy and Carlotta at once stepped back, hands raised in defence, but the attackers had focused their whole attention upon the old lady. The evening bag was snatched, a hand thrust a short broad bladed dagger into her throat, twisting and ripping the blade back in a single movement, and then the three figures were sprinting across the terrace and vaulting over the parapet into the gaping maw of the famous waterfall almost before the abandoned dagger had fallen to the floor.

Waiters, dropping their trays and wine bottles and pulling out weapons from underneath tables, rushed to the scene. Sandy reached the parapet in time to see three parachutes blossom open. Two of them filled and then abruptly faltered and spilled out their trapped air as rigging lines snapped and tangled, and the betrayed, superfluous, assassins fell to their deaths. The leader's device continued to fill with air, and he made a turn triumphantly holding up the evening bag, but Kurt, the pre-warned and pre-armed lifted his cross-bow and fired the bolt. The leader of the assassination squad slumped in his harness, and bereft of guidance his parachute swirled around and straight into the tumbling waters.

Carlotta knelt over the elderly lady, beyond any sort of rescue, but determined to make one last effort to communicate. Her voice was now no longer that of the south, but a cultivated English accent.

"I'm so glad that worked my dear! Your man will get it all sorted, I know he will, they'll be safe, the poor things, they'll be safe!"

…………………………………………

"Who was she?" Ruprecht asked.

"A Company agent, that's all I know. The papers she was carrying went into the falls, and unless you recover them, which is unlikely, we may never know what was going on. But she'd just given me the password when the hit-squad came in. I presume they were like the ones you told us about earlier? 'Invisible' ?"

"Yes, we'd only just picked them up when they made their move. We thought they were after you when they went for it, otherwise we might have been able to do something for the old lady. You've no idea who she actually was?"

"The company will know, and they'll make arrangements. But whatever she was carrying they weren't going to make any mistakes. That dagger was a horrible thing! Mixed metal blade so that whatever we did it would have made no difference, no way to save her, not even with a 'bite'. They didn't want her to talk. And, then, there's the fact that their leader seems to have sabotaged his teams parachutes, no one to talk or argue about the booty! It's very serious stuff!"

Carlotta was silent. Still recalling the old lady's final moments, her look of triumph. She'd known that whoever was after her, she had little hope of survival, and had been more than ready to die, if only she could pass on the information, and Carlotta had seen the small metal box. It seemed to be a powder compact, slipped into Sandy's pocket. She was still pondering the last words, '…the poor things, they'll be safe…', and the dying images from the old lady's thoughts of a remote village, stricken with poverty, and the sad grey faces of the inhabitants as they were herded away like cattle down a dry dusty road.

……………………………………………

The Ball continued. Guests were more than a little shaken, but the excellence of the 'champagne' and the glitter and sparkle of the settings went a long way to restore normality. Sandy and Carlotta danced, their minds carefully filled with thoughts of the here and now, skilfully keeping any ponderings over events tucked away in the dark recesses of the innermost psyche. The Ball Room might be safe from outside minds, but here in the swirling crowd of dancers who knew what intelligence was probing for a clue?

The American contingent seemed to recover from the incident much faster than the others, perhaps it is easier to be 'not involved' when you know you are going home soon to a place where your adventures are most unlikely to ever follow you! The French and Italian guests treated it as 'something that happens abroad', and there were too few English or other Britannic subjects present to make any general judgements.

The supper following the Ball took place at eleven, and by one o'clock that morning Ruprecht was saying good bye to his guests, graciously handing ladies up to carriages, shaking the hands of numerous gentlemen he would never meet again, and generally being the perfect host.

As the last carriage crunched off down the slope, the breath of the horses hanging in the air like streamers of dragon fume, the head of security came up to Ruprecht.

"Sir, we've found something that you need to see!", he raised an eyebrow and off handed placed his finger on his temple.

"Ah Kurt! Yes, of course. A...err… 'ticket infringement'?"

"Exactly Sir!"

The two men hurried in to the hotel and quickly ducked in to a small office. Kurt pulled the door closed and carefully connected a number of fine wires across the door jamb.

"Sorry Sir, but all our vampire staff are on edge and I'm certain I 'felt' something…err…you know, after all, it's in the family! Your great grand mother…"

"Yes, I know,….she was your godmother. I've always felt it was a bit strange, but she was an innovating lady….still is I guess, if we knew where she was…anyway, tell me what's happened!"

"Well Sir, firstly there's a Draculian hit squad, the one we were worried might be heading our way. Seems like they did come here, but somebody 'neutralised' them!"

"How? Where?"

"Right here Sir! We've just found the bodies, six of them. All been trussed up neatly, and then looks like somebody 'had a word' with them, Forsterite burns! We have no idea if they told them anything or even what it would have been, but when they'd had their way with them they finished them off. Pretty nasty business, injected them with finely divided Forsterite. I've read about it, but I've never seen the stuff used before."

"How did you know what it was then?"

"They left the syringes and the empty ampoules behind, like they wanted to sort of say what they'd done, otherwise we'd have just thought they'd had a dagger shoved into them. We've got them here for you to see."

"So, we don't know who they were after, but the trio we encountered decided they were in their way!"

“More than ‘in their way’ Sir! They wanted to be really, really sure they never got to speak! Not only will they be stuck in ‘the other place’, the shock from that stuff would probably put them out for a hundreds of years or more. No, seems to me that whoever it was killed the EA agent certainly wasn’t a Draculian and hadn’t a lot of love for them either!”

Ruprecht gingerly handled the tiny glass vials, and then turned the syringe over carefully between his fingers. It was the usual glass and steel device, quite unlike the plastic ones the American guests brought with them should they need medications. It seemed to have originated in Europe, and the ampoules were of the standard sort, not that you saw that many what with diseases being so rare these days.

“Err! Sir!”

Ruprecht came out of his reverie “Oh! Sorry Kurt! What were you saying first of all about the vampires being worried?”

“Yes Sir! Not just them, as I said, but anyone who’s a bit psychic. The werewolves are all OK though, not that much ever worries them! There’s a feeling of somebody eavesdropping as it were. It’s not a problem if you’re in one of the ‘wired’ rooms, only if you go outside, which is why…”

“Yes. Quite right. Make sure all the team know about it, and open up all the reserve suites for the staff to use for sleeping and leisure time, no sense in owning the largest thought proof conference facility in Europe if we don’t make use of it!”

Outside in the hallway the morning papers had arrived, transported from their various points of origin by the night train. The postbag would follow in an hour or so’s time.

Ruprecht looked at the stout solid front pages, good firm blocks of black print, a few black and white illustrations, the discrete formal looking advertisements, including one that always seemed to be there. A line drawing of a boy in lederhosen next to an alpine view, and an invitation to holiday in the Tyrol .These were the German papers. The French papers were a little lighter, and the English not dissimilar. There was a small selection from the world press, passed on by the Unsberg embassy in Atlantica, far away on the edge of things, where the world of electricity and flying machines began. These papers spoke of major disturbances, trade disputes, Sino-American negotiations and so on. The papers themselves were of a far flimsier construction, good quality paper though, for all their thinness. And the pictures! Such a lot, and all in colour! There were just so, so many advertisements as well, they seemed to make up more than half the paper, and surprise, surprise, whoever was trying to sell holidays in Tyrol had the same advertisement here as well! And still in black and white!

Finally he came to the last newspaper in the pile. The one he'd come to dread of late. Very grey paper, endlessly recycled, thick pages and a defiantly ancient gothic font. The New Transylvanian Times, official organ of the Empire. New, but not that new. There had always been an official newspaper, but it *had* suffered carefully controlled rivals. Now these had perished and all the majesty of the press was invested in this one paper.

Banner headlines proclaimed "King Kravitz the XXth to Recognise Archduke"

"So," Ruprecht mused, " they've finally decided which way the wind is blowing!"

The leader that followed seemed to have been written by a committee, and it probably was. Vampires had very limited patience with the written word, but would certainly not trust even *electifs* to get it right, so there would have been much midnight oil burnt over every edition, no wonder they were happy with thicker paper than normal, it hid the lack of news.

‘As a token of trust and mutual esteem our beloved Archduke has established his headquarters in the famous East, or Vesper, tower of the Kravitzen fortress in Prague. Audiences will be held every third day for the proper conduct of the interim government of the Empire…..’

Ruprecht took the ominous grey journal and picking up an oil lamp walked down the dimly lit corridors to the library. He threw the paper down on a reading desk and took up the speaking tube to the kitchens.

“A jug of hot strong coffee, a large glass of schnapps and some hot buttered toast please!”

A little later, after brushing buttery crumbs off of the paper and several bound copies of trade journals Ruprecht picked up the mouth piece of another speaking tube “Archives! I know you’re really awake! Please find me all the Armaments and Defensive Architects catalogues and brochures for as far back as we go please! Thank you, oh! And do you have any idea who last had Einkraut’s ‘Vampire Physiology’ out?”

CHAPTER 11

Carlotta was slowly and carefully opening and closing the window shutter, every now and then she leaned out, far across the sill, apparently scanning the street below for something.

"Comes and goes. The wiring on the walls cuts it right out, but it's there outside alright! Every now and then it's really strong, but it can't keep it up. Whoever it is, is pretty powerful, but….somehow….*not comfortable!* Yes, that's it. A very. very powerful presence, but without any self-assurance!"

"Could it be the Archduke? After all he must have got going by now, surely?"

"I really cannot tell. It's nothing like I remember all those years ago, that just sort of hit you between the eyes and if you didn't obey…well it wasn't very nice, no matter how far away you were. This is…weak, crippled….and yet it's got all the same, er…difficult to describe….the same *voice* as it were, but sort of wheedling, whining, veiled threats that don't seem to be made of anything tangible. That's about all I can say, but if we close the shutters there's no way it's going to be heard let alone hear anything. We're safe!"

Carlotta closed and latched the shutters and turned up the big oil lamp. Sandy had fetched out the small heavy metal object that had been slipped into his pocket and together they were investigating its contents.

It was in fact an 18 carat gold powder compact with a good Parisian hallmark, and although it seemed to have seen a great deal of service over its life, acquiring scratches and dents aplenty, it was still a handsome object.

Inside, nestling against a remnant of Du Barry rose powder was a small pellet of what looked like cosmetic tissue. Sandy carefully removed it and smoothed out the twisted and compressed paper. It unfolded to become a long ribbon of fine strong parchment covered in minute characters inscribed with Indian ink and the finest of nibs.

"We may need a magnifying glass for this!" he commented

""'Oh, just screw your eyes up a bit. If they've changed like the rest of you has you shouldn't have any problems at all!"

Sandy squinted a little, and to his surprise found that his eyes did, indeed now register even the tiniest details.

"Umm, straight forward plain message, at least to begin with I think….. 'Report on Mission to the Wastelands….previous reports are correct….large scale mineral extraction operation, sponsors unknown….local population being used as slave labour….only third hand information…site possibly old city of Kabul….exclamation mark….industrial installations reported, but dubious…..Draculian involvement…." Sandy paused and picked up the gold compact again, turning it over in his fingers and staring at its surface, its contents, its decoration.

"The message ends with her code name."

"So, somebody is after the fabulous natural wealth of the Wastelands. It's happened before, what makes this so special that an assassination squad was sent after her?"

"Well, perhaps it's the timing? Perhaps she just got caught up in events and they thought she was doing something extra?"

"Is there nothing more than that in the message? It looks a bit too simple and every day for all this effort, all the 'cloak and dagger'!"

"I think that there *is* more. Look, I have to deal with a lot of agent's reports, espionage if you like, as part of the job. You, that is all the different nations, all get the very best protection against threats because we identify the threats before governments become aware of them, design solutions and sell them to you. It's how we justify being Armaments Manufacturers, what we sell keeps the peace, and we have to know a very great deal indeed about everyone else's business if we are to do that properly. Now, the Wastelands represent the last unplundered mineral reserve on the planet, but, as you know the level of Revenantic Fall Out means that any non-European setting foot there will very shortly succumb to Zombyism, and any sane minded European won't go there because of the activity of the local population…"

"It's alright," Carlotta said, "You *can* call them Zombies!"

"Yes! OK! It's just….well I spent some time at EA's Field Station there, when we were working on the 'control wand'? Yes? They're such *sad* creatures, almost pure spirit, almost ready to leave, but forever pulled back…"

"Yes! I know! And they have lost almost all vestiges of humanity because they barely need a human body any more, which is why they cannot see the harm in eating anything and anyone who is available. *Don't you think it has been hard for us too!* Sorry! That was too harsh! Who knows what you will have to deal with in time….Forgive me….yes, the 'Wastelanders' have had a pretty miserable time of it, and if they are being used as slave labour, and if somebody has found out how to coerce them, then it must be pretty bad, but! I can sense you have something else from this message? Something hidden?"

"Sorry Carlotta, you're right, there are lots of different kinds of people all with their own special problems."

"That's alright. Please, if it helps, the old lady? She saw something, something awful in the wastelands? Reading that message makes sense of it. Her dying thoughts were of a long trail of grey faced people, led off in chains along a dry dusty road….now….tell me what you suspect about this message!"

Sandy fidgeted for a moment or two with the parchment ribbon, and took a breath. "It's like this. She wasn't one of our regular agents, but she was fully trained by us. I know most of the 'news gatherers', and the 'watchers' and a fair few of the 'messengers', but she would have been a 'special', anything to do with activity beyond the borders of Europe is a 'special', officially we don't carry out work beyond the border, but….well there are needs, hence the Field Station in the Wastelands. She wasn't part of the Field Station. I know that. So, she must have been recruited since it closed…oh…four years ago. So, she's been working on something that even the major representatives aren't allowed to know about. Then, she knows who I am, and makes for me, and has set it up with the Chief to tell me she's coming, that's makes it even more important.

Finally, she's given me a message signed with her code name!"

"And that's significant?"

"Very! It's a sort of last resort, drowning man signal! Something dreadful is happening, and she's trying to tell us to….look more closely."

Carlotta sat in silence for a moment, her thoughts lightly playing over Sandy's mind, her eyes set upon the middle distance.

"You know, people often accuse Vampires of being….inhuman…too logical….cold…it's not that really. We're just rather sharply focused. Please, think about this lady. She has passed you a message, you've read the piece of paper, the straight forwards part, and you're concerned that she wanted to pass on something else. What do you think it was?"

Sandy sighed and cradled his face in his hands, "I don't know! Perhaps it was the envelope that the assassin took and is lost forever!"

"No! Don't be silly! Women generally, vampires or not, are far brighter than that. The envelope was a decoy! She gave you the compact! What does it tell you? Come on! We need that quirky bizarre totally crazy human mind to work on this!"

"OK! Let's have a look. Du Barry Rose powder, and no powder puff."

"Stop! Even a vampire would think of that! Something else!"

"Ummm…grease marks on the mirror, dot code?"

"Good! But too fragile, you could have wiped it off just reading the obvious message."

"Right,…err…invisible ink message on the parchment?"

"Nice, but suppose the parchment was separated from the compact? You could check it out, citric acid's the standard, warm it over the lamp!"

The lamp failed to reveal any secret writing, and Sandy turned the compact over and over in his hands, then….

"Ah ha! The back has concentric engine turned rings. Look! Starts in the middle and runs outwards, and…yes….when we look closely there are old scratches, and *new ones*, with bright crisp edges, and they are of two, no three ,types, left oblique, right oblique and upright, and…well I never…its plain Morse code! Shouldn't be difficult…L…I…T…H…I…Lithium….K..I…Kirkuk Plan….Infiltration….Audit must be fake…Then she runs out of space and has just finished up with a name 'Stulheim' and the words danger repeated until the last part of the groove in the pattern is used up!"

"Is this one of your double bluff things? Ignore the paper message and just concentrate upon the little dots? Or the other way round?"

"I don't think so, I feel we are supposed to read the two messages with each other, and that any double bluff was the bit with the envelope that went over the edge. So, somebody is clearly attempting to mine the Wastelands using err Zombies….as slave labour. The Wastelands are a huge geographical area, the old Middle East in fact. If Lithium is the stuff they are after then we could, I guess, locate where they are operating from old resource maps…"

"I know just where they would be, if that was the case! But, I'm not so sure it's simply a matter of dealing with a headquarters. She mentions the Kirkuk Plan. Now that's before your time, but I remember it! It was in all the papers, and on every news broadcast, when I was a teenager. China was going to finally solve the whole Middle East problem by investing in infra-structure. They'd been buying up sites all across Afghanistan and all the other old countries that used to be. Their plan was to put in roads and railways, particularly railways. People at the time suspected that little by little the Chinese would take over the Middle East and it would no longer *be* a problem, and quite honestly it was *such a problem* that exchanging the total mineral wealth of the Middle East for a Chinese super-policeman to keep the peace seemed quite a bargain. Then of course there was 'the accident', and the Chinese had to write off the whole Kirkuk Plan, which in the face of the troubles they had to face with losing half their eastern provinces to RFO was the least of their worries. *But* the railway lines must all still be there! If they had access to the right materials they could, feasibly, be forcing the Wastelanders to provide labour."

"It's the 'right materials' that are the key, that and getting the Transylvanian Empire to agree to exploiting the Wastelanders. Technically they are subjects of the Empire and under its protection, not that they could do that much about it, but once the Americans heard what was going on they'd kick up a fuss, and not just on humanitarian grounds either, the thoughts of China getting hold of all those mineral goodies, especially right now with all known stocks of lithium about to run out…!"

"Well then! In addition to trying to get ourselves back to England to take part in a Transylvanian government in exile, escaping whatever the Draculians may have sent after us, avoiding any unfriendly German states on the way, and then coping with the political splits in England when we do get there, we are also investigating a Chinese plot to snatch the wealth of the wastelands!"

"That would appear to be about it! I'm sure that we are more than up to it, however we do need to consider just how the Chinese, if it is them, are controlling the Wastelanders. You see those control wands are quite special. I know that the letter from the Chief says they've been handed an example with Chinese ideograms on it, but they just can't have made one!"

"Why not? Surely it can't be that impossible, they'd perhaps captured one, and taken it to bits and so on?"

"Yes, you could do that. On first sight it looks easy. Very, very pure platinum and bismuth, not alloyed, just rolled together. Now, I'll give you the technical explanation. You've been to one of those EA briefings where they tell about Forsterite, and how it's made? You recall?"

"Yes, I recall, but please remember *we* have enormous problems with anything to do with craft skills, there isn't a vampire living (sorry!) that can sew on a loose button, or cut a slice of bread, so any of the stages along the way to how things are made won't stick in my mind, or not for long anyway! But, please explain it to me, I'll see the logic and commit the outcome to memory, but I'll be quite unable, by tomorrow, of telling you why!"

Sandy drew a deep breath and began his explanation. He reminded Carlotta that all of Europe and its immediate surroundings had no electrical or magnetic activity, this made all chemical reactions a bit different, it explained why explosives rarely worked, and also that a metal alloy would be completely different in how it behaved in Europe, which was why any specimen of Forsterite taken outside the continent transmuted at once into separate metal particles, and also why the metallic elements of a Zombie Control wand would, if taken into an electromagnetic field, suddenly corrode becoming non-functional, and what is more, totally unrecognisable and so incapable of being copied. Furthermore the metal purity needed for all the EA products could only be achieved in Europe's unusual conditions. At this stage Carlotta's eyes began to glaze over and fortunately a knock at the door disturbed the science lesson!

Ruprecht was there, with a bound volume of a newspaper and a large leather tome cradled in his arms.

"Glad you're both still up! Something very odd is happening!"

"Ah!" said Carlotta, "Do you mean the 'strange thoughts'?"

"Probably! Most of our vampire staff have reported somebody trying, not very successfully, to influence their behaviour. They were all on alert anyway with the current scare across the border. But, there's also some strange news in the papers!"

He laid down the huge bound volume of EA News, and lifted from between its pages that mornings copy of the Transylvanian Times, then he place Einkraut's Vampire Physiology on the table next to it.

"Firstly the Transylvanian Times reports that the Kravitzen have formally agreed to work with the Archduke, so constitutionally he's half way to being in control(though without the six Grand Dukes he's still stuck). Secondly he's only giving an audience every three days, today being the first occasion, the rest of the time he's holed up in the Vesper Tower."

Ruprecht paused, eyeing Sandy carefully, trying to gauge his expression. Sandy having shown a sudden interest seemed to be feigning indifference now! Carlotta stepped in.

"Sandy! Your professionalism does you credit! You clearly know something about the Vesper Tower, perhaps you should share it?"

"Oh! Alright! No secrets when you're married to a vampire I guess. But, it goes against the grain. However it looks like you, Ruprecht, have worked it out already. You've got the advertisement for EA's 'total psychic shielding system', and yes, we did install it in the Vesper Tower, and that's the 'anonymous head of state' referred to in the ad! Take that along with the really weird psychic presence that *might be* the Archduke, and something's up. If it were a human we were looking at, then they'd be camped out in the Vesper Tower to avoid a heavy psychic attack. The Kravitzen use it to plan and discuss matters, just as you use your conference facility, the difference is that when it was set up that sort of thing was still hush-hush, but now you find them everywhere (except in Transylvanian of course, where they are still seen as a little rude!) But who on earth would have the capacity to listen into and control the Archduke? Last time it was.... What? The entire six Grand Dukes (and good half of the other ranks*), and* a lucky shot with garlic wreath that took him down. We don't even know about any resistance to him at present, but somebody is having an effect!"

"Yes," grinned Ruprecht "Some of my staff who remember the Dark Days say it sounds just like the Archduke, but with something or somebody else! Is there some way he could have been weakened? I've been looking in Einkraut's book for some clues."

Carlotta looked thoughtful, then. "Not everything is in that book! It's been, erm… 'edited'….I was on the editorial committee…and I'm beginning to recall something that might be useful. You see, there was a particularly unpleasant Count, up near the Swiss border, who did some very strange things to his followers…in fact that is why he's not there anymore. Um….well…anyway once or twice when he'd got *two* followers who'd had an *accident* and had to be 'called back' from the other place he tried mixing up their remains. 'Just to see what would happen' he said, except he did it a lot more times for a laugh!

If you mix the remains of two vampires together and then 'call them back', there's a short period of time when they are a mixture of both personalities, and bodies, it was very, very distressing, and…well I was sent to investigate, and for the day or two that it lasted, in retrospect, it was just like the mind we heard calling out this morning! But, and it is the *big but*, is that it was impossible to sustain for more than a day or two…. so perhaps somebody got in the way when the Archduke was called back, and he's still sorting himself out?"

CHAPTER 12

Ernst looked down carefully, over the metal collar and down at his breastplate. The huge gilt letters K XX were suitably buffed, and although some of the gold was wearing off they still looked pretty good. Only another three months, and then back to the regiment! Thank goodness there was a service limit on palace duty, you felt physically and mentally ill being around the Kravitzen, but you got a really big bonus, and once the smell had worn off you could start spending it! He straightened up his pike, and adjusted the set of his arms and legs to allow the amour to hang in its most comfortable position.

'Just stand there!' the sergeant had told him, 'You're only for show, keep still, keep quiet, and we'll come and march you back out in an hour's time.'

The old boy was being brought in again. Some vampire swell! Perhaps this Archduke chap they kept on about! Well.... wouldn't want his job, not for all the beer in Bavaria! Actually in a wheelchair. An actual wheelchair! Thought vampires wasn't supposed to get old and shaky.

The little procession rattled past. Four Draculian Lords, a token werewolf and some humans, oh and a very minor Kravitzen dragging along at the rear trying to look as if he weren't really there.

The wheelchair's occupant was wrapped in a beautifully tailored black velvet cloak that came up high around the neck. A cyanosed bony hand , fingers encrusted with massive gold and ruby baroque rings gripped the arm rest, its nails carefully manicured, lightly pointed and with a darkly blooming sheen. Pushing the wheelchair was a non-descript, though clearly human, figure. Her face looked weather-worn, and an old scar crossed her forehead, vanishing into her grey haired temples at each side. At the door to the outer audience chamber she paused and adjusted the high collar of the cloak, apparently settling the seated figure more comfortably into the wheelchair. Before the little cavalcade restarted towards the newly opened door she turned to the following train of people and impatiently beckoned the Kravitzen from the tail of the procession to its front.

"Stop slouching around Claus, get out there and announce the Archduke, and don't forget to bow him in!"

Claus reluctantly did as he was told, distain registering in every muscle. The gaunt grey head was bent down low to the cowering figure in the wheelchair.

"Now Your Extreme Exaltedness, please behave and stick to the script we have given you, or I shall have to allow Gunther to wake up again. You wouldn't like that, would you?"

The figure made determined efforts to shake its head, the grey chicken-skin neck creasing and folding in its efforts to show compliance.

"I asked you a question Exaltedness. You wouldn't like Gunther to wake up would you?"

"No! Please! I would not like him to wake up!"

"Good! Then behave!"

The wheelchair trundled out into the Audience Chamber and the Kravitzen Claus announced

"His Extreme Exaltedness, The Archduke, Emperor of Transylvania!"

....

Once, a long time ago, there had been an elevator. That was before the 'accident' so it was indeed a very long time ago. Right now there was a staircase and a great many alterations, but it was an ancient building, and that gave a certain gravitas to meetings held there. Plenderleith, as he toiled up the endless flights of stairs, felt that one of the more modern buildings would have been equally suitable, safer too! He had a somewhat limited faith in the old architecture with its great glass windows and slender concrete supports. The really tall ones had all fallen down after a hundred years or so, and great swathes of the former commercial centre of London were now grassed over, informally landscaped and left as a backdrop to the much smaller establishment that was required for modern day activity.

Eventually he arrived at the board room level, and waiting for his panting assistants to catch up he regarded the polished wood of the doors and the distant views of London. It was worth the climb, he had to admit that, and you'd certainly not get any eavesdroppers at this height.

Far below the Thames ran as a silver streak between wide green banks, meandering it's way into the distance, small boats moving along its length. Far, far away was the hazy blue horizon, dominated by the interminable miles of reed beds and lagoons that made up the marshes. Somewhere out there, in the dredged channel that led eventually to Wilhelmshaven was the paddle-steamer with the next difficulty on board.

"Just what they hell are they?" he asked himself "And, what the blazes is really going on out there?"

The Ambassador had been perplexing enough! What on earth was she doing coming back home with a following of several thousand refugees? For goodness sake, they'd set up a complete self-sufficient Transylvanian suburb in London, just like that. The way that had fed into the Human League sympathisers and their conspiracy theories!

He felt that Their Majesties Government had been severely 'put upon', forced in fact to accept that they were hosting Transylvania in Exile rather than having a few month to chew it over. Well….all done now, better start trying to make some sense of it all.

His assistants had caught up now, their heavy burden of document cases and reference books having slowed them down over the past twenty floorsworth of stairs.

In the Board Room, around the great oaken table the other delegates were already seated, and sorting out their papers.

Essex Armaments, as hosts were at the head of the table, Universal Armaments were nearby, and the tiny contingent from Allied Industries had squeezed in beside them. There were three seats for the Constructivist's, The Beliefers, and the Human League, then the American and the Chinese ambassadors, each with a couple of assistants. Plenderleith took his seat at the foot of the table and waved a cheery hello to all present.

The Director of EA started at once on his introduction.

"Ladies and Gentlemen, please make yourselves comfortable. This is intended to be an informal meeting to help us chart out the way ahead. In accordance with recent agreements the three major Armaments Companies and the major political parties are represented, as are the two most significant Non-European powers. The purpose is to make perfectly clear to all concerned the Armaments Industry's position regarding current destabilisation in Europe. We wish to reassure the major parties and make plain to our international neighbours our *non-involvement* stance. Firstly, EA and our competitors are not under the direction or control of

TMG..." he paused at this point to take a question from the American ambassador.

"Do I understand correctly then, that your munitions and your own forces are not available to Their Majesties Government?"

"You understand correctly. EA's own three regiments and its various battalions etc exist purely for instructional and constructional purposes and will remain on EA's own property, a similar arrangement exits with our competitors. We do not supply munitions *in bulk*, but provide factories under licence to our customers, TMG included, so if a state of war develops, then our customers will not have supplies disrupted, and the principle of neutrality will be preserved."

Walker, head of the Constructivist Party raised a hand.

"What about your continental infrastructure. Sales staff, agents, construction battalions, advisors, training groups etc. How will they be affected?"

"As far as we can tell the hostilities will be restricted to Transylvania, and even there we anticipate that the new administration will rapidly make contact with us and wish to do business. You see, the thing about being neutral is that you *really do* have to be neutral, and if the Arch Duke places an order for our equipment, we will be honour bound to fill it!"

There was at this stage an angry outburst from the Human League representative who was rapidly 'shushed' by his assistant.

"Well," drawled the American ambassador, "I've got to hand it to you boys, and girls, you've really made something out of neutrality! Far than we ever did! If you can pull this off, then you'll have the respect of a fair few politicians around the world.

But what if the Arch Duke doesn't want to play? Can you get your people out safely?"

"Obviously I can't give any details, but, yes. We anticipate very few losses."

"What about your boy you had at the Peace Conference? The one we're all hearing strange tales about? Furthermore he don't seem quite so neutral as all that, *and* I hear he's gone missing?"

"I assume you are referring to Alexander McLomond. Yes, we are still awaiting definite news, however we have categorised his actions as typical of an EA advisor, assisting client's forces to make use of our technology rather than fighting on their behalf."

Rather abruptly the Chinese contingent started to confer, and the ambassador, catching the eye of the chair, unlatched the front of her face mask to speak more clearly.

"We would like to be more fully assured that Essex Armaments and its allies have not interfered in Transylvanian politics. We understand that the agent previously referred to now has a special standing with the so-called government in exile? That dual nationality has been proposed? We would like clarity on this issue!"

"When we have more information, then we can express a far greater level of clarity. It is very difficult for any Armaments provider *not* to take a hand in politics, since the purpose of our activity is to help ensure international political stability. However, we do take the point and will be doing all we can to investigate recent events, and if needed we will take action, please be assured of this."

The meeting went on for some time longer, though mostly it was now an opportunity for point scoring or vain attempts to set up future business. Plenderleith had heard most of what he wanted, and was amusing himself people watching, it was an old established habit of his to sketch out the table and its delegates and to then chart who watched who, who spoke to who and so on. He was getting some odd results, for some unknown reason the Human League assistant, not the main representative, seemed to be responding almost exclusively to the Chinese party. He was about to look into the matter a little more closely when the chairman called the meeting to order and wound up proceedings for the day.

……………………………………………

After Reichenbach the train line runs first to Dresden, and then strikes out north and westwards, becoming in a while a great deal more busy, gathering extra tracks, and carrying a considerable quantity of freight. Its passenger service is still excellent however, and it is without doubt the most comfortable way to travel, especially if you still have the loan of the Unsberg Royal Suite. Passport controls between the independent states that make up the Germanies are rarely observed, there being at least one hundred and thirty six states at the last count, so while import taxes and duties are a keen concern, movement of people is not, so it was not until Hannover that the occupants of the Royal Suite were asked to show their documents. It seemed a bit odd to the border police that the Unsberg Royal Suite was travelling with just a valet on board, but he explained that the carriages were going to be repainted at Bremen, so that was alright. At least it was alright for the border police, but very frustrating for the three gentlemen who had talked the border police into stopping the train and carrying out a check for Transylvanian nationals.

……………………………………………

Carlotta did not much like German cities. Too noisy, too busy, and too, too many people's minds all yelling and screaming at once.

There was the smell as well. The better districts had gas lights, but most of the poorer ones used fish-oil in the street lamps. She clung to Sandy's arm and accepted his pilotage through the crowds and the hubbub. The Germans seemed intent upon pushing steam to its limit. The factories had steam driven machines, steam powered railways perched upon brick viaducts moved goods from one place to another, and on the already packed streets the occasional steam carriage ground and snorted its way along. However, she did have to admit that everyone seemed to be having a very good time indeed. They stepped into another narrow alleyway that Sandy unaccountably knew the exact route of, and with a considerable amount of effort, by the time they had reached the other end of it, she had persuaded her dress to change from lilac to green. Sandy had managed a more prosaic alteration by simply taking off his coat and rolling it up.

"That should have thrown them off the scent. This is where we need to be."

"Is it some sort of safe house?"

"No, a lot better. Up this flight of stairs here, and, unless somebody's changed it, there should be a door….Good! And it's unlocked! This is the servant's entrance to the Metropole Hotel, and if we duck into here….we come out into the lobby…. looking as if we've just come down the stairs….and now we'll ask the lobby boy to get us a cab!

You see the cabs at the Metropole come close by under the awning, and no one can see from the street who gets in or who gets out. Very useful!"

"How do you know these things?"

"Oh just something you pick up. Here we are….Cabby! Swansdorf please!"

The driver hurried up his horse and the cab rattled off into the hurly burly of the street, its driver experiencing a pleasant emptiness of mind and not in the least willing to check the fare with the pictures of *people of interest* to the Transylvanians who had been asking questions that morning at the cab rank.

…………………………………

And so, by various ploys and ruses, both human and vampire it eventually happened that Sandy and Carlotta stood a few miles outside of Wilhelmshaven, once a great naval base, but now a pleasant little town from which the North Sea steamers sailed at regular intervals down the little river and out into the tangled sand bars and reed beds of the great estuary, and after pursuing a tortuous course for about a week, would eventually make landfall in London river.

North Sea tides had become notoriously sluggish and unreliable of late, so surprise extensions to journey times were to be expected.

The road into the town was busy with carts and strings of pack horses bringing goods in and out, though since England mostly exported small expensive things and the Germanies sold larger bulker goods there were often many empty carts and horses leaving. The railway line to Wilhelmshaven also did its share, but freights were expensive and local producers preferred to grow hay for free to feed horses rather than pay the railways to buy coal to burn in engines.

"I remember…" Carlotta began, and Sandy cut in "The lizards birds and the mammoth herds.."

"Sorry?"

"Oh, I guessed you were going to say something about the way the river and the sea used to be, and it popped an old poem into my mind about how the river Thames recalled being a tributary of the Rhine. But, I apologise. What were you going to say?"

"Well, just that really! How all this was the edge of a great sea when I was born. But, forget that for now, what do we do next?"

"Well, obviously certain people are likely to have made this location their last ditch stand to stop us getting home, so we don't relax vigilance. There is a really good frontier guard at Wilhelmshaven, so we'll have to declare ourselves in order to board the steamer at the dock, and it's pretty open there, actually on the dock, but with old warehouses and ruined buildings nearby that could conceal a crossbow sniper."

"Don't you know anybody here? You seem to be at home just about everywhere we've been so far!"

"I know all sorts of people, but to contact them would give the game away. No, we need something different. How are you feeling about water these days? You know crossing the running stuff and all that?"

"Oh! That's all old hat now! Not that it ever did do more than give me a few twinges. If I couldn't put up with water I'd not be volunteering to escape by boat…not that there's much in the way of alternatives!"

"Well, I think we can do something useful. First of all we need to get into town unobserved, and then we'll get ourselves hidden away in a suitable coign of vantage, and see what we can see!"

"You are being very mysterious again. You've really got this concealing your thoughts off pat, haven't you?"

"It may seem like that, but actually I not too sure just yet that I even *know* what we *will* do!"

....

It was coming on to rain, nasty thin drifting stuff that didn't take kindly to rubberised waterproof coats and took them as an insult, in fact it managed to find its way inside crevices and button holes and exposed seams, and soon the riders spaced out at intervals along the string of pack ponies were far more concerned with getting into the town and undercover than they were about the correct number of ponies in the string, and if there was one more rider than there should be. It was a blessing, it really was, how sensible and helpful the animals were being. Nobody shying at fallen trees, all staying at just the right interval, sort of no bother at all really.

The customs officer on the gate just asked which yard they were offloading at and waved them through. Another bonus, no head count, no papers. Soon be in the yards, get it all undercover and unload, then the tavern awaited. Food, drink, warmth. Just get the ponies bedded down first and then…."

So, the fact that when they did reach the yards a couple with two suitcases and a shoulder bag seemed to have become tangled up with the ponies wasn't really that much of a problem. The end was in sight.

....

"Quick! Down here! We need to stay as unrecognisable as possible, there could be any number of people on foot, but much fewer riders, so they'll already have been carefully checked up on! Come on, up you get!"

Carlotta sat stolidly in the saddle, and despite the fact she had no idea where Sandy was taking them she did her best to look as if she knew where she was going. A few stray thoughts from the crowd in the street.A sudden flash of what was clearly a vampire, but nothing to properly identify origins or intents. Sandy was slowing down and seemed to be checking side turnings. They appeared to be moving away from the built up areas now, and they were following the river just past the dock. The old naval base was actually lost in the low shrub-grown flats behind them, the sea having long since abandoned it.

Here on the level land beside the river was a terrace of old windmills, built to the traditional Dutch design. Carlotta grinned to herself, she remembered them being built, an attempt to speed up the draining of the marshes when the sea level started falling, and now here they were! Derelict and mouldering away. Sentinels to the great accident!

Sandy was clearly selecting a destination amid these towering structures. After a moment or two he trotted forwards, moving into the dark shadow at the base of the windmill nearest to the dock, perhaps five hundred metres away. He paused by a rickety wooden stair and waited politely for Carlotta to dismount.

"I think that the steps will bear our weight, if not, then I'm afraid it's another bit of stereotyping, you'll have to 'float'!"

But chance had it that the steps did bear their weight. As they passed through the doorway Sandy eased a few of the timbers out of their much eroded sockets.

"Mmmm! Clever!" commented Carlotta, "if you'd have broken it away people would have seen we'd been here, this way if they do try to follow they'll have it collapse on them and assume nobody could have come up this way!"

The rest of the structure was much better preserved, the outer skin of the windmill having kept the weather at bay. The pumping machinery sat in a semi-fossilised state, and was soon bypassed by a number of worm-eaten ladders. Soon they had ascended to the sail loft, the topmost cap of the windmill, where the enormous sails had at one time joined the shaft with its great cog wheels. The window still had a few panes of glass and the dusty wooden floor, though it allowed you to spy through holes on the levels below, was complete enough for comfort if you weren't staying for long!

"This one has a window facing the dock, and the glass is a bonus! But we need to make some holes in the roof, lots of big ones on the east side, knock out as much as you can, we can't start doing it in daylight, but dawns a long way away still."

"Why?"

"Well, come morning the sun will rise over there" he pointed vaguely to the north east, " and we need to pick up its light with my pocket mirror and flash it down at the steamer. It's the Doggerland, and she's got a captain *and* a first officer who are both err.... 'with the company', a helio Morse code message should escape notice since, as I say, there's glass left in the window and I hope it'll just look like the early morning sun glinting on the shards."

"It's a bit of long shot. What makes you think they'll notice?"

"There is a plan B, but it leaves us more open to being detected."

CHAPTER 13

"That's not Morse!" scoffed the Engineer to the Chief stoker. "Nothing like it!"

Anderson, the captain, however seemed to be dividing his attention between the crossword and the view down river. He suggested that the engine room should be getting itself ready for the journey, and the Engineer and the Stoker left to start raising steam. He motioned to the steward, " Peters, please get me Mr Wallace, and hurry up the crew with the last of the lading, I want to be ready to move with the tide, such as it is!"

Wallace came up from supervising the last of the cargo coming aboard.

"Yes sir?"

"Please take a P and a Q flag and run them up the forward hoist, then check the sea boat."

"Right-oh Sir! 'Business'?"

"Could be, keep it quiet, don't want our friends finding out." He nodded meaningfully towards the dockside.

……………………………….

High in the windmill Sandy noted the hoist of flags and turned to Carlotta. "That's the affirmative! I didn't want them to signal back with the helio, that'd have been a dead give-away. Once they start down-stream we need to make our move. Anybody listening in?"

"I don't think so. There's a lot of minds out there, but if you pry too much they get suspicious. Don't tell me too much, fewer minds the better on this. I trust you!"

"Thanks!"

…………………………………..

The Doggerland's paddles churned the muddy waters of the Wesser, using power to make sure the hull had enough clearance in the shallow channel to avoid grounding. Once they cleared the point then the worst of the sand banks would be behind them, and deeper waters would be available. But right now, outside of the main channel, there was scarcely room to paddle a canoe, if a vessel came to grief the passengers could almost, but not quite, have walked ashore. If it wasn't for the current, and the mud, and the ever present reeds. Anderson was aiming for a tiny patch of water just out from the hook of the point, where the current scoured around and created a deep pool that, with care you could remain within for a little while. The point itself connected via a series of broken sand banks to the shore, and with the telescope Anderson could just make out the signal. A white cloth hung on a stick with a second red cloth similarly displayed about twenty metres away. It was a shame that the sea boat was no longer serviceable, that schooner in the next berth but one had, unaccountably swung round and rammed her bowsprit right through its hull, and the life boats…well great clumsy things intended for open water, they'd have grounded well before they were useful for taking a party up from the beach, but he'd follow the plan anyway, and just hope they'd got something up their sleeves!

A horse suddenly broke out from the cover of tamarisk and heather and, its rider sitting low and tight, galloped towards the water's edge.

Anderson readjusted the telescope. Though with the speed the horse was moving the instrument soon became superfluous.

The initial gaps between the sand banks were mere plashes across which the horse sped, throwing up great fountains of spray, then as the gaps grew greater progress slowed to an energetic swim, and then a canter across the sand. Far behind, where the vegetation met the sand small dark figures were beginning to emerge, dashing forwards and converging on the base of the promontory. They did not seem that keen to follow beyond the first two gaps, and one was carried away by the current trying to cross to the third sand bank in the chain.

The final section of the point was good substantial sand, with strong clumps of vegetation, and even a small wood of scrubby trees at the furthermost end.

Anderson had scrambling nets lowered over the side, and a platform rigged with a linesman as well. He was edging the Doggerland as close to the shore as he dared, trying to get the blunt bows facing the sand, offering a safe boarding point away from the threshing paddlewheels.

The horse did not slow down as it approached the water, but plunged down the steep undercut bank and straight into the sea, swimming strongly towards the ship. A bare fifty metres, but the surface of the water was already ruffled with the turbulence of the current, and far from being a simple direct swim the horse and rider were having to accommodate drift; however they managed it!

The rescue party were somewhat confused at the sudden appearance of a second person and the mysterious disappearance of the horse, but being used to some strange episodes before with Captain Anderson decided it was best not to talk about it.Instead they helped the rather glamourous lady to support the exhausted gentleman on his way to a waiting stateroom. Surprisingly the gentleman was carrying a pair of suitcases, just how he had transported it across the water nobody knew!

....

The Wesser, accompanied by waters from the Elbe eventually opened into the North Sea proper, but the steamer followed the south shore until it passed the mouth of the Rhine, still a mighty river despite the much reduced rainfall of late. The way ahead was set in a wide wandering shallow inlet of the North Sea, veering southwards. Occasional inhabited islands supporting small populations of fishermen slipped past, making a change from the leaden water and the eternal reeds (wherever it was shallow enough). The voyage was usually six days, and to enliven the journey the Doggerland haled local fishermen and purchased fresh fish, while the passengers bargained for reed-work baskets and decorative mats. On the foredeck the ships carpenter was working hard on restoring the sea boat.

"Deliberate?" asked Sandy, standing there with Anderson watching the repairs.

"Pretty certain. The way it was, they had to have run up a trysail or something to swing round so suddenly like that, but I think it was fortuitous that they smashed the sea boat! I believe they were really after fouling our left paddle box, that would have really messed things up!"

"And you hadn't told anybody about the 'pick up'?"

"No, not even Walker, and I'd been trying to do the 'closed thoughts drill', but I guess I'm not very good at it!"

"Well, we're away now, they can't get at us until London."

"I hear that there are flying vampires again, mightn't they be a problem?"

"Not very likely. First of all no vampire, not even the old Arch Duke himself could manage more than a few hundred metres. Secondly it's over water, and the traditionalists are still a bit touchy about that. Distance helps as well. The further we are from any of their agents the weaker their thoughts will be, so they would have big problems finding us. Are you sure about all your crew though?"

"Hand picked. You know what sort of 'super cargoes' we carry.

It has to be that way. Plus I own a quarter share in the Doggerland and I have a very big say in who we employ, and who we carry. The passenger list is in my cabin if you want to check, it all looks clean. I think I actually know every passenger personally, and although I wouldn't say I trust all of them, I do know who they answer to! No….we're safe enough here for now, but we pass a few signal stations on the way, and they might let people know that we're on your way, so we might meet up with 'old friends' sooner than we think!"

"Hmmm! How soon will that sea boat be ready?"

"Soon enough, but it's a long way home , and you've still got to work out how to get ashore and past the coastguard! Surely you'll be alright once you are in the Company's safe hands?"

…………………………

Arthur Freeman, AKA 'The Chief', also known formally as the Earl of Sheerness, bearer of numerous Britannic and Transylvanian decorations and orders was nervously waiting in the ante-room of the Board Room. He was, ex-officio a member of the Board, but because of recent events had been asked to withdraw whilst certain matters were considered.

Development and Sales was his pigeon. The two went together naturally since it was the field sales staff who most often found out what was needed, and what was possible. A good run! As evidenced by his position, the peerage and the various 'thank you's' from home and abroad. He had stuck rigidly to the benevolent neutrality philosophy of the industry, and felt, quite justifiably so, that his time with the company had prevented a great many wars and had cemented friendship and cooperation between the major European players. His thoughts were, nearly always, on Europe, and the greater world was not attractive. He had once or twice given way to pressure to take part in missions to America, and had seen the murky shores of Atlantica, the American outpost at the edge of the 'zone' ,more than once, but he was always glad to be home.

He was known to have a werewolf mistress and employ revenant servants in his spacious mansion, so just now he doubted for his Country's judgement in its hard line controls on vampires.

Britannic citizens of all four kingdoms, (if vampires), and *all* alien vampires, were required to register their presence and obtain National Identity Cards. Persons of vampire ancestry were also to report to newly established centres to prove their status as human or revenant. It had been the result of public hysteria fed by the Human League and the popular press. Events at the peace conference which should have damaged the Human League beyond repair were now forgotten in the terror of the expected resurrection and ascension to power of the Arch Duke, *Dracula himself*! The return of the Dark Days!

The door opened, they were ready for him…

"Ah, Arthur! Thank you for being so patient! As you know we have had to deal with some very complex and difficult issues…" the Chair paused and fidgeted with some papers, "Err..", he began again, and then started to repeat himself "….as you know….ummm….well, the fact is that the Board, acting in the interests and at the behest of the err…shareholders….have asked, well…insisted…that for the probity of the company we investigate the commitments and loyalty…. the affections and attachments…in short the reliability of all members of staff. *If* it should happen that the err…Arch Duke, comes to power, in the manner that he did in the past, then, with the best will in the world….we would not be able to trust vampires. You are known to have strong links and sympathies with the revenant community, and until these are fully investigated we will have to ask you to take leave of absence, *on full pay of course*!"

The Chief looked slowly and thoughtfully around the table. There were the faces he was used to, the ones he had dealt with for the last twenty years in some cases, many of them looked embarrassed, unhappy, but perhaps that was his imagination! There were, he noted, many new faces.

"I see! Well, as a member of this Board, a person whose advice, guidance and experience has always been held in great esteem, I feel that I would like to make a comment or two. Of course you are pursuing your prerogative, as is only right and proper, however I should stress that the only threat perceived at the present moment would come from vampires, the rest of the revenant community are unaffected by the power of the Arch Duke, always assuming that he is coming back, in fact recent reports suggest that there is now active resistance being organised against the Draculian party by werewolves, werewolves I should add working in close harmony and collaboration with humans. There is in addition the very real threat to the probity of Essex Armaments from responding to TMG legislation in this way. The neutrality of the armaments industry depends upon the sovereignty of its properties and its freedom to employ whoever *it* trusts, *not* the government. It is a tricky pathway I will grant you, but the trust of Transylvania in Essex Armaments could well be lost by actions such as this, and with it the whole philosophy of the industry. However, I am sure that you have taken this into account, and that your investigations will be a formality, after which we can get back to work…but….before I withdraw could you please tell me Madam Chair, who these new members of the board are?"

One of the new members stood up promptly, and ignoring the offices of the chair spoke directly to him.

"Since you are suspended you are no longer a member of this board, and so we do not have to answer your questions."

There was a sharp rap of the Chairs gavel, then

"Mr Parker! Questions will be framed and answered through the Chair! I am sorry Arthur, it was rude of us not to begin with introductions. Following an emergency meeting of the shareholders the board of directors has been expanded, these ladies and gentlemen.." she indicated the new faces.. "are our six new board members bring the complement up to a total of twelve! I will have their names and resumes sent to you so that you can get better acquainted, and I echo your wishes that we will all, all, be able to get back to work as soon as possible."

One of the new directors raised a hand and was acknowledged by the chair.

"Madam Chair, may we please assume that the Earl of Sheerness'leave begins at once? And that he has no need to return to his office?"

"No. That has never been the company's way. Arthur, you may return to your office, please feel free to err…leave things in order, and then, indeed, please do go home. I'm sure we'll be seeing you again soon!"

Regular early morning runs with Jenny, a largely red meat diet, and lots and lots of healthy out door activities had made the Chief very fit and active for his age, far fitter than the two security guards sent after him by the board, who had the greatest difficulty keeping up as he plunged down staircase after staircase to the lobby, and then raced across the quadrangle to his office. In fact, by the time the two men had finally arrived red faced and gasping for breath, he was already climbing into his carriage with several document cases and dispatch boxes and telling the coachman to 'hurry off home'.

....

The Doggerland had rigged a couple of large awnings to act as sails and was making the most of the stiff easterly breeze, the steam paddles were now being used more for steering than propulsion in the narrow channel. The first signal station on the English shore had already been passed. They had seen it's helio station flashing the message Londonwards, the early morning sunlight and the clear weather conditions meaning that everyone would by now be aware of the progress of the Doggerland.

The forward lookout had been scanning the channel ahead with a pair of large tripod-mounted binoculars. He suddenly reached up and pulled the lanyard of the signal bell.

"Vessel in the channel ahead Captain!"

Anderson hurried forwards from the bridge and looked into the binoculars.

Tacking in a leisurely fashion against the wind and making slow headway towards the sea was a medium sized yacht. It's tanned red sails were being tightly controlled, and from the mast head a long extravagant pennant flew. At the times, when the wind allowed, it could be seen to be decorated with a silhouette of a running wolf and a naked man.

Anderson grinned and sent a messenger to rouse Sandy and Carlotta .

"Tell them" he said, "that the Chief's come out to meet them!"

……………………………………..

It was an exceptionally well found vessel! The Chief had been investing in it for many years, it was indeed his hobby, and Jenny (the werewolf mistress) was a very enthusiastic mate! It must be said that werewolves are the sportiest individuals that you could wish to meet, and that whatever activity a human will take to, so will a werewolf, only more so!

The yacht was named very simply 'Lupin', but was far from simple when you started to look her over.

The hull had an alarming multiplicity of bilge keels, stabilisers and lea boards that meant she could venture into the shallowest of waters, and yet still manage to heel over in a near hurricane with absolute safety. The broad beam had been dedicated to luxurious accommodation, and the unusually tall mast allowed the tiniest breeze to be captured and utilised. Beneath her copious coats of varnish you could just make out a maze of fine wires that meant she was as secure a base for conversations as anywhere in Europe, especially when she had been run well off shore. The galley and pantry were very well equipped, and if you had been inclined to risk the incredibly narrow (and shallow!) passages of the Dover straights you could have taken her out into the Atlantic and gone *anywhere*!

Today however, she was firmly fixed in the chilly and shallow North Sea, and having taken on her two new passengers was ready to go about and scud before the breeze!

………………………………………………

Hodgeson, Head of Security at the Essex Armaments main site was standing patiently, wondering when the 'dressing down' was likely to finish, and also if it was worthwhile brushing up his CV and posting it off to Universal Armaments before the weekend. He became aware that Parker, one of the new directors, was now addressing a question at him rather than just talking at him.

"Er, no sir, once he left these premises we had no jurisdiction over him. He went home sir, and unless you are going to make an accusation of theft and involve the authorities, then there's very little we can do."

"What do you mean? 'He's gone home.' I thought Essex House was a company property? It's got offices, and workshops, and a board room?"

"Ah! Yes, sir! Lots of people make that mistake. But, it's not company property, never has been. Lord Sheerness just makes it available to us as….sort of….overspill space I suppose."

"Damn inefficient! Why haven't we got space of our own? Is there a contract? And…hey! What about all our stuff that must be there? Can't we force an entry to retrieve it?"

"The arrangement has worked very well for the best part of twenty years sir. It all started when the company got into some temporary difficulties and his Lordship stepped in and helped us out. He even purchased all of Sheerness and beyond, after all it was no use to us anymore! But Essex House, it's only ever overspill, nothings kept there permanently" (except, he added to himself, the duplicate coding machines and the spare set of confidential books, but I not supposed to know that….so I don't!)

Parker redoubled his efforts to induce in himself either a coronary or a stroke.

"Why couldn't your men have kept up with him. He's got all the operating codes for the next month, he can listen in to any company helio, and goodness knows what messages he could send to people!!"

"You could always change the codes. But why would he want to do that sir? I understood this was just a routine security check on all staff with strong revenant sympathies . Perhaps I should be off the premises too? My boy's getting married to a werewolf girl next month, some folks might think that that means I'm a suspect too?"

Parker stared sullenly at Hodgeson. "And if you go on paid leave, who knows who you'll speak to…", then he thought better of carrying on and just curtly requested Hodgeson to get back to his duties.

Other new directors were out and about, attempting to throw their weight around, they were mostly disappointed.

The three company regiments had closed their gates and were 'engaged in confidential exercises'. but could be contacted via the Liaison Office at Kings Lynn.

The development department had had an 'unfortunate toxic spillage' and no one was entering or leaving this week.

Sales were suddenly all out in the field, and the helio office was having problems with its near repeater station so couldn't contact them.

The legal department seemed to have evaporated, which since it was staffed almost exclusively by vampires who should be reporting to registration centres was understandable.

Only Accounts was open for business, but nobody wanted to speak to them…and a jolly good job too!

The absence of 'The Chief' meant that very little active business was taking place, and there were only just so many 'Board Meetings' that could be held before they become 'Bored Meetings'. Decisions were taken, retaken, revised, modified, further discussed, but always at the end of the day nothing changed.

The company seemed to be running itself....the board were superfluous!

CHAPTER 14

Somewhere beyond the map make's art lies a wide reed encircled lagoon. The water is shallow, but not so shallow that the tidal range ever allows it to dry out, but still not so deep that in the brackish water reed beds and willow encrusted eyots have been deterred from making a semblance of land. The largest of the pseudo-islands boasts a small lake of fresh water, and somebody seems to have been 'improving' its banks with woven wattle screens of willow withies (tricky to say that!) A couple of what appear to be at close quarters to be watch towers, (but which at a distance just look like random accumulations of driftwood), are situated to the north and the south of the lagoon. In amongst the tallest of the willows, and connected to the shore of two separate islands by well secured gangplanks, is a very competent looking paddle steamer. It bears the name *Seapack* on its bows, and while unpretentious, shows all the signs of being extremely well designed, maintained and run. A heavily bearded Captain stands on the low bridge between the two paddle-boxes, the crew, such of them that are in sight, are either well rounded ladies or portly gentlemen with beards to rival or exceed the Captain's! Much of the deck space, especially if it is in a sunny spot, seems to be taken up by very, *very* large shaggy dogs of a wolfish appearance.

In the lagoon itself there is a rather special yacht, the sort of thing that costs a fortune and *still sails well*! Rather remarkable. It has a lupin blossom painted on its bows and the name '*WE FLOWER!*', which really ought to give you a clue to what is going on.

(surely you are able to solve anagrams!)

The skipper is talking….

"These are Jenny's people! We can trust them absolutely! Amazing that when all the other packs were going in for rugby and squash and all that sort of thing, that so few took up sailing and so forth. You see that smoke stack! Mostly for the galley fire, oh they've got a small steam auxiliary for when it's really needed, but I had this built for them years and years ago. The motive power comes from treadmills! You get the whole pack up for an extended run and it positively surges forwards….I'd back it against anything in the North Sea any day! Well, we won't intrude upon them any longer, we'll just get the dinghy out and make for the bungalow!"

The Chiefs idea of a 'bungalow' was pretty luxurious. How, or when, it had been built no one could say, but it was certainly a secret known mostly to himself, his Mistress Jenny and the Sea Pack. It was everything you could wish for in a hideaway, there being some amazingly ingenious devices, such as floating islands of willow trees, that could be moored across the approaches to the lagoon to completely conceal any evidence of the lagoon to passing shipping, while the top of the southern lookout tower was strategically placed so that a watcher could intercept signals from the helio station further up the channel. The Sea Pack were clearly running patrols around the perimeter, and every once in a while a huge wolf would doggy paddle up to the beach by the bungalow, haul out, shake itself dry, and mid shake, morph into a somewhat tubby mariner with a report on area security.

"So," said Carlotta, "have they given you the sack!"

"What a delightfully old fashioned term! Yes…the…er ...sack!…No! They can't do that, not easily anyway. I suspect that they need to find other ways of getting rid of me.

With the current climate, and I'm afraid it really has deteriorated since you've been away Sandy, if you can rake up enough scandal and enough intrigue you can do anything.

Do you know they're clamouring for you to be interned!

EA can't function without a very large staff of revenants, the future is clearly about us all working together, in every respect. I've been waiting for the right opportunity, but it was going to come very, very soon.

You see Jenny and I are going to wed, actually start our own pack! EA by next Yule would have had a werewolf in Senior management!

But, little chance of that !. The Arch Duke nonsense has put paid to it. But…but…the really big but! The papers here were more than ready for the news!

The Human League had all their publicity prepared…pre-prepaired! It was pre-printed! They must have known what was going to happen. The Constructivists, *and* the Beliefers were left out in the cold. The Beliefers even think that their presses were sabotaged so that their pamphlets, and so on, couldn't be got out in time to put other sides of the story. And it's still going on!

I get my own private intercepts, as you can see, and what comes *in* from the Continent *isn't* what's reported. You've been there, you've seen the confusion. There clearly isn't a monster controlling consciousness, the Arch Duke *is* there, but resistance is strong, and he's not getting it all his own way. Now, whether that's to do with the Grand Dukes, and all the others who've taken themselves off to the 'other side', I wouldn't like to say, *but* I'm certain there's something far, far more sinister than a Draculian plot! The poor creatures are clearly not in charge. I suspect the Chinese!"

Jenny returned at this stage bearing four enormous Steins full of German beer. The glass glistened with semi-frozen globules of ice.

"Oil powered fridge!" she commented laconically. "Darling, are you sure about the Chinese bit? It's always been a pet hate of your's."

"'Solutely dear! I even recognise some faces. The Human League delegate's aide at the conference was making eyes at the Chinese, and damn me if he doesn't turn up as one of the 'new directors'!"

"Why not tell Carlotta and Sandy about what has been happening over the last eighteen months? There's a lot more to all this, and they've been in the thick of it for a while, together we might all cobble something together?"

Jenny had a very calming, gentle, homely influence, a logical patient approach and an intense loyalty to Arthur. Carlotta smiled inwardly, and remembered why she always enjoyed working with werewolves!

"Right! First things first. Jenny will say I'm jumping to conclusions, but this is the way it seems to me. Number one, in the last ten years the sea level has dropped a further three metres, not much you might think, but it's not just an inconvenience for harbours and shipping, and dredging the rivers bit deeper….all that water has to go somewhere, and it's gone into the ice cap, and that's increased the spread of ice in Asia, in fact its wiped out several enormous Chinese mines. The Americans aren't affected because they've given up on the North decades ago and are using South America as their mineral reserve. Please remember this, it will be important later on, oh, also it's resulted in even less rain than ever in Africa, and almost all economic activity north of the Equator has ceased. Right. Well, the next thing is the sudden rise on the world markets of the price of Lithium, and certain other elements. Not much interest to Europe, eh! Lithium is only important if you are using electricity, which of course has no use whatsoever in Europe, so nobody is interested in the fact!

Now, where is the largest untouched reserve of Lithium in the world?"

"Afghanistan!" answered Sandy

"Exactly! And! What else is there?"

"Wastelanders!"

"Poor creatures!"

Carlotta and Jenny exchanged knowing looks as their respective partners looked very serious and solemn….it was amazing that despite *every* revenant having a major problem to balance their physical and spirit bodies, they always thought that Zombies had a raw deal!

"I believe," stated Arthur, "that EA has been infiltrated at a Director level in order to steal control technology that will allow the Chinese to exploit the Wastelanders as Slave labour to harvest minerals from Afghanistan!"

"It's a bit more than director level," said Sandy, "and it's been going on for a while now. We've got some fresh data of our own to contribute. Carlotta? Would you like to bring Arthur and Jenny up to date?"

Carlotta gave a brief and succinct account of their journey to Reichenbach , Jenny pressing for 'more details later', then went on to describe the events at the ball.

"So," she finished, "it all fits in, but after we dug deeper we found two key words KIRKUK and STULHEIM. Kirkuk I think I know about. An ancient infrastructure of railways and roads that could be resurrected to move materials out of not just Afghanistan, but the whole of the old Middle East. No need for engines if you have gangs of Zombies enslaved for the purpose. Stulheim I know nothing about, but it is clearly most important!" she stopped, and Jenny clasped her to herself, hugging her and showing her approval of her active role in events.

"Nasty! Very nasty!" Arthur said, shaking his head. "I thought that all that disgusting business had been settled a long time ago!" he looked pale and seemed to have temporarily lost his youthful looks.

"Stulheim isn't an it, it's a him! EA and Universal Armaments, plus some special agents from….well let's say 'good friends', got together and, we thought, eliminated the evil. Clearly we weren't radical enough!"

"What was it?" asked Carlotta, her mind already picking up Arthurs disquiet and deep disgust.

"Vampiric Essence!"

"But, that's a nonsense! It's a flawed formula, it doesn't work!"

"No? If you capture a vampire and inject them with the synthetic essence, then you can slowly drain them of their own, *natural* essence, the synthetic stuff keeps them alive for, oh…several months, during which time they struggle to make more essence. The genuine Vampiric Essence sells for more than you could ever imagine, and it extends life, cures all but the most serious injury, produces the most alarmingly healthy children….*and it works outside Europe*! It would be the most valuable substance in the world. No vampire would ever be safe again, and from what we found when we over ran Stulheim's establishment…… it was a horrific way to go! Urgh! But, what I also see is that a small shot of the essence would allow a non-European to work with impunity inside the Wasteland! This would be the key to allowing the Chinese to exploit the Wastelands! We lost three quarters of the team that took out Stulheim, that leaves four people who could possibly know about *true* Vampiric Essence!"

"That explains what Stulheim means." Said Sandy, " but there's the question of controlling the Wastelanders. They'd *have* to have the Control Wands, and I think you've seen the specimen sent back to you? Where do you think it was made?"

"Oh, I've no doubt it was one of ours! You could see some crimping marks on it that exactly matched the rollers on our production line, but, but the Chinese ideograms, they had been stamped on, and were done *during* manufacture, and, in addition, the ideograms had mistakes in them, mistakes that no Chinese operative would have made…err…the symbol for 'wand' had been mis-written as ' washing line'. You're right, it's not just the directors, somebody has been moonlighting in the workshops, but they haven't just been knocking out Christmas presents!"

The level of beer in the chilled glass steins dropped, and at intervals Jenny disappeared into the back rooms of the bungalow, and appetising smells began to arise.

"Roast goose!" she announced after one particularly savoury breeze wafted through. "The pack were concentrating on small game yesterday, so it's all wildfowl mostly. Next week it's time to visit the mainland, and we'll have venison and maybe a wild boar or two. We can be very, very selective, so there's never really a close season. Last week it was all fish! Very nice, but eels can get a bit monotonous."

"How do you catch them?" asked Carlotta

"If we're in a hurry, then we just dump down a whole lot of withy baskets with scraps in them, but there are a few lagoons where we have really big fish traps, and then it's fantasticfun! The whole pack just leap in and it's a free for all! Late summer of course, when the salmon are running….well we get all sorts of requests from land-based packs to come and join us for a week! It's rapidly becoming the werewolf equivalent of the Grand National!"

"You know," said Arthur, "I want to hear anything more you've got to tell me about these assassins, the ones with the metal wires implanted into their skulls?"

"We've told you everything that we saw, and were told by Ruprecht, but I understand that he sent you a sample?"

"Yes. I kept that very quiet, and got it properly investigated. Had to have been done somewhere within Europe because of the alloys that they used. It's a development of the old 'kriegshelm' that vampire commanders used to use to avoid anyone snooping on their battle-plans, but unlike the helmet, you'd not be able to take it off. I understand that anyone wearing one is functionally invisible to a revenant?"

"Well," remarked Carlotta, "I certainly wasn't aware of the three assassins that we saw until the actions of people around them prompted me. Very odd, sort of one moment they weren't there, and then they were. Ruprecht's security team did find out that the 'invisibility' bit wore off at close quarters. I've worn one of the old kriegshelms, and it left me feeling blind, deaf and very disorientated. The Grand Duke was wearing one as a precaution when he 'called us back', but I'm doubtful now it was necessary…"

"I don't know," Arthur pondered, "it would all be a bit too late once he'd got well and truly into your mind. Better safe than sorry! But if all the reports are true there's a very vigorous resistance movement out there, and vampires are playing their part along with everyone else. We'll know more once you link up with

Transylvania in Exile, however, to get back to business. If you put together the 'invisible' assassins, the Vampiric Essence, the control wands and the reports from the Wastelands there's a very coherent story emerging of a Chinese plan to seize the mineral wealth of what used to be the Middle East, ironically by using the very people who once made it a no go area for industry and led to the mineral reserves being untapped. So, that's part one. Part two is just what sort of mischief they got up to in order to lay their hands on the materials they needed. I have to tell you that Essex Armaments has been taken over at a shareholder level. No one was watching what was happening, and the share price suddenly rose, a number of eager buyers took everything that was going, and without any warning we woke up with the majority holding being with the leaders of The Human League, who I suspect are bankrolled by the Chinese. On the continent the Draculians seem to have been similarly financed and have been promised the resurrection of the Arch Duke. The assassins seem to be an enforcement arm, whether established by the Chinese, or as an independent organisation I don't know."

"That," said Carlotta, "covers most of the situation, but it must go back a lot further than there. Those assassins weren't created just like that. There must have been trials, mistakes, people who talked and were silenced, and then the surgical facility, that would be hard to keep quiet, I mean illness and things like that are so rare since the 'accident' and everyone lives to a much more than ripe old age quite naturally. It's made medicine a very rare science outside of military applications. Where would you hide your 'assassin factory'? Then again, the losses of weapons and formulae from EA, the message that the audit had been faked, that's all pre-take over, there has to be long term planning."

"I certainly agree, *and* I'd add that the Human League and the Draculians seem to be stooges in all this. I don't have fine details about the Draculians, but we've been keeping an eye on the Human League for a few years now, and they never had two ha'pennies to rub together, at least until eighteen months ago, but in the last six months it seems they've not just brought up EA but several national newspapers as well. They are whipping up public opinion into a xenophobic frenzy, that's why we couldn't have you two arriving by the usual channels."

"Just what are we going to do?" asked Sandy.

"I'll tell you after dinner!" Arthur replied "I think those geese are more than ready to eat!"

....

Essex Armaments was still in an uncertain state, not mutiny, not a strike, not a workers take-over….nothing in fact that could be categorised. However, given the enormous proliferation and employment of the military mind in the company there were plenty of opportunities for dumb insolence, wilful ignorance and plain honest mulishness that meant the new owners weren't making much headway.

Internal regimes still prevailed. Security had closed down Accounts, and further, the Third Company Regiment was having a rest day, so all business was on hold. The day after the Second Regiment was also 'on rest', and then field exercises with 'non-revetted' weapons meant that all non-military personnel had to be 'off base' certainly did not help. In vain the new directors decided to visit workshops and show their prerogatives of ownership off there, but it was even worse. "Sorry sir, you could well be the new director, but until the Chief sends me a memo I'm not letting you in….more than me jobs worth!"

In the midst of this calculated disobedience a small group of people had landed in a civilian marina at New Frinton, and were slowly, even leisurely, exploring the gentle valley of the river Stour.

It is a pretty place, even in indifferent weather, and the industrial archaeology of the defunct docks at Harwich and the stately remains of Felixstowe across the river are an excellent basis for a picnic. The party consisted of an elderly gentlemen and a very elegant lady of indeterminate years, she was riding a rather fine horse, and he was followed on foot by a very large, rather threatening dog. The horse had a pannier which seemed to contain everything the party could need, and then more.

After a long days march, where despite seeming to wander gently they certainly covered the miles, they eventually set up a camp on the wide green lawns of the river Stour within sight of the extremely ancient military site (long since abandoned) of Shotley.

"To think " Arthur intoned, "That that place was once at the hub of military technology, *flying machines* no less!"

"To which," Sandy commented, picking bits of grass from out of his teeth "we have still not aspired!"

"Oh, just let me see a steam engine light enough, old boy, and you'll be surprised, you really will!" then the pair of them went outside the tent leaving Jenny and Carlotta alone.

"I think it's best," said Jenny, "that we're beyond all of that. There's a beautiful balance in the way things are now, just enough technology, just enough belief, just enough uncertainty, just enough….well you know what I mean. I'd never go back….ever!"

Carlotta looked up surprised. "Are you…from the times before?"

"Yes. I've wandered about a bit. I joined the Sea Pack just as things were getting nasty in Holland….well what used to be Holland….before it got swallowed up and then regurgitated as part of a 'Germanic Principality'. I've, ... been an awful lot of 'things', with an awful lot of different people....I just hope Arthur's got the guts to 'take the bite' and let us start our own pack!"

Arthur was outside for the present, 'checking up', and Sandy was making a 'wide patrol' in his other persona, which meant it was a very wide patrol indeed. Between them they'd have a very fair view of any threats that were out there tonight.

"What are you hoping for?" asked Carlotta.

"What any of us hope for! A little ease, some fun, a chance to contribute to the future, and hope that it will last as long as possible!"

"Well....if Arthur accepts... 'the bite'...then it could be forever!"

"Forever is a long time! Your man there! I can see it....he's Grand Duke material...oh, I know he's not a vampire, it stands out a mile, but if he wants to control thousands, order the troops into battle, he's only got to click his fingers...you know that!"

"Yes. I do. And I also know that he's spent long sleepless nights, ones he hasn't owned up to, worrying about the risk he's put a few very capable, 'deathless' vampires to. I think I've got a 'good 'un', but I see your point....Where's Arthur going to?"

"I think he's going to be fantastic pack father! More, he's going to be the grandfather and great-grandfather of packs unborn, just as long as he doesn't sacrifice himself for some silly little something. I *need to look after him*, he's my pup, and I've had a few over the years, but this one is gold, pure gold, if he doesn't deserve a Barons badge no one does!"

"I know what you mean. In our luggage we've got a little package from the Grand Duke Orlov. It's got his jewel and a letter. He's bequeathed his gem and his rank to Sandy, actually made Sandy into a Grand Duke by standing down himself. Sandy doesn't know what to make of it, in fact he hasn't even told me about it, but I've seen it there in his mind when he sleeps.."

"Oh,." Said Jenny, "do you do that too?"

"Yes," said Carlotta, "it's the only way with humans!"

CHAPTER 15

"Are you sure we shouldn't all be going on this jaunt?" asked Carlotta.

"Quite sure! The guards will be perfectly happy as long as they only see 'old faces'. These are supposed to be reserve premises, in 'moth balls' as it were. There should only be a minimum guard, if there isn't we'll come straight back. We want to have a look at what's going on inside, this is the works where that crimping roller should be located that left its mark on the control wand. It's the obvious place for making some clandestine goods, and nearby to the river, so there's a route out for a consignment."

"Well….alright, but Jenny and I are coming with you as far as the copse of trees before the gate-house. We'll both be listening, and if there's any trouble we're coming in! Understood!"

"Absolutely!"

……………………..

Some little time later all four were assembled in the tiny clump of trees and Jenny was checking over Arthur's preparedness. while Sandy and Carlotta were whispering together about the forthcoming expedition.

"Don't forget," Jenny commanded, "your left knee will give way if you run too fast, try to pace yourself….oh I *do* wish you'd let me give you that bite!"

"Soon!"

Carlotta was warning Sandy about not being too confident and advising him to check what he thought he could see with what

Arthur was seeing "After all" she commented, "we still don't know all there is to know about those assassins yet!"

The plan depended upon getting in range without alarming suspicion, and making good use of Sandy and Arthurs very well-known features to help allay that possible suspicion.

A bottle of whiskey also figured in the plan.

The road took a sharp bend about fifty metres before the gate-house, and at this point there was a good deal of deep ragged shadow into which the two figures slid and vanished.

Sandy concentrated for a few seconds and then his night vision snapped into place. Every detail of the red brick lodge and its ornate cast-iron gates clear as daylight. There was one guard in an old fashioned sentry box and another making his beat along the road in front of the building. At his eastern-most point, when he halted and turned, he was about four metres away from where Sandy and Arthur were crouched.

Inside the gate-house, visible as shadows against a blind were two more men, they seemed to be at a game of cards. A light was burning in the window of the tiny room above the archway.

"Four!" said Sandy

"Standard procedure. Even if there is anything going on, they'll stick to what <u>ought</u> to be happening out here beside the road. I can't see anything to suggest more guards. How about you?"

"Umph! Let me concentrate, I'm looking for heart beats, that sort of thing. It only works at this sort of range, I've no idea what could be going on down by the workshops, but there's only four hearts beating just here!"

"Right. Well, let's be a bit more cautious, I'd never forgive myself if I did something silly and left Jenny all alone. Should have taken that damned bite really!....OK!....We've both sent out sentry and guard parties, what will this one have been told? You go through it.."

"Right! Leader of guard is given a list of names. A time and a location. When relief is due. How to signal for help. Weapons are checked. Supplies issued, transport, if needed, is arranged...am I missing anything?"

"Ummm. It's a night guard, any extra's?"

"Lighting. We've given up on oil lamps because a lucky shot with a cross bow and you've got an instant conflagration, so candles have been issued, and matches....and....and....*and there's never quite enough to play cards unless you're careful, so why are they wasting one in the upstairs room!"*

"I think you've got something there. Are you sure it's only four heart beats?"

"Certain, are you sure that rooms empty?"

"It looks it at first sight. I'm concentrating on the shadows, yes....a distinct flicker...could have been a breeze, but it's a still night...yes...again, and now *Look! Look! Somebody moved across the light!"*

"I was looking, but I didn't see it. Sinister! Seems we have an assassin, also seems I've definitely got a down-side to these 'vampire powers' the minuses as well as the pluses are there after all, just fortunate that it's only little things to worry about!"

"Invisible assassins are a little thing? I'd hate to have your major issues!"

"Alright, let's treat this as a bonus! A chance to investigate the workshops, *and* a chance to take a valuable prisoner!"

"Very good. How?"

"Well…….."

It was a good plan, and just because it did not go according to schedule and varied a great deal in content did not make it unsuccessful.

The sentry making the beat of the road had met with a sudden abrupt accident and was lying bound in the ditch. His colleague had fallen asleep after the most pressing feelings of lassitude had come upon him. As his head nodded forwards he had been gently taken, also placed in bonds, and laid in an out of the way corner. The assailants were just wondering how they were to extricate the two card players without arousing the attention of the unknown person in the archway room, when a jingling of harness bells was heard and around the corner of the road from a westerly direction came a small train of pack-ponies and their drivers. One of them, clearly expecting some sort of challenge blew upon a double reeded whistle and drew back the shutter on a dark lantern, waving it to and fro. The inside guards tumbled out and made haste to light a similar lantern and begin making a two letter Morse signal to the pack pony drivers.

In the confusion the missing guards were overlooked at first and then cursed for 'never being around when there's work to do'

Sandy and Arthur kept well back in the shadows, and Arthur had the presence of mind to take the last guards helmet and put it on as emergency camouflage should they be spotted.

The person in the upper room seemed to have been waiting for this arrival and came down with a bundle of papers and a small leather pouch of coins. Papers and coins were exchanged, and the two listeners in the shadows heard '….three nights time….password FX….no, we can't say when….just be ready to load up…..' then the pack ponies vanished noisily into the night, for a noisy pack pony train is a *normal* occurrence near the coast, whereas a silent one would have everyone talking for months to come.

Sandy was now able to see the strange figure from upstairs, clearly human and with a noticeable swollen line across its forehead, but if they moved a little too quickly they became faint and indistinct. Arthur was at the crouch, muscles tensed, and clearly about to do something a little less than sensible, but it was the ideal opportunity! The target in open ground, and distracted, the two guards still unaware of their comrades disappearance and the close presence of an enemy.

Arthur sprung, taking the whiskey bottle (that was to have been a prop for two drunks accosting the guard), and using it as a club. The assassin fell at once to the onslaught, leaving Sandy to deal with the pair of guards, both of whom now seemed to have picked up their crossbows and managed to cock them. He leapt in striking the first guards bow upwards and out of his grip, following through with a punch that hurled the man backwards into the railings of the gateway, but the second guard had sidestepped, and even now was tightening his trigger finger and aiming the bow unerringly at Arthur's heart.

From the outer darkness two shapes came hurtling forwards, one was a huge grey wolf that both blocked and pushed aside the bow. As the wolf sailed past, a crossbow bolt protruding from its shoulder, the second shape swept across the field of view and the guard fell dead at Arthurs feet.

There was an odd sort of flurry of fur, blood and a flash of bare human skin, and then Jenny stood before them wearing very little indeed and clutching at a shallow wound in her shoulder

"It's alright!" she said "If you can get the transformation right, and fast enough, you can sort of shrug an arrow out."

"You're bleeding!" said Carlotta, suddenly there from nowhere.

"It'll stop. It's a clean wound....but...Arthur....you could have been killed!"

She stepped over to where he stood, the crumpled body of the assassin lying in front of him, and put her arms around his neck, hugging him close to her.

"I said you were to be careful!" and she buried her face in his neck, stifling back the sobs, and repeatedly kissing him. Then there was a brief yelp from Arthur where the kisses had turned to love bites, and very shortly Jenny seemed to regain control of herself and they gave their undivided attention to securing the prisoners and investigating the gate-house.

It seemed to be being used as a store of small packages, all with serial numbers. Clearly a collection point for whoever the pack pony trains were organised by. A quick tear and rip of the heavy waxed paper covering revealed small wooden boxes, labelled in Chinese ideograms, and containing, among other things Control Wands.

"I think," said Jenny, "that this is evidence enough of where the items come from, and that illegal export is going on. We don't need to risk ourselves further tonight. Let's get to somewhere we can contact other people!"

....

The heliograph may well be the pinnacle of European high speed long distance communication, but it does not work very well in the absence of sunlight, though over short distances incandescent gas lamps can be startlingly effective. This night a much older system was in operation, and the beautiful lonely melody of a wolf's howl was drifting across the darkened landscape.

It started with a general 'is there anybody there?' note, and as other howls began to be raised went on into what was clearly an identifier and a request.

Then there was a silence of about a minute or two, then a single clear note from perhaps ten miles or so away.

The wolf that was Jenny seemed to be holding a conversation with clear questions and responses. After what seemed to be an age of lengthy pauses and once or twice a complete shift of 180 degrees to communicate with another wolf in another direction, Jenny stood away from the low mound she had been using as a kind of improvised podium and had a good shake, as she did so the dimly perceived wolf shape blurred, and seamlessly became the human version of Jenny.

"The Sea Pack are too far away to help us, but there's some good allies of ours about twenty miles away, they'll be with us within the hour!"

"Impressive!" said Sandy "Will they be able to take charge of our 'prisoner'?"

"Yes, and they'll deliver straight to our own people at Essex House, they know all the secret ways through. We've dealt with this pack before. It's the Havering Harriers.

Remember Arthur?

The affair of the so called Portuguese trade federation?"

"Oh yes!" chuckled Arthur "That was a 'to do'! Spies no less!

After our latest cavalry saddle design so they could sell it to the Americans.

Anyway, this pack are adept at moving people around without arousing suspicion. I think we can reasonably expect our mysterious 'assassin' to be safely under lock and key within a few days. Meanwhile we need to start using what we've found out."

"Who do we tell?" asked Carlotta, "After all, from what you've told us the political situation is a bit unsettled, and the press has doubtful loyalty and motivation, and the Company seems to have been 'taken over'. Who do we turn to?"

"We turn to ourselves, for *we* are the *they* who 'should do something about it', as people are fond of putting it. Sandy knows about the 'Freedom Plan', don't you?"

"That! I thought that was only for use in case of a revolution, or the fall of the government to invaders….that sort of thing!"

"Which my boy, is exactly what is happening. A political party, and although I hate say it, the Human League is now a major party, has attempted to take control of Essex Armaments by manipulating the Stock Exchange, it has also similarly infiltrated the 'free press', a national institution, and because of the very fragile multiparty government we have may well take over that government. There are violent Human League instigated anti-revenant demonstrations, arbitrary laws have been rushed through to seriously damage the long term culture and ethos of this island. And, across the way in Transylvania there is talk of the revival of Draculian policies, including war on Britannia. Human League politicians have been shown to be in collusion with the Draculians, suggesting that we may in fact be betrayed if it does come to a conflict. *I think* that counts as a National Disaster. I am putting the plan into effect just as soon as we have daylight and a helio station!"

"Alright" said Carlotta, "But you've been suspended from duty. Who will obey the signal?"

"Well, I rather think everybody will! After all I sent out instructions for everyone to avoid allowing the new directors any opportunity to make changes, view data or interfere with company running, and as far as I can see everyone has complied!"

"Yes," said Jenny, "you have really been rather busy for somebody who was supposed to be 'taking a rest'. As soon as the Havering Harriers get here you sleep! Properly!"

"Right O! Oh, does anyone recognise that 'assassin'? I think she looks oddly familiar, seen a picture or something somewhere.

But I suppose after all that surgery she might be a bit hard to identify."

……………………..

Jenny and Arthur were starting out for a cross country trek that would after a few days bring them to Essex House, and Arthurs stronghold from which he intended to take back control of the Company. The 'Freedom Plan' messages had been sent, and by the time he arrived should be nicely matured.

"Pity they couldn't have found a quicker way to get there." Sandy mused as the couple disappeared along a weed grown footpath.

"It might not take them so long as Arthur thinks!" Carlotta said with a grin.

"How do you mean?"

"Well, it's a good two day walk, but half a day's steady lope for a wolf will have it done."

"Well, that would get Jenny there but…"

"Oh Sandy! Didn't you see what happened? She nearly lost him last night! That cross bow bolt would have done for him, instantly at that range! She's been on at him to take the plunge. Didn't you see that nip she gave him? He doesn't know it yet, but he's a good solid werewolf now!"

……………………………………

"And now!" Carlotta was standing surveying their not very extensive luggage, "and now, it is our turn to join the battle. Should we go straight to Transylvania in Exile or report to Whitehall first?"

"I wouldn't rate our chances of doing that much good at Westminster. Don't forget I'm a citizen of both Britannia and Transylvania now, so either side can arrest me, perhaps even both at once, and I still haven't really got a clue about what we are supposed to be doing. My real skills are assessing the situation in the field and suggesting ways to make the situation safe."

"Don't under estimate yourself. You have the trust of a great many politicians on both sides, you are used to dealing with humans and revenants, you yourself are now a revenant, though just what kind goodness only knows. A great war leader who transforms into a horse is just a bit odd! Nice, but odd, nonetheless!"

"Alright, I have a role to play as a bridge between two cultures, and I've….got some very special….negotiating abilities and properties. I vote we get down to, where is? New Brighton? We'll introduce ourselves and see if they'll let us play!"

"Sounds like a good plan to me. How's your back?"

“Always broad enough to carry you my lady!”

There was a polite cough from the otherside of the nearby hedgerow, and through the gap in the hedge trouped six stalwart young persons. They had very sensible walking shoes on and very serviceable outdoor clothing,and each had a small leather satchel hung over one shoulder.

“Err. Excuse me sir and madam. The Baron said you might be needing our services!” He touched his forelock, “Havering Harriers First Junior Pack, at your service. We’re to go with you as far as New Brighton and see you safe to Werewolf Central Control. If it please you, we’re happy to travel either way round. Was you intending to transform sir? Only we’ve heard about it and would rather like the privilege of seeing how it’s done!”.

Sandy was somewhat taken aback. Of course people would talk, and in the werewolf community transformation was always a matter for intense, fascinated, discussion. Which way did you do it? The shake? Or the shrug? Or the dissolving view? Or even the very unpopular old fashioned morphing monster?

“Err, of course! Yes! I shall be…err…*transforming,* but as of yet I don’t have a preferred method…”

“ ’Course not sir! ‘Course not. It must be very early days. After all it usually takes those of us born to it, months to sort it all out!”

CHAPTER 16

In the end a little cavalcade set out along the old greenway that leads to the new bridge in the deep valley below Canvey. The bridge that crosses the broad stream and picks up on the causeway across to Sheppey.

Carlotta was very impressed indeed with the way English werewolves did things. Very different indeed from Transylvania! She knew that Sandy's firm made a great many products for the discerning modern werewolf, but at home the traditionalists still stuck to basic values and self-reliance rather than 'transformation technology'. Essex Armaments really had developed werewolf accessories to a fine art.

Each of the six wolves comfortably loping alongside the cantering horse was wearing a broad canvas collar and a brief harness, attached to which was a small khaki canvas pouch. The effect was very military, very functional, very business-like.

At transformation the collar and harness became the clothing, and the canvas pouch turned into the leather shoulder bag.

A perfect solution to the old werewolf-to-naked-human problem.

EA armourers had worked for years with vampire colleagues to find out the vampires transformational secrets that let clothes follow bats, and further more allowed changes in the *expression* of the physical form to occur.

The result had been exploited in England to allow werewolves to fit into a wide range of social settings and to now be rapidly on the way to be *expected* members of any work group, society or community.

The journey was progressing well.

Towards the end of the first days march two of the 'wolves' had accelerated ahead, vanishing over the horizon quickly and easily. A hour or so later the others caught them up, they were standing outside an Inn, ale mugs in their hands, and rooms and facilities booked for the main party for the forthcoming night. They had also run a wide patrol around the inn and could report no dangerous activity within ten miles. Local packs had been brought into the activity and would be maintaining a guard for the night. There were one or two hopeful young, local, pack members hanging around for a glimpse of the celebrity travellers!

Sandy took the leader of the junior pack aside.

"Are there any humans you can trust here, and who will help?"

"Yes, one or two."

"Good. Get them to join your guard. You want them to double check places where you *don't* think anyone is!" and he explained about the *assassins.*

The bridge below Canvey posed a minor problem, but one that could easily grow into a major problem.

It was guarded!

One of the young werewolves had come back with a report.

"It's a military guard sir! I left Fred up on the ridge and ran down to have a closer look. An infantry detachment, six privates, a corporal and a sergeant. They've got a couple of big telescopes trained on the road coming down to the crossing. I heard what you did sir, in Transylvania, making your transformation change so you was a different sort of horse, and I thought, well, let's give it a try. It feels real funny sir, being a Dalmatian! But it let me get right up close and listen in. They've got descriptions of you and the lady sir. They're watching and waiting for 'an elegant lady on a strong horse'. I wanted to listen some more, but my tail kept on going bushy, so I got out sharpish!"

……………………..

"So, what have we got?" asked Sandy. He was involving the junior pack as much as he could, their enthusiasm and ingenuity were inspiring. Carlotta was already talking about some kind of exchange visit scheme with Transylvania once the difficulties were over.

"Well sir. This is the town of Canvey Bridge. It isn't over large, in fact it's only here because of the bridge and the stadium. This is the best crossing point between Essex and Kent, so it's the natural place for the Rugby stadium. Mostly werewolf rugby, but some human matches to! The town's mostly hotels, hostels, inns, eateries (best steak tartare in Essex!) Oh, and there's lots of souvenir shops and sports shops. The population live a bit further down river (much quieter on match nights).

"Normally there are no controls on the crossing, tolls were discontinued years ago, so this is something special, and I guess they are not used to doing it, which may be helpful.

"Next, usual daily activity. You see we spent a month here supporting the pack team last year.

Most travellers make the crossing between mid-morning and early afternoon. You see a fog often builds up, and the causeway on the Kent side is miles long, has poor banks, and sometimes people have been known to get tired, mistake their footing and tumble off the causeway and into the marsh. Looks like a good fog building up today, should start rolling down river at three-ish, you might be able to make use of that, I don't know how, but you might!"

"An excellent summary, and it's already given me some ideas. When's the next rugby match due?"

"Oh, not for months sir, but there's always practices going on, and amateur teams visiting, but not an actual match, sorry!"

"No, that's OK, you say there's visitors? Tourists sort of thing?"

"Yes, that's why the gift shops do so well."

"Right! Then here's what we'll do. You know those souvenir rugby outfits they sell, the err…*strip* I think it's called?"

"Err…yes….they're a bit daft really…"

"Yes, I know ! No real player would be seen dead in one, but I want you to go down into town, well in fact I want several of you to go, and buy us eight over-sized sets of…err…*strip*…got that ?"

"Absolutely Sir! You have a plan?"

……………………………………

The dense sticky grey fog was rolling inexorably down river. Warm air from the upper valleys of the Thames was now cooling and strolling downwards to the sea, taking with it a burden of moisture, and available soot particles and dust from the nearby roads. The bridge head, with its long abandoned toll booth and bar was just starting to feel clammy. The Private currently in charge of *telescope one* completed his transit of the upper road, then paused and swept the great brass barrel back for a second view.

"Sarge! Sarge! Lady on a horse! It's a big 'un too!"

Third false alarm this day! He'd be glad when it was just too thick to see, that way they'd be able to shut up shop early and go back to base for a cuppa.

"Let's have a look them! It's not another kiddy on a donkey is it?"

The sergeant wiped the murk of off the lens and applied a large bloodshot eye. "Oh, it's just another of your….no…yes…..it's them…must be…turn out the guard!"

In the misty circle of magnified light the lady and horse seemed to make their way steadily down the street that descended the valley side towards the crossing. No doubt about who it was. A very elegant lady on a very powerful horse. They were coming up to the cross roads, the cross roads where the huge banners welcoming the forthcoming county champions drooped and obscured the view.

"She's turned off Sarge! At the cross roads!"

"Quick! Corporal, get your squad up there at once! Follow the Southend Road, catch them up. Hang on, leave two men here, just in case!"

The two men left, just in case, with only six crossbow bolts each (you won't need any more than that!) sat in gathering discomfort, dampness, gloom and dissatisfaction.

"Serve 'em right if they do catch them up and get their blood sucked out!"

"That don't happen any more!"

"'Snot what the Human League says!"

"Oh that lot!"

Figures loomed out of the fog.

"Bridge guard! Bridge guard! Come on! On your toes! We need to be across before nightfall! Come on! Is it papers to stamp?"

The first guard looked worriedly into the gloom. He decided on balance that it was better not to level his crossbow at the figure, after all there were so many revenants about who took exception to damage to clothing from arrows, and people had actually been fined for causing that sort of damage, and *some* of those shirts the *really fancy* vampires wore would be a week's wages just to get the stains out.

"Who is it?"

"Dengie Junior Werewolf Pack and Pack Parents on a running holiday of Kent. Come on, we haven't got all day!"

Ah! Well! Yes! Pretty decent types those werewolves. If only a few more human families took the time and care to raise youngsters in a health outdoor manner.

He waved the group across, noting the awful souvenir National Werewolf Rugby Squad strip that *even* the pack parents were wearing. He even watched as they noisily vanished into the fog enveloping the bridge, making it difficult to see more than the white line painted down the middle.

"Shouldn't we enter that in the book?" asked Number 2

"No!" replied the older guard. Something in his mind was suggesting that even talking about the event any more was a bad idea.

"Let's get the gear together and pack down those telescopes. When the others come back they'll thank us for being ready to go home without any more mucking about!"

"Oh! Yes! Good idea. I'll get the boxes."

A reasonable distance across from the bridge the appalling Rugby strip suddenly jettisoned itself to the ground, though in one case the wearer had to spend a moment or two sorting out the buttons. The whole caboodle was bundled together, weighted down with stones and tossed into a black pool of fog swathed water.

"That was not very classy!" commented Carlotta, "Not classy at all."

"And that," said Sandy, "is why if it is reported they won't think it's ús!"

"Yes, but having the pack sing rugby songs as we ran off!"

"Just a finishing touch. Now, we need to keep our eyes open. The Kent side comes up after a few miles. Would you like to ride?"

"Yes please!"

………………………………

"Kent shore ahead sir!" reported the scout.

"Very good." Sandy replied. "Is it guarded?"

"Yes sir! Regrettably so. Two humans and four revenants and something that we don't quite recognise."

"How do you mean?"

"Well, if you sort of, err…put one hand over one eye and sort of squint, you can make out an indistinct shape. I wouldn't have given it a second thought, only I remembered what you told me at the inn on the first night."

"Ummm! Looks like trouble, might be nothing but….have you ever seen anything like it before?"

"No sir. And we were all taken to meet old Mrs Besom, the shape-shifter at Saffron Walden, and she was a right mystery!"

“Alright. Our first task is to get through, and then to get away. But…we do it properly. You know….*the right way!”*

“Absolutely sir. Revenants can come back, so do your worse, humans don’t get a second change…so *we’ve* got to give them one…if we can!”

“That’s right. *If* you can stun or wound do it, don’t risk your own life, but don’t take theirs unless you have to!”

“Our first lesson sir!”

“Good, but no silly risks! Have your pack got any ‘special weapons’?”

“Yes sir. Issued with two Forsterite daggers, and told not to use them without your express permission!”

“Very good. Right, if we have read the signs correctly we might have to use them! Let’s get back to the others.”

Carlotta was speaking “Yes…yes…I can see them. You’re right, two humans, both very frightened, four revenants, all vampires, but…something odd, they don’t belong, I think they are *from home*, from Transylvania, and…and, and an empty space! Wow! I’m quite pleased with that! I can see something that isn’t there! There is a seventh member of their party, and I know they are there *precisely because* there’s nothing there. It’s almost as if there’s a poster saying ‘empty space’!”

“Ha!” said one of the werewolves “I think I know what you mean. In scent trials, when you are a cub, they set up very complicated trails, with missing parts, but the *spacing* gives it away, there has to be something in the gap, and that way you find the hidden object. Is it like that?”

"Very much" said Carlotta, thinking to herself again, 'These English Werewolves can teach our people so, so much!'

Alice and Edmond had ownership of the daggers. They also had ownership of large pocket handkerchiefs with which they carefully wiped the blades every minute or so. "Remember" Sandy had told them "Once we have a *fallen* enemy you plunge in the dagger, anywhere, and hold it in place for a long count of five seconds, then out, wipe, and look for the next target. Five seconds and they are out of it for two days, longer and they might not come back! Remember!"

The Vampire mind is a wonderful thing, fast, complex, resourceful, packed with data, all easily recalled, and at speed….BUT multiple processing is something it lacks…surprising, but true, which is why humans at the end of the day tend to win out (not that the vampires admit to this, but little piles of dust do tell their own story.)

Hundreds of years ago some fool invented the word 'hoplitophobe' or something like it. It was supposed to imply a pathological fear of weaponry, which is a dubious condition. The term however does come some way to expressing the horror, fear, complete terror, that comes when a vampire is required to wield a Forsterite dagger! The two, so armed, vampires at the Kent Shore had put on kid leather gloves, then gauntlets, and then wrapped heavy velvet sheets around their hands and forearms as an added precaution. It was additionally terrifying that when the vampire lady, for so she clearly was, rode up to them she reached out a hand and snatched the blade from the first guard, the edge clearly cutting her hand and raising a thin bead of blood. She distractedly viewed the damage while the four children of the night stood transfixed. She raised the dreaded dagger to her lips and daintily licked her own blood of the metal edge.

"Waste not, want not! The taste is very strange indeed, but not as unpleasant as you would think!"

She turned to the leader of the Vampire Guard "You Sir! Would you like to sample the alloy?" and she plunged the dagger into his throat. His features suddenly set into a horrific rictus as she slowly counted to five and withdrew the blade. The other three vampires, as if released from a spell began to activate, to consider attack, but the great horse reared, and boxing deftly with his hooves punched the remaining three into temporary oblivion. Figures hurried out of the mist, stabbing and counting as their weapons ensured that the three did not have the capacity to return to active duty for several days!

There was the usual transformational flurry of form changing, and the Kentish Shore bridgehead had four corpses, two tightly bound bundles that wriggled vainly against their bonds, and a strange, more-or-less human shape enclosed in a handy tarpaulin and bound with ropes.

"That's good" said Sandy, "We've got another one for questioning!"

....

Onwards, ever onwards! Across hill top pathways, through forgotten green lanes that ran through the bottoms of suburban gardens, sudden emergences into village greens and gentle pastures, but always southwards and to the west, until after less than a week they were standing on a prominent hill top over-looking Old Brighton.

New Brighton was still on the southern horizon, far out on the plain that led at last to the trickle of water that made the frontier between Britannia and France.

The old gap in the ancient cliffs that wound down to Brighton drew all the roads, paths and bye-ways to it, so that any traveller intending to visit the new lands beyond the old shore line was obliged to pass through this natural checkpoint!

And this natural check point had been recently augmented by coils of barbed wire, picket fences and a standing guard of cavalry. A mile or so beyond the 'gap' the lands of New Brighton began, where the temporary realm of 'Transylvania in Exile' exerted its presence. A shaky territory, not quite mutually agreed, but agreed nonetheless, and allowing a national entity that Britannia wanted to acknowledge (in case of events working out that way) but also wanted to be able to disown if things went 'wrong'!

There was a certain strangeness to the border guard. Two distinctly different units were present. A dowdy, utilitarian detachment, bearing national 'English' badges, and a second, larger and much better equipped group with a far better discipline and much more élan! The 'Company' troop seemed much more in charge of events, and when the great crowd appeared on the road ahead they actively shepherded the 'other' detachment off the highway and into the fields nearby, gently relieving them of their weapons as they did so.

A vast crowd of wolves flooded through the check point, and, in the very middle a somewhat bemused lady upon an enormous white horse rode onwards surrounded by a honour guard of great grey mature wolves.

CHAPTER 17

The road from Old Brighton runs initially across a causeway, there having been in distant times a deep long-shore channel that still supports a marshy tract of land, but soon it relies upon the firm ground of the New Brighton plain. It then runs straight as an arrow through pleasant green pasture lands grazed by great herds of russet coloured cattle until the spires and ornamental turrets of New Brighton come into sight. Beyond that there is the narrow strip of water that is the remains of 'La Manche', the English Channel. True it widens quite respectably as one goes westwards, but to the east you can see the shore curve around and extend, past the marker pylon with its huge flags that indicates where England ends and France finishes (depending upon your direction of travel),and becomes the French shore. The land at the pylon and thereabouts is swampy and of uncertain probity, it is a border that polices itself!

New Brighton started out as an attempt to recreate a seaside resort when the seas began to recede, but it itself is now situated a lengthy walk from the water's edge. Perhaps the isolation of the town and its purlieus from the rest of England, and its rather restricted economic value explains why the reactionary politicians of the time of our story decided it would be the best place for the Transylvanian Exiles, and transferred them there from London .

That they were happy with the result was obvious, there was hardly any local population at all, and the few people that there *were* welcomed the incomers as a chance to improve their livelihoods.

"So, exiles in exile!" Carlotta quipped.

They were sitting on the broad south facing terrace of the Grand Hotel, which looked out across a gently falling series of lawns and picturesque shrubberies to the quarter mile distant streak of silvery sea.

"Sort off." replied the Baron. He'd been obliged, since werewolves were now running Transylvania in Exile, to qualify his position as *Senior* Baron. He wasn't happy about this, and stressed that the current hierarchy of werewolf barons was 'strictly for the duration'.

"Actually we remain in close contact with London, and other major cities, and with our agents and sympathisers throughout the land, and across the water. Officially we use the helio station here to communicate with Old Brighton, and then our messages, in and out, are relayed to us. Unofficially we have friends on Beachy Head and other high points and a comprehensive private network courtesy of the English Werewolf Pack Network. We really do have a lot to learn, the packs here have done so much! As for news from abroad, well, it's quite amazing just how many French packs of Loup Garou have contacted us and made life a lot easier. We get the continental papers a whole lot faster than London, a pack on the French Shore send us over a bundle every two days by boat, and the papers often arrive from Transylvania just four days after they are printed."

"So," said Sandy, "Just what happened in London?"

"Mobs! Didn't think that sort of thing still went on, especially here in England. We know that it was Human League behind it, and our friends inform us that a lot of the 'protestors' had been paid, quite handsomely, to take part. After three days of rioting there was a decision in Parliament to offer us the New Brighton district as a 'realm in exile'. I don't know if we did the right thing in accepting it, because the Human League press and their politicians are now accusing us of a clandestine invasion of English territory! We still have an embassy in London, but there are questions being raised about the legitimacy of the staff. The Human League leaders seem to have periods of inactivity followed by bursts of intense action where they pull strings, buy off opposition, and when their enemies have 'accidents', it's as if they are waiting for instructions all the time and have no real on-board leadership. We suspect the real organisation comes from outside the party."

“So just how secure is your position here?” asked Sandy

“Pretty good! It suits the politicians at Westminster to make a distinction between the ‘Realm in Exile’ and The Transylvanian Empire!

Whatever happens they win!

If the Draculians do get the upper hand, then we become an enclave that gives all sorts of political benefits. If as we suspect, the Draculian uprising fizzles out, then they can say how generous they were to us by granting land.

However the situation in England is the real worry. You may not have noticed, having been adrift for a while, that Their Britannic Majesties government is having problems asserting its authority. Questions were asked in The House yesterday about Plenderleith’s ability to control the military! Your friends at EA have become a third force in the land.

They’ve completely rejected the High Court’s orders to allow the shareholders access, via their directors, to the company’s assets. The Court can no longer enforce its demands since the EA regiments have taken control of the civil authority on and around EA property. EA has made the claim that since the major companies were accorded party and even state status they must use their own judgement. Now, that was a clever turn around, because we found out that all the lobbying to get the Industry that special diplomatic status came from the Human League, and it looks as if they intended to use EA’s resources to take over the country, except EA beat them to it….sort of…well, I don’t think they want to take over, just restore the traditional system.”

“I hope so” Carlotta murmured, and Sandy echoed her comment.

“What’s your summary then?” Sandy asked the Senior Baron.

“Transylvania *and* Britannia have both been infiltrated by a foreign power with enormous resources. We have both been destabilised by an appeal to extremist traditionalists in our population. Money did the job here in Britannia, and in Transylvania the promise (or the threat) of the Archduke, plus some very long prepared…err…*inhuman resources?"*

"Long prepared is certainly the word. Are you up to date with these, err, *assassins?"*

"EA keeps us very well briefed, and I have other sources as well."

Sandy had a brief mental image of the place 'in between'. He nodded to the Senior Baron, and lightly touched his brow where you would expect horns (if you had them) The Baron looked startled, and then smiled. "Yes, of course! I heard that you had been there, as you must have to be able to…do what you do!"

Carlotta seemed miles away, distractedly staring at the waiter who was winding up the gramophone and attending to the records.

The Baron leaned forwards so that he could whisper in Sandy's ear. "*They* do not enjoy being 'in between', it is a very dangerous place for them. Do your best to protect her from having to go there unless it is really the only way."

Sandy nodded, and reached across to take Carlotta's hand and press it to his lips.

"Dearest? You were very far away from us just then?"

"Oh! I'm sorry. I had a sudden feeling of dread, but it is past now. What were we talking about?"

"Whoever is behind all these problems. Who has made it all happen?"

"Oh! That's easy. The Chinese, well some of them, perhaps the big people who own all the factories, not necessarily the politicians. I know Arthur has a 'bee in his bonnet' about it, but I spoke with Jenny for quite some time you know! You can trust a werewolf's judgement. She laughs at his intensity of feeling, but she understands his logic, she checks his facts, and she's quite convinced that he is right. It's what we do about it all that's the conundrum!"

"Well," the Baron began, "Some people might say that we are half way there. The EA have thwarted the Human League here in Britannia, and back home it looks as if the Arch Duke is proving to be a spent force."

"This is true," Sandy commented, "But, there's more to it than that. I can't see any direct profit to a foreign power, maybe China, in just destabilising two countries that they neither rely upon for trade, or who can do very much to them on the international stage. I'm more concerned with finding out what it's all really about, and what we've been cheated out of!"

"Does anybody have any idea of the *depth* of support Human League and the Draculians have had? Just how long will they be paid to be a nuisance for example?"

"We actually have a handful of agents within the City of London." said the Baron. "They were supposed to keep an eye upon werewolf interests, look out for suspicious activity, big purchases of silver for example.

Now, they did tell us, that the attempted take-over of EA by Human League seemed to come out of the blue. One minute absolutely no involvement by Human League (we do keep an eye on them), then suddenly they are at meetings, and generally without the slightest idea about how to behave or how to make their point. You see most of the security at conference centres is werewolf, so we get a chance to keep tabs on them all. Whoever paid for the Human League coup didn't give them any warning, any training, and doesn't seem to have been too worried about how successful they would be. There's been no sign whatsoever of any kind of rescue for them, they've been left to sink or swim. Whatever *they* wanted from Britannia, either they've got it…or they've missed the boat and can't be bothered to catch up. Transylvania's another matter entirely. Those *assassins* were decades in the making, and to locate and bring back the Arch Duke must have been a major project. Whatever they want from the Old Country doesn't come as easy as what they are after here."

"How can we both best help?" Carlotta asked. "It seems that Britannia is sorting itself out without us. What can we do for Transylvania?"

"I'd hoped," the Baron said a little shamefacedly, "That you two would be telling us what to do…"

………………………………………………

Little Mythering is a pretty, a picturesque, a scenic, village. It has ancient 'pre-accident' elements, and lots of good modern rural architecture. The 'Scout Hut' is particularly worthy of attention, being as it was, built jointly by all three major sections of the community.

'Bat Pack' Wolf Cubs started generations before. A very liberal and humorous Scout Mistress having decided to integrate elements of the three cultures. The construction and design of the building is unique, offering three levels, above and below ground, and chances for everyone to show their ability, strength and comradeship. Which is why the community have now taken their stand around the building, and a joint taskforce of werewolf, vampire and human members has taken the defence of the village upon itself. They have already set up a helio mast and tried to attract the attention of the station up on the Dunstable Downs, but the village lies in a fold in the land and attracts more than its fair share of fog at this time of year, so the messages might or might not have got through.

The column of Human League 'Liberators' completely blocked the sunken lane that was the only approach to the village from the far off highway.

The front of the column was held back behind a great banner made from complexly stitched cloth and depicting a rather unbalanced human figure set beneath a huge radiant sun. Beneath its feet were broken bones and a smashed coffin. The closely packed rabble marching behind the banner sported a rich variety of weapons that ranged from impromptu spears and halberds made from scythes and billhooks all the way up to silver tipped spears looted from government forces that had decided enough was enough and it was time to go home.

The Human League leader was wearing a fearsome helmet with dense festoons of wiring to protect his mind, and had a crossbow that was both un-cocked and unloaded (its string also looked very frayed indeed, and the trigger mechanisms urgently needed oiling if was to work without seizing up at a critical juncture.

He stopped and surveyed the flimsy barricade set across the lane ahead of him, then remembering his instructions he pulled out the printed card from his waistcoat pocket and addressed the 'rebels'.

"Hand over all those miserable revenants sheltering in your midst, and we will be merciful to you!"

"Go home and sober up!"

It was probably an accurate comment, bottles were being passed from hand to hand,silver rings and cloves of garlic were being fingered in pockets.

"We have our sacred duty to rid this land of evil.."

"Then take yourselves off somewhere else, that should do the job!"

"We have warned you! You can expect no mercy!"

"We know that, but I dare say we'll be merciful to you and let you choose between living and dying…or any other choice you may want!"

The Human League leader had wisely placed his trusted officers at the rear of the column, and had also equipped them with some very serious weaponry. The result in the narrow way was an uncomfortable and largely unwelcomed advance.

Ahead, at the barricade set across the lane three worried faces peered at the advancing horde.

"Do you think they'll get here in time?" asked David the village council leader.

"Bound to!" said Peter, the local werewolf organiser "It's the Third Chiltern Pack, confirmed by helio and by howl. They'll not let us down!"

Edwin, the village vampire contact, spoke next "It will work! It will! Our people are there as well, waiting as a back-up. If they have to….act….then they will, protecting the village is everything, even if we have to spend half the night calling them all back!"

The mob, driven forwards by an absolute guarantee of being speared or shot down by cross bow bolts from behind, against the almost certainty of the village defenders taking them prisoner and then returning them to their communities, began their advance, carefully dropping weapons at the critical point and politely kneeling and bowing to the dozens of great grey wolfen shapes that began to appear from the bushes around the sunken lane. It only remained for the half dozen or so vampires that had shown up to snatch the weapons from the rear-guard and deal with the odd one or two who had decided to sell their lives dearly, only to discover that the vampires were not in the least interesting in taking lives, in whatever way, but merely neutralising the attackers and sending then home unharmed!

So ended the siege of Little Mythering, and so began the 'Chilterns Alliance', a confederation of villages from Dunstable to Aylesbury determined to celebrate diversity and solidarity and keep the buggers from the big city out of the villages!

………………………………………………

New Brighton was abuzz with lights and music. A steam fair had made the long and laborious journey down from the ancient coast line, across the causeway. Traction engines hauling great carts and complicated waggons with gilded woodwork projecting from beneath stiff weather stained tarpaulins.

Now properly set up, and with the carbide gas-light flares illuminating the scene the whole site was thronged with happy people.

Three separate mechanical organs competed with each other for musical dominance, while smaller steam calliopes shrilled out tunes as roundabouts twirled and various sideshows shouted out their attractions.

Sandy and Carlotta wandered arm in arm, pausing once in a while to watch the crowds trying their luck at the side shows. Given the very specific nature of the area the fair had, had, perforce, to bring out some very special attractions. Ancient traditional favourites such as hoopla and shooting galleries were a born looser with a werewolf and vampire clientele, so there was the Blindfold Cross Bow range, where potential participants had to wear a large wrap-around metal visor and sight through a small keyhole shaped aperture.

Sandy picked up one of the visors, turning it around and closely inspecting the construction. The stall holder hurried over. "S'all right guv'ner. Safe construction no lasting effects. I can see….Oh Gawd!....I'm sorry your Serenity!...I really am…err…'ave a free go!"

Sandy looked puzzled, but Carlotta intervened. "It is alright! Please do not make a fuss! His Serenity is here *incognito,* but your deference is noted and admired! Thank you."

Carlotta took his arm and steered Sandy away from the stall and into the noise and hubbub of the roundabout.

"Sandy! That was a 'Tizzy', a descendant of the Szgany!"

"What! I've never been sure that legend had anything in it. A tribe of gypsies with….a…symbiotic association with vampires!"

"Yes…it has been a bit of a secret. Imagine if EA got wind of a genetic defence against the undead! But…it's all a bit complicated. The Tizzies don't have any sort of immunity, but…they are seen as *useful,* so useful in fact that no orthodox vampire would ever *inconvenience* any of them, or their allies. They drifted into becoming show-folk, which is why so few of them are still in their homeland. BUT they can *see* vampires, and that *is* hereditary. He *saw* you, and saw you as a Grand Duke. You've got to face up to Orlov's gift to you, and what you've inherited. This meeting tonight is critical!"

"Yes. The TIE committee and then, what is it? The European Werewolf Youth Alliance?"

"Yes, and they will be hanging on your every word!"

"Oh dear! I see myself as much more tactical than strategic!"

"Be that as it may, you still have to address the audience!"

……………………….

The tide, spring tide as it was, did it's best, and flooded up to the jetty at New Brighton. It would, indeed, float off a heavy ferry (if it had to), but it seemed to rather hope that nobody would expect it to do such things.

On the jetty Rath Conwy, the leader of the steam fair, spoke to the ferry master.

"We want to be across to the otherside as soon as you may! There are fetes, occasions, 'happenings' that we need to be part of….and we do not need hindrances!"

"Ah! The hindrances! The 'uman league puts all sorts of obstacles in my path, but….other people put clearances! Is it not so difficult, after all, for a friend, especially one who takes such delight in assuring my well-being, to be accommodated!"

Rath Conwy carefully and pointedly took out a small leather purse full of gold coins and dropped it into the ferry masters hand. "Remember," he stressed, "the Tizzy do not forgive! Any problems, and….something….will be back!"

"Oh! How could you think that of me! Of course it will all be perfect!"

"Good! Only Miksha Doblish said his pick up was late and there was only cheap Polish Vodka, not Slivovitch in the salon!"

"I don't know he was talking about!"

"Good, let's hope I don't either!"

………………………………

Back in their suite at the hotel Carlotta and Sandy prepared for the evenings schedule. The two meetings followed on, the one from the other, with the formal address to the committee of Transylvania in Exile, and its guests.

The former ambassador to Transylvania, now TBM's minister for Transylvanian affairs (and living a life of constant shuttling between London and New Brighton), and some senior members of the Britannic Kingdoms revenant communities.

In the lobby downstairs attendees were arriving, on foot, in carriages and occasionally on four feet! Werewolf security was very much in evidence, though the possibility of interlopers in such a community as New Brighton had become seemed unlikely.

The werewolf youth alliance was still dining, and its members would make their way to the conference hall once the committee had finished it's business.

Have you read the briefing papers? And the ones from the minister? And what about.."

"It's quite alright!" Sandy replied, cutting across what he knew would become an endless list of advice. " The key stuff is actually in that last letter from Arthur, the reports from the companies agents in Prague. With that sort of information we can demonstrate to the minister that we are significant players in the game and can start outlining what everyone should be doing next."

"Transylvania will listen, but will London? Is Plenderleith really still in charge of things? Or is it now a coalition of minor parties? Also, does London now control things again, or is the civil state still shaky?"

"The briefing papers *say* that the government is still in the hands of Plenderleith's administration, but that in rural districts there is still unrest being fomented by Human League activists, also a few, a very few, towns are also, err…. 'unsafe'"

"What about the *armed forces?* We saw them clearly following Human League instructions!"

"According to the official briefing that was due to infiltration at Whitehall (though Arthur reckons there have been Human League sleepers in most of the regiments for sometime) *Officially,* Plenderleith is back in the driving seat, but EA and the other companies have made sure all the government troops are confined to barracks. There's also been a huge desertion rate. Most families have some sort of revenant tie in, and a lot of the 'desertions' happened, *en masse*, when orders were given to arrest and detain werewolves and vampires."

"Umm! So in reality there's the tail end of an unsuccessful uprising still to be disposed of.

What about the Chinese dimension?"

"Arthur's got a lot to say about that, and the minister has been very helpful as well. Plus, the company has its own sources within Whitehall. Briefly, the Chinese have vanished! Sold off all their holdings in Britannic companies, pulled the plug on all banking arrangements, cancelled leases, contracts and so on, all over a 48 hour period. Whatever it was they wanted, I guess they got it, and had no use for the Human League any more. The organisation they set off was very, very expensive, and long planned for. So, much effort went into it, so much that this sudden withdrawal *must* mean they got what they wanted."

"Which was?"

"Essentially a chance to plunder EA, and the other companies, of equipment and secrets. By the time we found out it was all virtually over. That consignment we personally intercepted seems to have been left-overs. The main staff had left days ago. They seem to have covered their traces pretty well, clearly took some things that were of no real use in order to cover up just what it was they really and truly wanted. As a final snub they've closed down their embassy in London and advised all their nationals to return home as they can 'no longer be confident of law and order and the continuance of civil society in Britannia' !"

"Small loss!"

"Oh, they'll be back! Once they find Europe's got something they want, the big companies in Hong Kong will start making overtures, and the Chinese government will apologies for the former administrations serious errors!"

"So, they've left Britannia, but what about across the water? Still there?"

"Not officially! All the embassy people left at the very beginning, but Arthur says their infra-structure is still intact. Information gathering, transmission, a little light sabotage and the odd useful assassination, but *no easily identifiable agents!*"

"Are they still funding the Draculians? That surely must give them away?"

"Now that they've got their hands on the Treasury funding is not a problem. It's getting jobs done that's the real trick! Only a handful of Draculians, most of the aristocracy have slunk off to the 'otherside' and the one's who've stayed may or may not be in favour of the Old Days, some could be self-designated 'sleepers' on our side. Who are they going to trust? The *electifs?* Arthur says our agents can only confirm three cases of *electifs* being 'honoured', but they look like window dressing, all three quickly made up to Count and then hurried off to somewhere inconsequential and invisible!"

"Ye gods! In my day you had to do your apprenticeship first before you even got a 'ladyship'! They aren't exactly living up to their promises to bring back the Dark Days!!"

"Exactly! And there's more! The agents confirm that the Archduke *is* in the Vesper Tower. That is what makes their government legitimate, constitutional in fact! Which means that international support has, perforce, to be with them and not us! Orders in council, decrees, proclamations, are all being made. The Draculians, the Kravitzen, the Congress of Commoners even…"

"What! That hasn't been assembled for over a hundred years!"

"Yes! Someone has done a good job of finding out exactly what sort of rigmarole is needed to get technical legitimacy for the new leadership…but…has this come from Dracula, the 'fountainhead of darkness'? No! I think not! Everyone still says, that even in Prague, his mind is weak, wandering, disabled. And, it's *not* a sham to get everyone onside. Agents reported that a week or two ago there was a minor crisis, a rebellion against the Draculians by a small group of vampire guerrilla's. The old Archduke would have just frazzled them without straining an eyebrow, but they only backed off when the Draculians brought in Romanian mercenaries armed with Forsterite arrows (and that in itself is strange because the Draculians have been rounding up every bit they can find and dumping it in old mine shafts!)"

"So, a very much weakened Dracula, who can now be controlled. A puppet! Who would have thought it, ever!"

"Somebody! The clue is in what you were saying about that Count scrambling two of his followers together! I'm sure of it. Someone has taken the Archduke and blended him with, oh, I don't know. It doesn't even have to be a human. Can you get were and vampire forms of non-humans…err…animals?"

"It's possible. I knew a very progressive Duke who was trying to create, well I suppose you'd call them Vam-cows! Animals with enough vampire characteristics to make them a more than acceptable substitute for humans. It was going quite well until the donor programme started, And then, well it just wasn't needed any more!"

"So, the Archduke plus a very biddable creature, maybe even a Labrador Retriever, and that's it. Total control of Transylvania!"

"I see what you are getting at, but I'd suggest it's still a human they've blended him with. Somebody very susceptible, very vulnerable, severe learning difficulties maybe….who knows?"

"If that's true, then the answers simple! A commando mission to 'Free Dracula'! Get the old boy out of their clutches, and then skilfully dispatch him back to the 'caves of waiting', and the rebellion fails because they've lost their President!"

"Simplistic! I wouldn't mind betting they've set up some new statutes that allow for a successor ! It might be even worse!"

"OK, but, it may sound a bit romantic, but I can see ourselves taking arms to ensure the personal freedom of the very individual we both most detest!"

"Quite! That's what being civilised is all about! And now, if you've really finished putting the world to rights, you need to decide if you are going to wear the Grand Dukes jewel when you address the committee…I think you should!"

……………………………………………..

"Ladies, Gentleman, Strangers and Fellow Countrymen…… it all gets a bit complicated, please can I just call you all companions in adversity?" Sandy paused, and took a swig of water from the glass and carafe set in front of him. "I represent both Britannia and Transylvania. Our two countries have for a long time been partners, each supporting and aiding each other, We can return to this, the current climate is transitory! The biggest difficulty, the greatest test, of our two nation's faith is the shortage of information about what we are both doing! Yes! Really! If we base our decisions on what we read in the newspapers we get stale news and the journalists direction of our thoughts! I cannot share with you all that I know, BUT, I can tell you, don't believe all you get from the papers, or even your official briefings…..please, please ask questions, talk to the people who have been there. The ordinary people who have been running the fairground stalls this evening have only recently returned from the Continent, how many of you have asked *them* what they have experienced over the last few weeks? I am now going to tell you about things that I *think* I know about. For goodness sake use your own sources to check what I am telling you…" and Sandy began to explain what he thought was happening.

……………………………………

"Oh! Well done! You've really inspired them!"

"Yes, but I've got to talk to the werewolf youth of Europe next! I'm sure they are a much more discerning audience!"!

"It's alright, you'll do it! What are you going to tell them?"

"I thought that I'd tell them about the attempt at a Peace Conference and how, in time, we can get back to that. I don't know just how much I can say about how well TIE is working with both Britannia and France, because all of that co-operation is between willing individuals, not national governments."

"That's a good start, but you need to remember that you don't have to be so careful about stepping on peoples toes! Consider! You are a very senior member of EA, you have the personal friendship of the de facto Director, Arthur. You are ,also, a citizen of two nations, and in Transylvania you *really do* hold the rank of a Grand Duke, and that means, whatever happens ,you are one of the six members of the Cabinet, the core of the government of the *true* Transylvania! And that's what it is all about! *You* are a World Leader, and you need to start throwing your weight about. *You* and only you, have been gifted with the authority to do something about this mess! Start doing things, but don't think *too* much. I know you, you'll dither, and try to be fair, and prevaricate! Just act, we'll sort out the details later!"

In retrospect Sandy wished he'd not followed Carlotta's advice so closely….but it did lead to exciting times!

....

The conference chamber was filled with young(ish) people, men and women. A werewolf doesn't come of age until 45, so the youth movement were from a fairly wide age range, however within these limits werewolves always look (and behave) in a very eager and youthful manner!

"The future," Sandy stated "belongs to imagination, to vigour, to doing things differently, and breaking the rules without breaking trust!" this had gone down very well, very well indeed!

"It is up to those with the energy, the motivation, and the courage, to make the new world! To bring harmony, progress, friendship! Our resistance to the Draculians, and to the Arch Duke, if indeed it is he, are due entirely to co-operation. Vampires, Werewolves, Humans, and everyone else! We can have a truly wonderful time together! There are people in our wonderfully mixed community who recall a time when we were all pitted against each other, each believing we had to eliminate the others for our own survival.

All, all, terrified about the consequences (or even possibilities) of the afterlife, locked into the morass of suffocating, blinding, sterilising, religious beliefs, and then! The great 'accident'! Was it a disaster? NO! Not for those of us who live within its wonderful perimeter! We, each and every one, know now that all three, (or more!) of our kindreds continue, survive, and do not have to worry about being good or bad, but just being ourselves, *and* aiding each other! Truly the ancient admonition 'do what thou will, but do no evil!' has been realised!

People, people not so far away, both here in Britannia and in Transylvania, and elsewhere will try to resist this, to say that the old ways were better, were in some way sacred! I know, I know from actual experience, that it is in no way as easy for a vampire to contemplate the infinite as it is for a human or a werewolf. So! We support and comfort each other! The future, if we help, support and aid each other, is rosy! All I ask of you, *all of you* here tonight, is do your best to help make a world where each, every, and all of us has a chance to live a full and happy life that does not hurt others and enriches and ennobles us all!"

Questions followed. Sandy (and Carlotta) were somewhat surprised by the questions, and their intensity! The werewolf youth of Europe (including pack members from as far away as Tenerife and Lusitania) had pertinent and unusual things to ask.

"Excuse me Sir! But is it true that your transformation is a horse?"

"True indeed! I prefer to be thought of as a pony, but yes…equine!"

A fetching female werewolf, wearing an evening dress a high studded collar… "I understand that you are able to transform into…well different kinds of….err...equid?"

"This is the case. However, I must point out that one of the young people helping us make our way to New Brighton managed a very similar alteration to their, err...traditional appearance…in fact managing for a significant period to be a *Dalmatian dog!*"

A wave of hushed admiration ran through the audience. Ideas were being born, new thought patterns engendered. The very concept of laying powerful and controlling hands upon your view of what you actually were, were being considered, possibly for the first time in werewolfdom!

It was growing perilously close to the time the meeting was due to close, and werewolves are sticklers for doing things by the rules, a spokes werewolf stood up, raised an arm, and everybody rapidly grew silent.

"Please? Everybody! His Serenity has been more than generous with his time, and has given us a closer view to his thoughts, his fears, and his hopes, that anyone in the past! He has shared personal information with us as no one ever before! I trust we will all act upon his suggestions, his example, and his advice, but for now let us allow him, and his most excellent lady, to retire. Three rousing cheers please!"

CHAPTER 18

"Your Serenity! Your Serenity! Please! Please wake up! The Steam Fair have left on the morning tide!"

"Oooh, urgh, err .What on earth is going on?"

"I'm sorry! I've been told to tell you that the Steam Fair embarked for France this morning…*and*…a party of thirty young werewolves left with it….after raiding the armoury!"

"Oh Bother! I never meant them to do *that*!!!"

………………………………………

"Nothing is so hard, or so difficult, that thinking does not make it so!" That is how the Bard would have us believe it to be, and it is largely correct. Sandy had, quite unconsciously, removed the critical barrier to varying werewolf transformation, as indeed he had already done to his own transformational capabilities.

The ferry arrived in France and delivered a complete Steam Fair *plus* a great many other odds and ends that French customs and excise, not to mention border control had absolutely no jurisdiction over whatsoever!

A distance of five miles or so beyond the port the force assembled, gently morphing out of the shadowy foliage and into functional reality. The only real problem was the lack of a plan beyond crossing the Transylvanian border!

…………………………………………..

"Why us?" asked Carlotta as Sandy hurriedly packed the two leather travelling cases

"Because I should have thought a lot more before addressing and enthusing such susceptible young people, because I have all the contacts on the French side to sort things out, because I'd rather be in the field than in the conference chamber....and...just...because!"

"Alright! But, once we've caught up with our party of hotheads, what happens next? Do we take them home? Or do we....carry on?"

Sandy paused, stopped wrapping a box of small glass vials in the middle of a pair of socks and put his mind to feeling for Carlotta's thoughts. She was a little upset by Sandy's immediate decision to follow the werewolf expedition, but he sensed, far more because she felt she had not been consulted, than from not *wishing* to be involved.

"Sorry! I should have talked it through with you first, but I just felt so responsible, especially since there are parents here, of some of those youngsters, and they are asking where their children are."

"They are werewolves! They take far less harm than humans!"

"True, but you don't know just what could be waiting for them on the southern shore."

"What do you mean?"

"There are plenty of *Loup Garou* in France, but they have to obey very strict rules, border controls tend to be very severe and often very, very final!"

"So. And your contacts?"

"The usual, EA contracts. The coast guard commandant owes the company a favour or two. I can send a helio when the fog lifts."

"A good start, but once we catch them up?"

"All depends upon circumstances…" Sandy paused and once again probed Carlotta's thoughts, she seemed to be recalling their escape from Transylvania and the Germanies, there was an actual glee in her thoughts.

"…they're probably well inside France by now, always assuming they've not been intercepted, by the time we catch up we could be within striking distance of the Transylvanian border. Us two and thirty odd enthusiastic young werewolves determined to do their bit, and with half the contents of the armoury hidden about their persons? We could find out *exactly what* is happening in Prague and *then* report back to New Brighton!"

"We would, of course, report back?"

"Well….if we did go over the border it *would* only be for reconnaissance….so we would have to report back…"

"You've convinced me! When do we leave?"

"There isn't a boat for another forty eight hours. I'm afraid I've thrown my weight about, and officially you and I are in conference with the committee until then, and won't be seen outside the official suite. In actual fact, if you're up for it, we will be on the southern shore by tomorrow morning. The werewolf network will have a local pack ready to help us across the border, and once on the otherside we'll see what's going on and plan accordingly."

"Very good, but *how* do we get there?"

"It's all over land, except the narrows, and that's where the network comes in, they'll sort something out!"

…………………………………

The carriages made their way along the sandy coastal track and followed it into the dune slacks and scanty birch forest that ran southwards for as far as the eye could see. Eventually the picnic site was reached and the party debouched onto the dunes, spreading out rugs, lugging picnic hampers and attempting to put up parasols in the stiffening breeze. The hotel had advised against a picnic with a storm gathering, but everyone had just laughed and carried on packing the food and the rugs into the small fleet of carriages.

Seated in a carriage somewhere in the middle of the group, and trying to look as werewolfish as possible, Carlotta was in fact agog with eager anticipation of the expedition. The fears that had assailed her in the days leading up to the fall of Prague had now vanished. She had a confidence in Sandy's leadership and in her own new indestructability, and it was becoming clearer with each and every day that the Archduke was no longer a psychic force to be reckoned with. The thoughts of a return to Prague and finding out what was really happening became increasingly attractive. She had borrowed a dress from a very sporty werewolf lady, it was constructed mostly from glossy black leather and had a choker collar with brass studs. She contemplated the fact that following Sandy's prompting werewolves had now discovered that they need not *always* transform into wolves. Sandy's example of *different* equines was enough, it seemed, to open the door to a whole range of possibilities. Of course, ever since the *accident* there had been the odd shapeshifter, mostly following ancient traditional forms (lots of people able to change into hares in East Anglia, a few bears in Bavaria and so on) But, she'd already seen one of their earlier escort hold the shape of a Dalmatian dog for a good ten minutes, to the general applause of the pack, and since then all sorts of canine alternatives had appeared, some better considered than others, but all quite, quite revolutionary.

'Do I have to remain a bat?' she asked herself, then remembered that Sandy had in fact given her her freedom, and an irrevocable ability to be herself and do whatever she wanted. 'Well,' she thought, 'I'll just have to see!'

The carriage door opened and Sandy looked in, he also was wearing werewolf gear, tight black leather waistcoat and bare arms with slim leather breeches that left little to the imagination. The only thing out of place for a werewolf picnic was the fact that rather than a picnic hamper he was carrying two leather cases.

A watcher, if indeed any would have been foolhardy enough given the combined nasal power of the picnic party, would have seen the unloading of picnic equipment and the gradual disappearance of the figures into the dunes. A werewolf picnic usually includes an overnight stay, and so the departure of the carriages was in no way remarkable. Soon the wind had blown fresh sand across the carriage ruts and across the foot prints left by the picnickers. The slight and infrequent disturbance of wildlife gave some indication that they were making rapid progress through the dunes and heading for the distant white line of breaking waves that showed where the narrow, shallow waters of the international border lay.

Apart from the small company of government troops who maintain the beacon (and normally remain ensconced in their block house) nobody officially lives on the sandy wastes. That does not mean that nothing is going on. The straights can be swum with ease at low tide, and even at high water, if you choose your jumping off point carefully to exploit the currents, is not impossible. Swimming the English Channel has now become little more than the equivalent of running a half-marathon. All along a wide front individuals come and go between Britannia and The French Republic. The company at the Beacon is supposed to monitor this, but there is little point. No big cargoes can be run and both countries now have such small populations and such abundant resources that warfare and espionage are consigned to ancient history.

The look-out on the Beacon tower commented, off-handedly, that it looked like ' The doggies were off to France again!'. The watch commander scarcely looked up from his novel and muttered something along the lines of 'Lucky for some!'

Down on the sandy beach that seemed to run on forever in both coastwise directions Carlotta was watching while Sandy took a hand with manoeuvring the light, woven wicker platforms that had been stacked up in the dunes. They looked like extremely long treble thickness hurdles, and with a person at each end they could be speedily moved down to the water's edge and linked end-to-end together. Eventually they became a safe pathway that crossed the shallows and the quagmire of quick sands that lay beneath, extending out to where the sea deepened and a dozen or so small pontoons floated allowing access to water with depth enough for a boat to moor.

A middle-aged looking werewolf lady came over and sat down on the sands next to Carlotta.

"Of course, not so long ago we just used to swim out to the boat, a lot less fuss, but nowadays everyone thinks that's not 'dignified'. I blame it all on transformable clothing." She paused, running a finger around the edge of her black leather décolleté bodice. "Mind you," she continued, "It is a blessing to still have some clothes on when you change back....err...is that a *Delia Darkwolf* top you've got on?"

"Sorry, I wouldn't know, I've only borrowed it for the trip."

"Ah! Suits you, all the *DD* range is good, transforms down into collars and nice easy to wear harness. Doesn't get in the way when you're.....ummm...*au natural* as it were!"

All werewolves just love talking shop, and she was about to go into a detailed account of how her latest outfit worked, when Carlotta saw Sandy toiling up the dry sand of the beach to where she was sitting. He reached down a hand to help her up from the sand. Totally unnecessary of course for a vampire, but she appreciated the courtesy. It was a slightly damp, and even unsettling journey from the beach to the awaiting boat. The wicker hurdles seemed very insecure, and frequently dipped just below the surface of the water, but the passage was brief, and soon they were walking dry shod across the pontoons and then stepping over the low gunwales of the boat. It was surprisingly comfortable with light screens to keep spray and the weather away from the bench seats. Motive power was mostly the tidal currents themselves, though long sweeps allowed the boatmen to both steer and propel the boat through any difficulties. The werewolf pack-leader explained:-

"For many years the south coast packs have been in communication with the *loup garou*, when the sea levels really started to fall we saw the chance of unregulated crossings, at first it was a challenge to swim across, and then as transformable clothing became an option, and things became a little more *chic,* well we developed our own private shipping line! A great many packs now have at least one *breath of French air* each year. We know all about the way of life in France, we have our own stopping points, partiċular restaurants that are werewolf-friendly, which towns we are welcome in, what routes to use. We will set you on your path, in fact we intend to see you all the way to the border with Transylvania, and perhaps beyond! What plans do you have to find the runaways? And, maybe you think that this is a chance to go a little further? A reconnaissance in force? Whatever you decide the 3rd Brighton Pack is with you!"

Sandy and Carlotta chatted politely for a while. There was little chance of giving their plans away, since beyond getting to the French side and gathering information about the errant pack there was little advance planning that was likely to be of much use.

When the couple were alone once more, and the gentle spray was expending itself against the woven screens Sandy opened one of the cases and took out a bulky brown envelope.

"The latest dispatches from EA. Arthurs last chance to brief us, though I doubt he thought we'd be reading it half way to France!"

"OK, open it up and lets have a look, there might be something we need to know before we land!"

The boat continued to ride the tide, and by degrees the French coast came closer and closer. Soon the outlines of buildings emerged from the haze, and the boatmen were taking extra care to guide the craft into particular channels, not heading directly for the port, but for a sandy promontory a little way before it.

The pack-leader returned. "We will be ready to go ashore in about half an hour. There's no problems, no customs or anything, but we do need to be quick because the tide turns soon and the boat has to get off before the water shallows too much. They've got a proper landing stage so you won't have to get your feet wet!"

As promised the landing was a smooth affair with no official interest. The situation in France was very different to Britannia. The *Loup Garou* were more than just tolerated, but the ever closening integration of werewolf and human society was not happening, and as for Vampires, well as long as they stayed in the Chateaux and kept themselves to themselves they were politely ignored. Both of the revenant classes were expected to take part in military service however, and The French Republic had a very effective integrated field force to patrol its borders with the rest of Europe.

Carlotta was making heavy weather of the soft yielding sand. Most of the werewolves had transformed and were scampering across the beach, miniature saddlebags on their harnesses bouncing up and down as they sped towards the waiting transport.

"Sure you don't want to ride?" asked Sandy

"Seems a bit of an imposition given how short the distance is."

"Actually it would be a blessing. These cases are heavy, but transformed they weigh a lot less!"

"No, I'll struggle on. It's a vampire thing. Makes us feel a bit superior I suppose, which now I come to think about it is downright silly....no we're there now!"

The pack were smoothly transforming back to human shapes, and the seats on the charabancs began to fill with very svelte leather clad figures carrying fashionable small leather handbags and travelling cases.

The pack-leader re-appeared at their side. "We're going to Dieppe Neuf, it's as good a place as any to pick up news and prepare for the next stage. The local pack will up-date us on any route restrictions and unusual activity. It's got a decent number of werewolf-friendly restaurants as well, and a 'special' hotel that we can use as a base while we're waiting for information."

Dieppe Neuf (New Dieppe) did not disappoint. Built on the low sandy flatlands of what was, in times past, the bed of the English Channel it was a much more successful settlement than its counter-part on the Britannic shore, New Brighton.

The restaurant they settled upon was obviously an old favourite of the pack, and waiters and the manager turned out to welcome them and usher the pack to a comfortable side room equipped with both dining tables and large overstuffed lounge chairs. Large glass mugs of beer arrived, and the tables were being laid up for a werewolf banquet. A few local *Loup Garou* tentatively entered and exchanged greetings. The pack-leader drew two of them to one side and seemed to be having a hurried and urgent conversation. After a brief period of these hushed exchanges he brought them across to Sandy and Carlotta.

"These young people of ours! They are very resourceful. So many different nationalities were at that conference, and such wide experience too! The local packs know they arrived, and that they moved on, and all without the authorities realising anything was happening. They have made use of their own youth organisation network, and they didn't just take weapons from the armoury, they've got a mobile helio station and a set of emergency code books, they can listen in and even send their own messages. Oh, and they've mastered the whole transformation thing perfectly, the only effective road block the authorities managed to set up was ridden down by a herd of what looked like wild horses!"

"So! Where did they go?"

"That's the problem! Three roads lead to the frontier, and all were blocked, more or less, and all were challenged! These youngsters are a clever lot! The stampede of horses took out the whole road block on the route to Lille, and then there was a very odd incident on the old Boulogne road. Huge amounts of local werewolf activity, a great many packs deciding to travel and swamping the waystations with quite legitimate movement orders, absolutely out of keeping with normal conditions, no one could quite keep up. And then… on the Valencienes highway…. a very discrete party that only attracted attention because they 'forgot' to include an extra 20 members who were 'delayed by illness', most un-werewolf-like!"

"OK! Which exit from the port had no reports to make?"

"Well, none really. Absolutely every gate out of the port had something to report, *and* the towns for quite some way downstream. It was almost as if everything that could go wrong that night did go wrong. Just about every border guard or town sentry *just had* to add something to the record book….nothing like it for years!"

"Yes, well that's what any well trained group would do. It's only that no one's seen anybody do it seriously for years!"

"How do you mean?"

"Oh, EA have written the definitive textbook on confusion and delusion, and these people seem to have been following it to the letter!"

"So?"

"Well, start thinking like a vampire! What are they doing? What do they hope to achieve?"

"Oh Dear! You know you've learnt more than I thought you would!"

"Thank you! What did you expect?"

"Sorry, I didn't mean that to sound bad. You've picked up more about how we work than anybody I've met before. And….you're still not 'giving way'. It's amazing!"

"Sorry?"

“Well. A classic Grand Duke would by now be insinuating himself into the minds of all the vampire community, and badgering the werewolf pack and clan leaders, and forcing his will upon everyone. You could do it if you wished, but you don’t, and not because you can’t…the way you seem to know just how *we* should be thinking, and then you don’t use the power you have….! It’s….just very, very different! That’s all.”

“Well, alright! What I’m after now is, which road have they taken. I’ve got my suspicions, what I need is your unbiased analysis of the situation to give me an independent view of the situation! Got it?”

“Right! It’s difficult in a moment of crisis, because that’s when all the innate things click in. But….I know what you mean, you’ve reawakened lots of human features of my mind. For years I thought I had become entirely Vampire….it was a sort of comfort that I was no longer human….I’d escaped that frailty and weakness…but it’s not really like that, is it? Humans are far, far stronger at the end of the day. They can, and have, destroyed everything and anything that has threatened them. For all we vampires, and the dear old werewolves, talk about our control and domination….it’s humans that decide what’s going to happen at the end of the day!”

“Yes! And this human wants Humans, Vampires and Werewolves to have a brilliant time together. And it *can* be done!”

“Yes, yes…I know. But right now….cut with the psychology and just tell me where these kids have got to.”

“Paris. It has an express train over the border, no checks after leaving Paris….but a refuelling stop just outside the terminal , I know that sounds silly, but the journey time is set after leaving the service stop, *not* the terminal , that way delays are not part of the journey time, and the train operators won’t stand any interference to their schedule. If you slip aboard at the service facility no one is going to strain a muscle to stop you….it'll damage their bonus!"

"So, they travel to Paris, cross the city, and then stow away on the train. Seems unnecessarily complicated, but I do see that nobody in their right mind would consider it as a likely route to take. If you want to get across the border quickly and smoothly, then it's a northern route from here. But there's so many of them. More than a normal pack, and with weapons and gear. How are they doing it?"

"Well, so far we don't have any first-hand information. Only what has come in fourth hand (at least!). There's the reports of their diversions, things like the stampede of horses, but nothing about how they left the port. Everybody, on both sides, has been looking for a super-sized youth pack on the road, maybe fifty or more individuals, and their gear. They've seen a few of them, but not the main body. The people who would really know are the local youth packs, but they've all vanished away on field trips and the like and are making sure no one can find them. I've got to hand it to them, it's the up-and-coming generation that's showing everyone the way!"

"So, do we follow your hunch and just start for Paris?"

"Not without some sort of solid evidence to back us up. How are they moving their equipment?"

"Well, the mobile helio alone needs a small cart and at least one horse, and the weaponry just can't be carried once they transform. Somebody is assisting them, and if it involves horse transport it's likely to be humans." Carlotta paused, "Of course, the Tizzies aren't just friendly with vampires, they fit in with werewolves as well. Perhaps we need to see which way *they* went?"

CHAPTER 19

Beauvais is still a populous town, and has plenty of opportunities for travelling shows and the like. There is a large open space just outside the urban area designated for circuses, fairs and the like. The side show stalls had already established themselves and as the twilight faded into the true darkness of night the lights were lit and the steam organs started up.

At the edge of the showground, and at carefully planned intervals very small groups of youngsters were setting up bivouacs. It looked at first like the usual hangers on of a travelling fair sorting out temporary accommodation, but when you started to calculate just how many of the little groups there were and how each and every one seemed to have set a watch for the night, it became apparent that the whole site was now being guarded!

The leader of the gypsy company that ran the fair was sitting on the steps of a living van with a young and athletic looking man and woman.

"So, how long before he catches up?"

"Very soon. He's so brilliant he's sure to be able to follow our trail."

"I don't know. You set up some very good false trails back at Dieppe Neuf…. That road block…! Ha! That was fun!"

"We are certain that they will have started out by now, and tonight there may be news from some of the youth packs along the way."

………………………………………

The elegantly dressed werewolf lady was listening intensely. Somewhere, a few miles off the beautiful music of an extended wolf howl was rising to the clear starlit sky.

The howl came to a perfectly tailed off finish, and the lady relaxed, and then turned to Carlotta.

"Of course it would be very much easier to both hear and interpret if I was *changed,* but there wasn't the time. If you change then it's almost like listening to speech, but not quite. The closest thing I can say is that when you listen to a Shakespeare play you know they are not speaking proper English, but you understand it all, it's a bit like that. Anyway I couldn't get much out of it, it's almost as if they are using code! The main thing is it was a very young voice and it was talking to another young voice about twenty kilometres west of here. Youngsters often talk to each other by the howl, here and at home. It may be no more than a couple setting up a night out next week!"

Sandy wandered over with the pack leader.

"Is it news of our runaways?"

"Can't tell. We must be hard on their heels. There's two travelling fairs both within a days journey now, and both could, feasibly be moving on to Paris. Beauvais seems most likely, but if they aren't there then we've wasted a day."

Carlotta seemed to be considering the matter deeply, then, "You say we can't make a run over there tonight? Local movement restrictions? Yes?"

The pack leader nodded. "Yes, I'm afraid it's not like at home , and they enforce laws quite rigidly here. I'd be happier if they went straight over into the Germanies, things are much more relaxed there, even if the restaurants aren't as good!"

"What will they be looking for? Wolf shapes?"

"Largely. They can't recognise a transformation, but the guards shoot first at anything vaguely canine. It'd be far too risky to anything until first light, and by then they could be anywhere. You'd get through quite easily, but how would you let us know what you'd found? You can't howl!"

Sandy shrugged, "Looks like we're stuck!"

"You know," said Carlotta, "everyone is making such sacrifices, and doing things they thought impossible. I'm going to try something. If Sandy and I can get to Beauvais in say, two or three hours we can find out if they are there, then it's a simple matter to either turn them back or carry on."

"Yes, but…how will you let the rest of us know what's happening. If you find them just gone you can't follow without waiting for us, you'll be isolated, vulnerable!"

"At first light," Carlotta said "you will have to listen very carefully for a howl. I can't promise it'll be very clear, but it will be there, and you'll know whether to follow us to Beauvais as fast as possible, or get across to Clermont and the other travelling fair."

The pack leader and the other werewolves looked puzzled. "How? If there's nobody there you won't be able to send a howl!"

Carlotta looked a little embarrassed. "Look, I've been thinking about this for quite some time. It's really, really difficult, but it amazing what you can do if you try. Just don't ever, *ever* tell anybody, especially another vampire, but I think…."

Carlotta stood very still, her face began to contort, her features to lengthen. Her clothing started to distort, her sleeves to become more like a cape, her skin texture seemed to be having problems deciding if it was smooth or furred, for a moment the features of a great bat seemed as if they would triumph, and then be sheer force of will her customary transformation gave way to her inner thoughts and by a rapid series of step changes shrunk downwards and outwards until a magnificent golden coated wolf stood in her place. It sat back on its haunches, raised its muzzle to the starry sky and gave a perfectly modulated howl that brought every pack members hurrying to see what was happening.

The transformation did not last more than ten seconds or so, and with a flurry of merging forms Carlotta was back, looking flustered and grasping Sandy's arm for support.

"I'm not saying," she gasped, "That I'll be able to keep it up and listen for a reply. But you'll get news of us! Oh yes you will!"

....

Gomez was a young werewolf from the deep south of Spain's Mauritanian province. The Youth Conference at New Brighton had been excitement enough, but to be involved in this clandestine mission to discover the truth about the Archduke was adventure beyond belief. He had the middle watch, and was scanning the darkness for any signs at all of anything whatsoever! He'd already had the briefing about the 'invisible ones', and was very proud of having spotted the sentry two days earlier thus saving the pack from an unwanted entanglement with the authorities. A simple detour had left the concealed checkpoint safely behind. Right now he was aware of several things. A small group of wild boar three hundred metres to the right. A couple of rabbits grazing only a few metres away, and two large, decidedly revenant bodies about a quarter of a kilometre dead ahead. Likely to be friends, but you never knew. He picked up the mess tin lying on the grass beside him and gave it a sharp flick with a finger tip. The distinctive note cut through the sounds of the night and was shortly answered by similar noises. The picket was alerted!

The pack leader was suddenly by his side.

"Over there, dead ahead moving quite fast. Pretty big, can't make out if it's one or two!"

"If it's McLomond he'll be transformed and probably with Her Ladyship on his back, it'd look huge and have two heart beats. Does it seem like that?"

"Very much. We can travel a whole lot faster if it is them. No more hanging about to let them catch up!"

"Lets hope you are right. I suspect they'll use the situation to push on to Transylvania, but you never know."

"After what he said at the conference I'd be surprised if they didn't back us up."

"Alright. Hold the position, I'm going out to meet them."

....

Sandy and Carlotta's conversation had been somewhat limited for most of the journey. Sandy had been intent upon the dark pathway ahead, Carlotta was using all her powers to look ahead for enemies, and mind reading, while a very useful revenant ability really needed much less stressful conditions to be much good, plus there was no indication of just who might be listening in. Eventually Sandy signalled for Carlotta to dismount, and transformed back into a more accustomed form, the saddlebacks slumping of and into their conventional luggage shape again.

"I think we are nearly there. What can you pick up?"

"Well, it's handy the winds coming towards us. Lots of werewolves, a smell of oils and coal, a great many horses, and, ummm….canvas!"

"Sound like a travelling fair alright. If they are wise they will have set up guards, we don't want to blunder into a picket line."

"We won't! Friendly werewolf one hundred metres ahead!"

"How do you know its friendly?"

"He's waving at us! It's Hans from the Youth Conference team!"

....

The travelling fair had its own commissary area, with cooking fires and trestle tables, but the werewolves had set up their facility. It was a lot better organised, with a night staff keeping fires banked but ready and with a great cauldron of meaty soup at hand to keep sentries comfortable during the watches of the night.

"We are very glad to see you sir!" said Hans, who seemed to be in charge at the moment. "I do hope you'll approve our actions. You did say it was vital to gather accurate information, not rely upon third hand material!"

"Very true, and although I expect the people back home will have a great many things to say about the way you have acted, it cannot be denied that *now you are here,* and undetected , going back would be counter productive. What did you plan to do next?"

"Well sir, not that you and her ladyship are here we thought we would press on to Paris and find a way to take the express train to Metz and then move on across the border at Salzburg by whatever means presents itself. Within a week or two we could work our way up from Vienna and into Prague."

"How?"

"Well, we had rather relied upon you both joining us and giving us the benefit of your experience. I thought that perhaps we could do something with the Szgany…..” he tailed off with a hopeful look on his face.

“Yes, well, let me think about it. Who’s running this travelling fair, and where are they headed?”

“Oh, they call themselves the Children of the Danube, but that’s just a sort of trade name, none of them have been south of the Germanies before, they are already well beyond places they are comfortable with. The work mostly around England and France. We’ll have to say goodbye to them soon anyway, but they promised to get us as far as the huge showman’s camp at St Germain outside Paris.”

“That’s good. Should cover our traces nicely, and be so hard for the authorities to manage that they’ll largely try to pretend that we aren’t there.”

“Thank you for your confidence in us sir! I’ll let you both get some sleep, it’s a few hours still to dawn.”

There was a sizeable dry space underneath one of the living vans, and Sandy spread out the saddle cloth, popped the cases underneath to make a pillow and gathered up their two cloaks to act as a cover. Carlotta snuggled up close in the friendly darkness and together they settled down to enjoy the last few hours before the new day began.

……………………………………

For a small fee at the office by the palace gates it is still possible for tourist to purchase a ticket to visit the Royal Palace of Westminster. Of course if you don’t want to spend so much of your valuable and limited time in the queue for this attraction you can easily wander around the largely deserted and partially derelict

Buckingham or Whitehall Palaces or a short train journey will take you to the truly ancient historic site of Hampton Court.

Today however, there is a large sign in place informing the public that the palace is closed to visitors due to state business but will reopen next week. Visitors are frequently misled into asking if they can view the Throne Room. It is in fact The *Thrones* Room.

Their Britannic Majesties were all in place. The Prime Minister, Hugo Plenderleith was seated at his desk before them, and a crowd of assorted party leaders, ministers, secretaries and deputies stood behind him, awaiting permission to be seated. The ritual was by now relatively ancient, and never varied. The Prime Minister would enter first, take his seat, then each of the four monarchs of the realms of Britannia would enter and sit down, finally the actual apparatus of governance would enter, and at the Prime Ministers signal would take their seats.

When the changes first happened there had been a confused period of a developing threat from the 'accident' in Switzerland. That something catastrophic was happening was certain, and as much as eighty percent of Europe's population were evacuated. This led to doubts about the continued viability of many nations, and strangely to the emergence of numerous nationalistic and independence movements, hence the fragmentation of the United Kingdom. As one of the most prolonged catastrophes of recorded history the unfolding effects of the Hadron Collider accident took twenty years to fully develop. The rapid emergence of an increased polar ice-cap and plummeting sea-levels meant that Scotland became a tiny strip of wintery landscape bordering a snowfield that extended from Hadrian's Wall north to the pole. Its population moved south, but Scotland remained a territorial entity. Wales kept her borders, but with the mountains now the home of quite considerable permanent glaciers. Ireland by contrast now had extensive new green and pleasant lands running west and south, though Ulster was under a hundred feet of ice. England, apart from loosing viable land in its very frosty north began to extend westwards and eastwards, now having a more-or-less land border with Ireland and a sizeable population happy to move into the new lowlands or even migrate to the sunny climes of the deep south of Ireland.

The changes to the physical laws of the new Europe and the altered reality that allowed the easy and general existence of revenants had a remarkable effect on all those left inhabiting the critical area. Life spans increased considerably, and illnesses became most uncommon, however these beneficial effects were exclusive to individuals born in the area, incomers from America and the like slowly became unwell, and ultimately contracted Zombyism. The protective effect upon Europe was astonishing, and soon the Old World and the New became permanently divided, leaving an astronomically large second generation refugee population in America and elsewhere that could now *never* 'go home'.

Of course the first hundred years or so was far from easy, and as has been indicated elsewhere the alarming growth of the Transylvanian Empire posed a real threat to peace, however along with the realisation of Vampires and Werewolves there came also for Humans some very positive absolute proofs and evidences of an afterlife independent of religious belief. Revenants became fellow travellers on the great shared journey to the infinite, and although some significant sections of society remained antipathetic to integration many countries, Britannia in particular, found that a society that had active participation from all its members had a lot to recommend it, and although there was still a long way to before Vampires would sit in the House of Lords there was a steady developing groundswell of support for having an inclusive society. Werewolves in particular were reckoned to be good neighbours and excellent parents! But, as ever, there are those who object, and the Human League Party was a constant source of headaches! This will give you some indication of the background to the forthcoming meeting in the Royal Palace of Westminster.

Wales (Margaret the 3rd), as youngest monarch opened the proceedings, happily handing over to England and Ireland, who were to jointly chair the meeting. Scotland remained aloof and sulky.

"Mr Plenderleith, could you please give us all a summary of the situation."

The Prime Minister gathered up his papers, half turned and bowed to the crowd behind him, who now took their seats properly and also started to sort through papers.

"Your majesties, assembled members of parliament and colleagues. I am very pleased to report that the insurrection led by outside forces has been foiled and that the attempted manipulation of our national press and major companies has also been effectively countered," he paused to consult his papers and in the brief gap Eleanor III of Scotland seized the opportunity. Scotland had little to say, and her advisors had already briefed her on the issue.

"Prime Minister! Is this not a lie? The armed forces of Britannia do not in fact hold the country, their place has been usurped by the mercenaries of the armaments industry! What do you say to this?"

Plenderleith continued to shuffle documents for a moment or two, and then looked up with an almost bored expression on his ample face.

"Majesty, I am sure you remember the orders in council some eighteen months ago which *you* in particular supported! The major Armaments Firms are now afforded the status of independent nations....our retaliation against the insurgency has been aided by our international neighbours, not by mercenaries. Essex Armaments has an Ambassador at the Court of St James, we are in regular daily contact."

"BUT! He's a werewolf!"

"Yes Majesty, he is indeed, and the Transylvanian Ambassador, whichever of the two persons you consider him to be, is also a revenant. It is no longer an issue"(there were a few raised voices from behind the PM, and he pointedly paused and half turned before continuing) " despite what a few minor, discredited factions persist in proclaiming!"

The monarchs of England and Ireland made eye contact and rose together. A rare use of protocol, if the monarch rises they have the floor, no matter what. It is a privilege rarely if ever used. Wales, lagging a little behind also joined them. There was a very hurried, whispered consultation, then as eldest monarch Ireland became spokesmonarch.

"We wish it to be known, that while the situation must still be reported and debated by this assembly the Prime Minister has our complete confidence, as do the recently re-selected cabinet. We ask however, that you all do him the courtesy of hearing his report without interruptions. This is the majority decision of the monarchs of Britannia, Prime Minister please continue!"

Eleanor III remained seated, though tight lipped. Even a monarch is not immune from a majority decision!

Plenderleith resumed his stance took a moment to adjust his glasses, and then resumed his speech.

"As I was saying, with the aid of our immediate neighbours civil order has been restored, and rebel elements within our armed forces have been isolated and dealt with. The national press is once more free from any level of political or commercial interference. The recent behaviour and conduct of our greater political establishment, especially the Human League and its allies is currently under judicial review. The results of this review will determine whether charges of treason are appropriate. The review will be conducted openly, in public, and before a committee drawn from across the political spectrum. The recent sinister manipulation of our financial institutions, particularly the clandestine purchase of voting stock by foreign powers is also being investigated. In the interests of international peace and co-operation we will not say any more at this time.

……………………………………

Arthur put down the pen and leant back and stretched. The letter to Sandy and Carlotta had every chance of reaching them with a month. Using the werewolf network it would have , possibly, been a lot quicker, but then everyone would know all about it. Better this way. Things were much more settled now in Britannia, and now the last pockets of the Human League activists had been cleared public safety was restored. Plenderleith had assured him that the legislation covering the 'independent nation' status of EA and the other major companies was now thoroughly embedded in the constitution. The role of the companies in dealing with the insurgency and returning democratic government to the four kingdoms had more than convinced the doubters. The difficulties vis-à-vis Transylvania looked to be more a matter of time than of conflict. Once the question of the Archduke was resolved, then all the signs were that no doubt, the Empire would have its own fresh internal convulsion and the Chinese facilitated Draculian uprising could become a matter for history books not newspaper reports. He mused that development projects for the next few decades would probably concentrate upon portable psychic screening, and of course how to circumvent it! There was still the very worrying matter of Vampiric Essence! But once the Empire was functioning correctly again there would be more than enough resources and resolve to eliminate interest and investment in that horrific commodity.

As EA's Ambassador to Britannia he got a very interesting post bag these days, and even more interesting unofficial briefings from the PM. He'd still trust EA's intelligence and espionage system over the Whitehall operatives, but the official communications outside Europe, that EA had largely been able to ignore, now gave him a wider world view. The lithium crisis was a whole lot more important than he had imagined, even to the extent of a few tentative expeditions to assess the viability of Antipodean ventures. However, revenantic contamination and completely unknown local conditions had meant an untimely and frequently unpleasant end to the matter so the old Middle East workings were still the only likely option. Well, Sandy and Carlotta just might sort out the situation in Prague. It looked more a matter of exposing the Draculian conspiracy than doing anything by force of arms. The letter he was committing to a werewolf courier would make sense to Sandy, but just about no one else, and he'd made three copies and was going to engage three independent couriers to do the job (and given them the run of the EA 'toy room' for any tools they thought might make the task easier!)

CHAPTER 20

The Showman's Ground at St Germain is considerable, both in extent and content. It needs to be. Paris has become the centre of the industry, and the railhead alone is the size of a small town. Transylvania always felt that, what with the gypsy connection and the glamour of culture it was the natural home of circus, the Germanies thought that as the most enterprising steam technologists fairgrounds were really their forte, the Lusitanian plains of Spain produced superb performing beasts from elephants to big cats, England was renowned for its clowns and jugglers, but they all had a lack of something that would give a reason for a European centre. France however contributed the most vital aspect of circus imaginable! While they did not make equipment or train animals or perform, they had the most enthusiastic and knowledgeable audiences of all, and spent the most. Since they had few natural barriers with the majority of countries and a good railway network (and considerable organising power and excellent hospitality) Paris was now the Fairground and Circus capital of Europe.

The site is, of course, well fenced, and the gates guarded, it is for the trade and not the general public. Indeed, once you have entered, there is no need to leave (in the short term) since everything you may need is available without going outside the gates. There is a considerable hay market, numerous forges, farriers shops, dealers in livestock, training schools for performers wanting to gain new skills, costumiers, van builders, an extensive livestock market and most of the performing animal agents have premises.

It takes the best part of an hour to walk from one end to the other, and the broad perimeter track acts as an exercise and training ground which is more than sufficient for the needs of the showground.

As we have said, the gates are guarded, but to be perfectly honest the sheer volume of traffic means that inspections are often superficial. The travelling fair that came in from the north arrived in such disorder that it was easier to just wave them all in, after all they must have been show people, they looked just like it!

....

Sandy and Carlotta were standing looking at the elephants. There must have been fifty or more, beautiful Lusitanian giants from beyond Gibraltar.

"They never fail to impress!" she said, gripping Sandy's arm and pulling him closer to her.

"You know, when I was a girl they'd all but stopped using them in circuses. People were just too cruel. Some of the old Ring masters were down right evil! I ate one once!"

Sandy was taken up a little sharp by this.

"Oh well, not ate, I suppose 'consumed' is the right word. It was back at the beginning of things. Circuses are a wonderful way of entertaining people, and just after all the upheavals of the 'change' lots of companies set up and toured across the new countries. Transylvania wanted to show it was cultural, so it invested in circuses, just like the Soviet Union hundreds of years ago. Anyway this was before people had begun to catch on to what *actually* happens when you die, and that a good one in ten folk reincarnate into various animal, so there wasn't the sympathy for animals there is now…anyway, to cut a long story short I was sent to 'assess' a new circus, and the ringmaster was an absolute tyrant, so….he perished!"

"Well, happier times now! At least there will be if we do our job. It must have been rather special, living in those times when it all started to leak out about the after-life!"

"Oh you don't know the half of it! Ten years of a total embargo on any communications with America until they got their heads around religion being totally wrong! And had a civil war about it! Though even today there's some backward areas where they say Europe is just a bad dream , and that one day we'll all wake up from it in the arms of Jesus!"

"What was it like in other places?"

"In those days the only 'other place' where there was any real religious fervour was the Middle East, and of course they caught the full force of the Revenantic Fall-out, and Zombies don't take part in international discussions. They can see the afterlife, but they're doomed to be pegged down in the here and now until somebody does the decent thing with an axe and a stake!"

"That's a bit harsh!¬"

"Sorry! I just think we pander to them too much. Anyway, the elephants are perfectly splendid, and they are all on short term lease to each company with a huge deposits paid against their safe and comfortable return. So I'm not worried about them anymore, and the Ringmasters are safe….for now!"

"I'm glad that that's sorted out. Now then, which of all the companies here should we approach with a view to entering Transylvania?"

"Ummm, I've been giving that some thought, and I think none of them!"

"What?"

"Yes, all not quite what we need. We should spend a week or two setting up our own company."

"But how?"

"I know it was three hundred years ago, but things don't change that much. I used to be Transylvania's chief circus licensing officer. Two thousand credits a month and all the Ringmasters you can suck dry…sorry that's in bad taste, I won't extend the joke…You are more than adept at organising, logistics, physical activity, setting up camp, …all the sort of things circuses do. We run our own show, and that way we keep our own secrets. But….I do suggest we take on as many 'tizzies as we can."

……………………………………

There were 4 of the Euro-youth pack and three from the 3rd Brighton Pack and one local Loup Garou. The camp fire had burnt down to a cosy red glow, and the shadowy figures of werewolf guards beyond its glimmer gave confidence of security. Sandy looked up and spoke.

"Thank you for offering your services. It is much appreciated, and if there ever is a time for honours and medals, well….they will not be slow to arrive, if I still have anything to do with it. The problem we face is crossing the border. Current intelligence tells us that all the emphasis is on crossing barriers, the international frontier, moving from one province to another, getting an (and out) of a walled city. The maximum effort is concentrated at the border. Once across we can always go around difficult places, but the trick is to get across!"

"M'sieur!" the Loup Garou spoke "

"I know the area well. The railway ends a mile before the border, and the crossing itself has had to be expanded in recent years. Most travelling shows enter by that route, and congestion is the normal state of affairs. Anything that saves the border guards time is welcomed, often at the expense of doing a good job! Now, if as you say you will putting the show together yourselves that is an advantage, they will be looking for smuggled people, not the whole outfit being the target! However, let us try to divert them, even so! I suggest that, as planned, our packs staff the travelling show with a few trusted hired extras to provide the 'acts', but that we also include a large number of people who *will arouse suspicion*, but that they will have instructions to conspicuously *vanish* between leaving the train and arriving at the frontier. If the guards are made aware of the event at the right time, they should wave us through to create space and resources to investigate the diversion! A good plan, no?"

"A very good idea! We still have to assemble our show itself. So far we have had offers of tents, sideshow stalls and a reasonable sized 'big top'. There is a limit to what we can afford to purchase without attracting too much attention. Any day now I expect that we will be back in communication with New Brighton. The helio has been set up, and we should be able to break into the local network. Any news from the local packs?", he looked up at the Loup Garou again."

"The authorities are making half-hearted attempts to find you. It seems to have become very political. Your presence has been reported in the press, but only as rumour. The French government has denied that you are here, and that, anyway, they would not permit their neutrality to be compromised, this may explain why the police take great pains *not* to find you. It also may explain why several strange persons of no known state, and travelling incognito have been held indefinitely by the local police. We tried to get a closer look, they seem to be further examples of your 'invisible agents', the ones with the wires embedded in their skulls! I think that that is about all, except that there are reports of some strange Loup Garou. They are seen, and then they are not there! They move with speed and secrecy but do not seem hostile in anyway, but they are heading this way. At least three of them, but not moving together. The outlying packs have sensed them, smelt them, felt them in their dreams. It is very odd!"

"Hmmm! Well, we'll deal with who they are if and when they arrive. However, no immediate problems for us in this camp or just outside it?"

"No! The show folk know something interesting is happening, but they are very good at not interfering with other people's business. We will be left alone. They clearly see we won't be competing with them for business, and there are quite a few who are itching to offer their services, if it looks like some excitement!"

"Good. We are going to need a 'top dressing' of old hands. We won't have to actually put on a show more than once or twice, and when we do get clear of the border we can ditch the vans and the equipment and start to move a lot more quickly. But, we will need enough people to take the outfit off on a false trail, just enough to give us a start if we do get rumbled!"

....

Carlotta, assisted by several senior pack members was holding an audition. The 'big top' small though it was, gave just enough space, and total privacy now that the panels were securely laced.

"Can you hold that pose again please! Yes....raise the left front...good....now we're going to use the limelights....OK with that? ....good, and one more time!"

On the bruised and trampled grass of the makeshift arena a dapple grey circus pony struggled under the sudden glare of light from the lifted shutter of the carbide lantern. Its form flickered for a moment or two then became more distinct.

"Thank you! You can rest now!"

The large dapple grey body swirled around a bit and then resolved into a large dapple grey wolf, and then an energetic, and very sweaty, young man.

"That's good! You're in!"

Carlotta ticked of another name from her list.

The elegant lady werewolf to her left nodded. "Yes, I can see it'll all work, but how do we account for the absence of a string of dapple grey ponies when we are on the move?"

"Hopefully no one will look that closely. But all the draft horses we take on will be small, dapple greys, that way it looks even more impressive that we can put on such a good show with everyday beasts! We just have to keep anybody who looks at us a little confused, lots of milling around, a few runaways, that sort of thing. Nobody, but nobody, has managed this sort of transformation manipulation before, it's our 'secret weapon'. But, everyone has got to be very, very good at it. Hence the bright light test, and not using anybody who can't hold their shape."

"Well, we certainly do 'live and learn'! I must say your 'wolf' is pretty convincing. Has Sandy tried anything like it?"

"Well, no, apart obviously, from being able to adjust size, colour and so on. I suspect that more is possible."

"Yes. But, little by little. For years it was considered most impolite to pause mid form, the 'wolfman' image was really not our thing. I suppose that's put us off of experimenting. Anyway, we have a novelty act next, a young lady who thinks she can transform into a zebra!"

....

At the main entrance of St Germain the gate guard saw one of the local gendarmerie approaching with two large muscular police dogs. This was quite normal, nothing to remark about. The police man touched the brim of his kepi, and one of the dogs sniffed the guards boot, seemed to consider lifting his hind leg, and then thought better of it. The gate guard was about to pass a comment, but his attention was diverted by some small activity on the roadway, and when he turned back the gendarme seemed to have vanished. He thought of asking the Gypsy with the two lurchers if he'd seen him go past him into the camp, but there didn't seem any point really. He turned back to checking the roadway.

The Gypsy with his two enormous hounds strolled of and in his turn disappeared amid a temporary encampment of living vans., a little later on three very large wolfish looking dogs with khaki harness came scampering out and chased each other wildly around the encampment, their joyful barks fading into the distance as they ran off in the general direction of the railhead.

Sandy was sitting on the wooden steps of a living van, enjoying the sunshine and wondering just how everything was going to work out. News from home would have been welcome. Despite the support and enthusiasm of the packs they had brought with them and the very vigorous Loup Garou contribution he did feel like he was now at the limits of a supply line, working beyond the furthest outpost, and very much indeed like a climber who has now reached the end of the safety rope and now ventures out without support onto the raw unforgiving rock face. He was aware that something was going on a few yards away. Some of the Youth Pack were on a very unobtrusive sentry duty around the encampment, and were currently talking to some new comers. Something quite odd was happening, and to Sandy's senses he saw a mild confusion of identities, and then it seemed as if the newcomers faded a little, and the Youth Pack Sentry seemed to become two people, and then one. He concentrated and put a hand up to cover one eye, always a good ploy when psychic senses started getting complicated. All the thoughts from the sentry were positive, almost jubilant. The 'doubled-up' werewolf walked across to Sandy, gave a nod and sat down on the step below him. He seemed to be, physically, the same youngster who had been on guard, but ,at the same time he wasn't.

"Sorry sir, just being cautious. EA special messenger. I was told to pass the word 'cloudy sky'."

"Umm. To which I reply 'daybreak'," said Sandy, seeking in his own head the thoughts of the newcomer. He was immediately successful and now quite at ease with the messenger. "how was your journey?"

"Not too bad sir. The French do like their werewolf curfew to be observed, but they are generally good enough to shout a challenge before they shoot at you. All three of us got here at about the same time, the others are sorting out some lodgings before we go back. Here's the documents, and I was asked to let you know that 'The Old Man' is having a good time each full moon!"

"Ah! How's he taking to it?"

"Oh everyone says it's quite wonderful, the PM is getting everyone used to the idea that EA is now run by a werewolf, but on the whole people are more than happy!"

"What about the Human League ?"

"Oh, that lot are very much discredited now. The last of their MP's stood down last month once the full story of the Chinese involvement was made public. Err, we need about twelve hours rest and then we're going back, if you've got a reply to send that should give you time to code it up. I reckon we should be back home in about two weeks." And with that he was off into the general crowd, his own persona resumed. To any casual observer nothing remarkable had taken place.

The door above and behind Sandy opened and Carlotta stepped out and down onto the steps, and then settled down beside Sandy on the sun-warmed wooden step.

"Visitors! That seemed a very accomplished young man. Didn't he want to stop a little longer?"

"Oh, I guess he was being sensible. Werewolf couriers are very good at avoiding being noticed, and part of it is to never stay in the same place or the same shape for longer than they have to. What we need to do is read through these papers and have any replies ready before they start for home. Let's go inside for a moment."

CHAPTER 21

The next planning meeting took place shortly after the three visitors had left. The news of a politically secure Britannia and an end to the attempted insurgency had reinforced their resolve. In addition to news from home and an indication that Their Majesties Government would attempt to back up what ever good things came out of the reconnaissance EA had included the required passwords and permissions for Sandy to approach local financial agents for additional funds to assist the expedition. It was therefore with considerable high spirits that Sandy announced the 'Travelling Company' would be hiring a train to take them to the border within the next week. There were however still some details to arrange.

"How many of the Szgany are willing to join us?" Carlotta asked

"There are very few of them anyway, but six have agreed to assist. They didn't need too much persuading, in fact they were willing to work free of charge in consideration for helping a Grand Duke, for so they see you," the Loup Garou nodded to Sandy, " They are very perceptive, but we still need a couple of, err, 'regular' humans. So far there are no reports of the 'invisible' ones around, the people with the wires in their heads, none since we left the area around the coast, but I suspect we will come across them again nearer the border."

"Well, we must all keep our eyes open. The extra funds we now have available may help us attract somebody. I don't know. Tomorrow I go to the Bankers Camp to arrange the gold."

....

Although each and every species, human and revenant has a particular metal or combination of metals to which they are antipathetic everyone agrees that gold is a good thing and has no objection to handling, wearing and owning it. The small cluster of tents that made up the Bankers Camp was not far from the rail-head and was enclosed by a wooden palisade with guards on the gate. Just outside of it a couple of Taverns offered rest and refreshment for those wearied by financial transactions. Seated at a table outside the smaller of the two taverns were four Americans, each was wearing a Forsterite ring with a leather guard over its surface. They were travel stained and weary, but seemed to possess a cheerful optimism. One of them had a small leather camera case hung over one shoulder. It looked as if it had been through a war-zone .

"How much we got left?"

"Time or money?"

"Both!"

"OK, lemme see." He pulled out a small notebook. "Altogether we got ten grand US in the account and a thousand in gold, mostly French. Jim, you got six months, all but a day or two, George and Hiram, you both run into trouble five months from now. I got thirteen weeks, then its Zee Time. We got to either split up or agree a strategy. We going back to the Motherland and risking the Draculians or try to buy a ticket to Lisbon and see what the Embassy can do?"

"Sorry Martin, I had no idea it was getting so close for you."

"'S'all right. My plan was always to stay, just the uprising rather got in the way. If we split up I'll just wander off and see if there's some sort of deal I can do locally. Got to be the right sort of people around, but I had rather sort of settled on joining the Grand Duke in Strelsau! Never mind, can't be helped. I know you boys always planned on getting back to the US."

"Not so sure now," said Hiram, "Folks were so kind to us all, getting us out to safe territory. I wouldn't mind staying there now. But I guess we should really call it a day and head for Iberia."

"Let's give it another month. Somethings bound to happen to make up our minds by then."

Another round of drinks were ordered, and as they arrived so did a rather elegant though practically dressed Englishman. He had an odd air to him, which made Jim think about the old Grand Duke he'd made such friends with before the uprising.

"Good day gentleman. My banker says that you might be interested in earning a little something to help you in your travels?"

The little group looked up with guarded expressions, many strange things had happened on the trip from Prague and they had learned to be very, very cautious.

"Could be, could be. I told old Durance we could do with a little work."

"Really? I had it from Fromeister, I guess he told his friends."

"No that sounds about right. We trust Fromeister. So what did you have in mind?"

"Oh, quite simple. I just need some watchmen, well something like that. We are a travelling show, going to make a tour of Austria, might do some other parts of the Empire as well, but really our plans are only made until we reach Austria. Light work, but it needs, umm, shall we loyalty?" Sandy drew open the top of his jacket and briefly they saw a nine-pointed enamelled star.

"You're not are you!" gasped Jim, "I thought, I mean we were told you'd all gone into hiding?"

"I am, and again I'm not! You see that waiter over there? The one with the hoop ear-rings. He's a Szgany, you know? The ones who can…see? Call him over, say you want to order a drink for me. Watch what happens!"

Jim beckoned the waiter hurried over. "Err. M'sieur can we please have another glass…", but he got no further.

"You are fortunate to have such a guest gentlemen. I will bring another glass and a fresh bottle. It will be the pleasure of the house to treat your guest, and of course yourselves as well. Such an honour!" and away he scuttled.

"Well," said Sandy you have some evidence to judge me by there, but…." Here he paused reached a hand down to the table and on buttoned the leather guard on Jims Forsterite ring. He pointedly pressed a finger to its surface, which he then withdrew, moistened with his tongue, and then replaced on the dull metal surface of the ring. "You see! How can I be a vampire and not be affected, and yet….the Szgany see me as what the start says I am. I am Sandy Lomond of Essex Armaments, and I purpose to enter Transylvania illegally to gather information about the current status of the Archduke. Are you willing to help me? Fromeister says that you are to be trusted and may well support our cause."

"What's the pay?"

"What do you need? I understand times running out. Help us and we'll pay(and arrange, which is a lot more) for you to get straight to Lisbon once its all over and onto a boat for the US."

"How long's it all going to take? Some of us have got very limited time."

"If we aren't all done within a month, then it's all over. EA agents will take over and get you out. If there are any complications and we can't fulfil our promises we can offer anyone who wishes it a 'no obligations' bite to avoid, err *zombification,* your choice werewolf or vampire, assuming that that appeals, but we can other wise guarantee final results. Its all a risk, but I'm thinking that the news team that got actual pictures of the installation of the Archduke are accustomed to risks?"

"How'd you know that? Mind reading?"

"No, its much harder than you think to read minds. I've just got more than a few contacts. I'm sure you'd prefer to sell your story directly after its all over. Help us and you'll have an even bigger story!"

"Right, so suppose we have a talk about it among ourselves and agree to sign up. Just what do we have to do?"

"Well, that's the really interesting bit. Have you heard about the 'invisible ones'……?"

……………………….

A major highway, about sixty miles south of Prague. The circus caravan has finally come to a halt. The great road engines that have been hauling the wagons are still smoking gently and occasionally a whistle is being sounded to let off some of the surplus steam pressure. There is a cordon across the road. The Burgomaster is arguing with the Draculian troops that make up the cordon. He doesn't want to get on the wrong side of them, but, there again he doesn't want to let them get their own way.

The troops, as is the case these days, are mostly *electifs*, there's one very harassed vampire officer, who truth to tell would just as easily opt for spending the next few decades in a pickle jar as a handful of sapient dust as lead these….oddities! And he'd always thought of vampires as a bit obsessive, no way beside these creatures, he'd even stopped seeing them as humans, oh of course there was a decent meal or two, if you liked that sort of thing, but to be honest, perhaps the Grand Dukes had been right all along, time for change. Still, couldn't be helped. He was pretty certain that Gregor was a police spy, certainly he had a Forsterite collar under his tunic, that or a rather special taste in underwear. Eventually he settled for it being a Forsterite collar, *electifs* weren't as trusting as they had been at the beginning of the revolution, too many had complained, and then simply vanished. Not that he could blame them, the promises of vampirehood had not been fulfilled apart from a tiny token few, paraded around to encourage the others. He brought his mind back to the present and tried to recall just what he had been talking about. It all seemed to be getting a bit foggy, vaguely reminiscent of some time long ago, long ago when he'd been different, and….something had happened. With a start he pulled himself back again from wherever he had been.

"Umm, errr, the Road Engines, they run on steam, they will not be allowed within the city. You know the rules!" it was clutching at straws, something he knew he had jurisdiction over.

The Burgomaster was all conciliation, as was the negotiator from the circus.

"Do not fret Captain. Do not fret, the show will be set up outside the north gate, on the green used for free markets. The company always follows the rules, no actors mountebanks or travelling people within the city after nightfall. We will camp a quarter of a league away from the gates and only enter the city during daylight to distribute our posters and handbills. Perhaps some of your troops would benefit from complimentary tickets?...."

A wad of stiff pasteboard tickets were produced. In small smudged print they stated that the bearer was entitled to free standing space at the back of the grandstand (subject to availability)

"Oh for goodness sake! Yes! I suppose so! But you'll have to go around the city walls, can't have you going through the streets."

"No problems Major, no problems. Wouldn't get the wagons through the gateways anyway. We'll make our way around there right now, then we can get set up before nightfall and be up bright and early to visit the burghers!"

The Vampire captain was left clutching the wad of tickets and scanning the landscape for the *electifs*, most of whom seemed to have obtained pottery jugs of strong liquor from one of the circus vans and were even now seeking solace from their unrewarded attempts to join vampiredom.

The circus caravan huffed and puffed its way around the city walls, the compacted gravel road surface crushing downwards to its foundations under the unaccustomed pressure of heavy vehicles. The occasional farm cart or merchants wagon went past in the opposite direction or was slowly overhauled as the inexorability of steam countered the pauses and faltering's of draft oxen and heavy horses.

Sandy sat directing one of the circus' horse teams pulling a light cart loaded with fodder. There seemed to be far more animals in the traces than any reasonable person would have considered economic, and very oddly the reins, and the long carriage whip, were not being used at all.

"You know," said Carlotta, "for the sake of authenticity you should at least hold them taut. You never know who's watching!"

“Ah, but I do! If I’m not having to bother about things like putting on a show, then I’ve got time and enough to watch out for other peoples thoughts and take evasive action.” He picked up the reins briefly and nodded to the driver of a light carriage speeding past them.

“Take that for example! A local man, no doubt, and so exempt from gate tithes, and yet he takes a long detour around the city, when with a narrow manoeuvrable equipage like that he could cut through from north gate to south gate. He needed to see things looking normal!”

“But! Hang on a minute, I never saw him until you nodded at him! What’s going on?”

“Hiram and his chums are at various points throughout our caravan. Hiram, and the werewolf with him (its Jessica) are constantly comparing notes, that way they pick up anything, even the ‘invisible ones’, I keep my mind just a little bit focused upon Hiram and Jessica, and that way I’m prepared. As you can see!”

“Why didn’t you explain this to me earlier?”

“I did. I have, four times in the last four hundred miles! The Vampire Thing, remember? Too much technicality and it doesn’t stick? Simple straight forwards mind reading is easy, but this is needs technical considerations and measurements, all the things that don’t work in a vampire mind. If you were to just read Hiram’s mind it would be easy, ditto Jessica, but you need both up at once, like reading two pages of a book at the same time.”

“Yes. OK, I see now, or I will for a while. How did things get so complicated?”

“How do you think we ended up with a reasonably well distributed balance of power in Europe? Vampires are so single minded that it just isn't true! But give them a complex problem or ask them to understand technology and it all falls to pieces. All part of the rich, diverse and varied tapestry of life!"

"Right, I'm going to be single minded. What are we doing about the man on the carriage? The one who's just gone past us?"

"Nothing. If we did anything at all it would give us away. Chances are we have escaped attention, but we'll double the guard tonight. If he's suspicious then we should have somebody looking us over and taking notes. We'll follow them and find out whose spotted us and if there's anything to worry about. Anyway, we've now got past (almost) the outer ring. You'll have visited this mighty burgh before I guess, I know I have, and going around it is much better than going through it, quite apart from the garrison the drains here are disgusting!"

Some say the city , now called Rosenblaustat, used to be called Tabor, but that may have been some nearby settlement, certainly it is on a major crossroads, just as Tabor was, but three hundred years and the forging of a major new Empire do strange things to places. Suffice to say that if you ever visit the military architecture is exactly the same style as everywhere else, being designed by either Essex Armaments or one of their close competitors. Once you get inside the magnificently towering city walls there is all that you'd expect from a city of the 'outer ring'. Transylvania went through some very difficult times until warfare became more civilised and economic, and rebel states within the Empire frequently combined forces with foreign adventurers to attempt the down fall of the Arch Duke, and action ultimately managed from within the highest levels of the vampire establishment. To guard against repetition of such eventualities the Empire had in the last century provided the capital with an outer ring of fortresses intended to delay any emergency until the inner ring, the smaller fortified structures within a mile or two of the capital, could be fully garrisoned and put in readiness. It must be stated that this plan was devised right at the end of the 'exciting' phase of Transylvanian history and at the start of the 'dull' or sensible phase of co-operation and collaboration and as a result the outer ring was more of an obstacle to trade than a strategic necessity, hence the great by-pass road around Tabor to keep trade flowing.

To the north of Rosenblaustat (a fanciful name derived from vampire slang for jugular veins) the circus was now fully encamped. It seemed to have a plethora of canvas screens and eye high dodgers so that no out-sider could get any more than a tantalising glimpse of the delights to be viewed in exchange for a few coins. Ticket sellers and poster stickers had scurried off into the town, and a lengthening queue of local merchants hoping to sell hay, fuel, replacement animals, and just about anything else that might be needed was building up outside the entrance to the site. As ever a few hopefuls from the younger end of the population were making enquiries about auditions and if a jugglers apprentice might be required. In short a perfectly normal circus or fair ground scene.

"The Herr will be needing forage for the onward journey?" the man from the haymarket beckoned a couple of assistants bearing great baskets filled with forage. "Or perhaps this sample would be more to your liking?" he scooped the layer of hay from the top of the basket revealing a large haunch of beef. "That team you were driving look to have a very special appetite!"

Sandy looked up quizzically and motioned for the doorway to be guarded. After a moment or two of activity clearing the waiting queue further back from the tent he prodded the meat with his pencil.

"Ummm! We might find that useful. Who are you?"

“Well, I really am the largest local hay dealer, but that is because all the upland pastures of the Bohmerwald are my peoples hereditary hunting grounds, but today we prefer to harvest the grass and not the deer, unless of course it’s the first week of the season and it doesn’t interfere with the rugby! Baron Vlkvlad Von Bohmer at your service and that of your pack! When do we march on the capital!”

....

It certainly was an amazing circus. Three evening performances and two matinees, not to mention escorted tours around the equipment and the menagerie. Hardly surprising really that the whose establishment stated it would be closed for 36 hours before final performance. There was even an entertainment at one of the city’s largest hostelries, paid for by the circus, to thank the people for their generous support.

“I’m a little fed up,” remarked Carlotta, “Being the only vampire round here. It’s always me ends up with the ‘messing up minds’ bit. I know you’ve got to do other things, but…”

“Yes, I know,” Sandy commiserated, “ I did think about offering one of the Americans an early transfer, but we really, really do need their special talents, and anyway I’m pretty sure they each fallen head over heels for their werewolf co-workers and are set upon becoming part of the pack. Anyway, it’s just this one time. I’m co-ordinating the operation, you just need to take care of the vampire officers, I’ll send the *electifs* off on a very long journey, the Baron’s people will deal with any regular human troops and the Americans and their werewolf partners will sweep up and ‘invisibles’, then the real fun begins. Have you ever been in the field with werewolves?”

“Well I’m sure we’ve both had plenty of experience….”

"No. I mean did your job ever take you into an actual *battle field* situation. You know. The ones no one talks about afterwards?"

"Did yours?"

"A couple of times, plus I've done enough theory and weapons training for a whole regiment. No. This is the last leg. Fifty, sixty miles and we are up against the inner ring. If they don't know we are coming we can get over the walls and find out just what the Vesper tower is actually hiding! Is the Arch Duke really there, or is it a Chinese plot?

Imagine what it's going to be like if he's not there? If he's been dead and gone for years and is just an imaginary threat? Can you conceive what it's going to be like for the Draculians and the *electifs?"*

Carlotta sat very quiet and still for a moment, tyhen as if gathering herself together from some far off realm of the mind she took a deep breath and began.

"Yes. I can. I've been there. Twice."

"How so?"

"The benefits of being far older than you'd readily imagine. As a child, a very small child, I saw the Berlin Wall come down. That really was an event! All those people who'd thought the USSR was a workers paradise, a source of political perfection, only prevented from achieving paradise on earth by the corrupt west. What happened? It was all suddenly exposed as a sham, a cynical, inoperable nonsense. But people recovered and put their trust elsewhere. Then again. After the accident, the way all of Europe suddenly became aware that there certainly *was* an afterlife, but no God! Oh, gods a plenty, but no supreme being. There are places outside Europe where they still don't want to believe it. Parts of

America where they insist we are just an illusion, despite what travellers tell them when they return.

I've been there, twice. And now, whatever we find in Prague, whatever secret the Vesper Tower is concealing, it's going to be another major change, a liberation or a disappointment, depending upon your outlook. You haven't been a vampire, haven't met with others and gloried in the power, the control. No, you've just stepped straight in, all sensible, reasonable, kind and considerate, and suddenly you are at the pinnacle of vampiric power, but with none of the guilt. If the Arch Duke, well, lets give him his true name, if Dracula, the fountainhead of vampiricism, is shown to be *dead,* or under some sort of control, no longer a threat, capable of being *absorbed*, pardoned, nowhere as dangerous as we thought he was. It makes a difference. No vampire can say 'It wasn't my fault' anymore, no vampire can have justification for refusing to consider tackling the 'golden mist', and as for our powers, perhaps we've just been selfishly keeping them to ourselves rather than going out there and benefiting humanity . Don't get me wrong. I want to see *him* gone forever, no one having to go what I went through, even though I did volunteer for it and knew what I was doing. No one being *driven* to evil and then feeling tainted, poisoned, worse than worthless, harmful…"

Sandy took her hand and held it between his, he looked deep into her eyes.

"Do you know? I think our big problem is that we have names for all sorts of people, Vampires, werewolves, Zombies, Shapeshifters, but no words at all for creatures like I was and Hiram and his friends are.."

"But we do! Humans!"

"No, no. You are a human, so is Jessica over there, even though she is in the form of a big furry dog at the moment, so am I, but we need more words so that we can all say that we are humans! Everything you've described about being a vampire is about being a human! You really are lucky to have had so much life experience, perhaps that leads to remembering too many of the bits that didn't work! I've spent all my working life trying to help people stave of disaster, but….on the understanding that eventually I'm going to make it possible for one party or the other to do the most awful things to their neighbours. It's what the armaments business is about. Look! When I first started out I had a commission in an independent training regiment, there were a lot more companies around in those days, it was rather slipshod. My first job was training new recruits for the old Spanish government, down on the plains south of Malaga. I didn't have a clue what it was all about and I ended up teaching a cavalry platoon how to butcher helpless peasants. I felt pretty sick about it, but….one of the rebel villages (I didn't know they were 'rebels' at the time, had hired a military engineer to construct defences. They survived, and they were the ones at the negotiating table, with all their stories, once Spain had to address the issue rather than attempt to destroy it. It decided me to *try* to be on the side of reasonableness. I knew I couldn't change things, but I could work for the people who wanted things to be better. Of course I still made mistakes, and after a while I had problems in sorting out who needed the help and who didn't. But….key thing…I got there, and so have you! No one's keeping score! There is no recording angel, there is no final account to pay. You've stood in front of the 'golden mist', just as long as you feel you've done your best, that's all you have to worry about!"

Carlotta looked downcast, but brightened up a little. "You didn't mention love. That's traditional at these times." She said, trying to make a joke.

"Absolutely true! Don't you feel that even the smallest bit of trying to do the right thing, of love, of care, or pleasure in other people's happiness, all that sort of thing far outweighs the nasty bits?"

"Yes."

"Alright, well….right now we are going to do our personal best to put things right for millions of people across Europe by, at the vey least, proving just what is going on vis-à-vis the Arch Duke. Lets rest on that and get busy. You are going to suborn the entire Draculian Officer Corps of Rosenblaustat, they are to hold the city against any Draculian force, unless over run, in which case they are to flee…"

"Because that way they can't be questioned."

"Correct. Any you will join us…?"

"At the little spinney two miles north of this camp, I will arrive as a wolf and join the muster….are we really using a 'zulu muster'?"

"Yes, the next fifty miles is all under cover. We meet up at Ravensdorp, well two miles north of it, in the pinewoods on the ridge. Local packs will join us bringing up-to-date information, more people and supplies, then we will have about one and a half thousand werewolves to play with. The way in is going to be," he paused and wrote the name down on a scrap of paper, showed it to Carlotta, and then burned the slip in the candle flame. "Right! Sure you will remember it till then? I can tell you it all again anytime you find it slipping?"

"That's alright. I'll do my best."

CHAPTER 22

Ravensdorp turned out to be one of those strange places that is clearly within town, but at the same time is countryside. The vast spiders web of roads converging upon the capital had taken of late to merging with one another, so that now the traffic was squeezed together in order for travellers to see the great granite ramparts of Prague displayed against a verdant leafy landscape. Ravensdorp on its miniature ridge looked very pretty in the evening light, there were no local inhabitants to admire the immediate view since the landscape feature had been planned for effect rather than utility.

Fifteen hundred werewolves (and a handful of others) had been channelled down through the intervening countryside into this picturesque pine forest. The American contingent had already abandoned its horses a few miles away and were now puffing away as they toiled up the pine needle coated slope and under the cover of the great trees. A white horse cantered up the slope from the road, easily leapt a low fence and vanished into the forest gloom, various other shadowy shapes flowed through the bracken and the heather to accompany it into the recesses of the woodland.

A visitor to the tranquil sylvan scene would not have easily seen much, perhaps one or two wolves taking their ease, as is normal in such places. They would have needed to penetrate the dense bramble patches and the over grown twiggy bases of the trees to find the sheer numbers of wolves in this wood. Every hidden spot was packed with them! Rest was the order of the day, or perhaps late afternoon, and silence reigned. Apart from some occasional bird song not a sound, not even the gentle cracking of twigs or rustle of leaves that betokens animals moving around. The whole wood was waiting, patiently, for instructions.

At the cardinal points of the woodlands margins well concealed figures lurked, four pairs of watchers, eyes scanning the vista in unison, minds so in tune that the merest nod, murmur, grunt had meaning. The landscape, however, remained free from any threat. A further cordon of deeply hidden werewolves ensured another deeper level of security. Once in a while a small bat with curiously golden fur swept over the tree tops and back into the shade of the pines.

The great clearing in the woodlands heart, originally planned as a holiday gathering area with stone build barbeques and bench seats started to fill with great grey wolfish shapes, and into the centre of them moved a very powerful muscular white horse, then the whole close packed assembly seemed to quiver, to dislimn and then reform in a whole array of shapes, forms ,colours and energies, then the situation seemed to settle, to resolve, and without undue fuss became an orderly open air meeting of well over a thousand lightly clad energetic looking humans(for want of a better word), some clutching small leather satchels and others with light weapons and small pieces of equipment.

The human who now seemed to occupy the space that had held the white horse raised a hand in greeting, and beside him a burly bearded and moustachioed figure did likewise, as they turned slightly to recognise the whole gathering a tall elegant lady seemed to materialise beside them, she leaned closely to the man who had been the horse and whispered "All clear, and I've checked up with our American friends, nothing to report. You have about twenty minutes!"

The burly figure spoke first.

"Thank you all for answering my call. Thank you for being so discrete, for being so urgent! I will not waste time, we have so little of it. We are safe here for a short time, a short time only. I only ask this of you. Listen to this man. I believe all he has to say, and I have many proofs and instances of his sincerity, his ability and his worth. If you will support him in what he asks I believe we will move away from the crisis that besets Transylvania, if you do not I fear things will get worse. I only *require* that if you do not support what he plans to do you will just withdraw to your home territory and not hinder his endeavours. Now I ask him to speak, there is little time for questions, and for action!"

Sandy stood forwards, bowed to the Baron and then to the packed forest glade.

"As you will all know the Draculian faction has sought to reinstate the Arch Duke, many people believe that this will destroy the happy life that so many of us enjoy. The situation is confused, some think that the Arch Duke is alive but unwell, some that he is still in the 'other place', others again that he is being controlled by foreign powers, and again that perhaps he never re-awoke but that the effects of the last year are a sham, a decoy. We believe that the Arch Duke, if he does indeed still exist and is in this world, will be the cause of great suffering and pain for us all. We also believe that to act upon the supposition he *is* once more alive is also dangerous. I intend therefore to conduct a reconnaissance in force of the Vesper Tower. If the Arch Duke is there then I intend to take whatever action I can, either then and there or at a later date to…ummm…..inactivate him, by whatever means is appropriate. I do not say that I *shall* destroy him, for that is a vain boast, but I shall do all I can to stop him ruining all the good things that every human and every revenant of any worth has toiled so hard to achieve. I am no longer strictly human, so I can't say I'm willing to lay down my life for this with the sort of sincerity I could have done a year ago, but….if I have to stay in the 'other place' for an age of the world, well I'll have considered it a reasonable price to pay. If you are with me I will tell you what I intend to do and how you can all help me. If you are not with me....well I know how you feel, please leave now and no hard feelings....anybody still here in one minute is on board!"

The whole forest glade seemed to be under a spell of immobility. Total silence, total frozen inaction. The minute moved past, and then every figure with uncanny precision and unanimity raised a right hand, focused their gaze upon Sandy and spoke in unison.

"We the pack, acknowledge that for now the whole is greater than the individual, we pledge that, even though it leave us depleted or no longer in existence, the time has come to say stop. The enemy of the pack is the enemy of us all, of the pack, of the friends of the pack, of all who impinge upon us, all who aid us, all who value us, all who rely upon us. We shall now act, even though as a result we are no longer in this world with its skies, its trees, its grass and its waters. All who oppose the pack shall be given warning at this time and then they shall be destroyed."

The Baron looked across to Sandy, and to Carlotta. "That," he said "has not been pronounced for many, many years. Many of the younger pack members have never heard it except at an initiation. You are privileged, I did not order it. You have your force!"

....

Forlorn hopes and last stands and all that sort of thing are generally wasteful and unhelpful, so it was with considerable thankfulness that Sandy found himself briefing an intelligent and sensible series of werewolf groups, most of whom had never done anything more exciting than a Scout and Guide weekend, there was however a small and slightly secretive group, the leader of which whispered to Sandy that they had 'been in the alps recently'.

....

The enormous increase in numbers now that the party was nearing Prague brought with it not just an abundance of werewolves! The packs travelling the shortest distances had felt that to encumber themselves with weapons would not be a bad thing. Now, under normal circumstances a werewolf prefers to use the weapons that nature has endowed them with, but when tackling stone built fortifications projectiles of various sorts begin to make very definite sense. As a result there were a goodly number of crossbows, throwing knives and javelins available, and these plus the small party of werewolf *alpinerie* now formed the spearhead of the attack.

Sandy had, mostly due to inside knowledge, settled upon entering the capital via one of the artillery forts that punctuated the city wall. The forts each had a broad thirty foot high platform on which catapults and ballestas would usually stand in times of war. Currently the great lily-pad shaped structures were unmanned, their enormous iron bound doors that gave a route for the machines of war to be trundled out were heavily barred, no chance of breaking through those! Instead one of the empty platforms was now over-run, the result of a number of human pyramids of athletic werewolves swarming up and over the walls. Crossbows were being levelled and javelins readied for the possibility of a guard on the battlements high above noticing the activity. In the event the precaution was not needed, and the small party of rock-climbers quickly dealt with the swollen overhang of the masonry and were letting down lines to their comrades below. Soon the entire section of wall was in werewolf hands (or paws perhaps?) and the fort's point of contact with the structures either side of it was being controlled by the invaders. The tiny garrison of the fort had largely succumbed to their attackers without offering any significant resistance, such was the size of the onslaught and its complete element of surprise.

The local werewolf Baron was bursting with pride and excitement, "What do we do next?" he eagerly asked.

"Well, now we've consolidated our position we need to take steps to neutralise the wall either side of us for a good two bowshots, but that has to done quickly and secretly. I'd like to leave that job to your local packs. When we come to leave they will be the last away, so the easier it is for them to melt into the countryside the better. I'm moving on with the people we brought with us, and a few of yours as well, if you don't mind, to breach the Vesper Tower. The best way to let you know what is going on will be by runner, if we get rumbled then it'll be by howl, but if that happens the chances are we'll all be getting out as fast as we can. No one's picked up anything significant from the Arch-Dukes thoughts for a week or two now, but we do still need to be wary."

After a few more minutes arranging passwords and final details the reconnaissance party set off.

A modern tourist guide to New Prague will show you the ruins of the Vesper Tower, unfortunately the tower, when it was newly built, was regarded as of such importance that accurate representations of it were banned from guide books in case they should fall into enemy hands, such was the climate of the time. So, we must rely upon a verbal description.

While called a tower it was far more a citadel that just one tall narrow structure. It housed at its peak the Kravitzen royal household and the Imperial staterooms. It was never intended as an administrative centre, more a secure abode, refuge and council chamber. As Sandy and Carlotta viewed it from across the roof-tops it seemed to have become blind, its tremendous fourth floor windows heavily shuttered and vast rose window in the end-wall of the great hall obscured by boarding.

"Hmm, not taking chances are they? No windows there for somebody to come in by."

"Very true, but I'm afraid that the window is such an obvious route to for espionage or assassination that a good head of security should always think twice before spending too much material on shutters."
"OK Mr Armaments advisor. What's your suggestion?"

"Well, since they have spent so much time on putting up shutters it would be a shame to disappoint them, it's just that I'm planning some other things as well. Good job we've got those rock-climbers with us!"

....

The Captain of the Guard (who was only a sergeant)was looking worried. Goodness only knew what had happened lately. All those extra heavily armed men that he'd started to become reliant upon just weren't there anymore. Not since most of the Chinese had pulled out of the Tower. Oh, of course there were still a platoon or so of them in the inner chambers, and those weird grey-faced people with the scars all over their faces still seemed to be about, but you couldn't but help notice that the establishment was being run down. The Arch-Duke was still wheeled out every three days, and the Kravitzen were in their own apartments, but it felt as if things were running down. It had it's good side, however, those damn *electifs* had vanished, along with most of the Draculians. He was startled out of his reflections by a very out-of-breath corporal bustling into the guard room.

"They're throwing rocks at us Sarge, bloody great big ones, must have a bloody catapult!"

"Calm down lad, and less of the 'bloody's'. Who's throwing rocks? Where?"

"Number six postern gate. It's next to that inn that was shut down. Bloo…*very big* rocks. It's damaging the paint-work!"

"All right, get a party of four men together and take them down to gate five. It's probably Claus from the Dog and Bucket trying to get his own back, he knows we spent all last month re-doing the paint. Give him a good thumping!"

The corporal rushed off, gathering up men as he went, his place was quickly filled by one of the upstairs servants.

"Ah, sergeant, can you do something?"

"What sort of something?"

"The shutter in one of the ante-rooms has been knocked down. I can't see how it could happen, but it has. I know they're supposed to protect us against attack, so I thought you ought…"he tailed off and looked hopefully at the flustered Captain of the Guard.

"Oh, all right, tell two of the men in the guard room to go with you. They'll get them back up, 's probably just someone not putting the bolts in properly. Oh no! What do *you* want?" this to yet another worried soldier bursting into the room.

"Angry mob sir! Angry mob! At the draw-bridge!"

"Well, that's easy! Take a squad and get the portcullis down, the bridge up, and few cross bow bolts shot into their toes! Bloody peasants!"

He rushed off after the man so that he could hurry-up the crossbow men, so five minutes later he missed the corporal and his four men being returned to their guard room gagged and bound. They were placed carefully and politely in the cell of the guard room and the room then filled up with a large party of werewolves who had not yet started to raise a sweat!

At the main gate the ‘angry mob’ seemed to have evaporated, and after loosing of a few bolts at shadows the Captain of the Guard decided to call it a day, “Alright me lucky lads, let’s get back to the guard room!” But, there were no lucky lads. Instead he was firmly but gently relieved of his weapons, and a very elegant lady with snow white skin and raven black hair was asking him if he would like to give them the passwords for the Vesper Tower. Of course it was up to him. Oh, yes. But….it was so much better to do these things because you *wanted* to help your country rather than because you *needed* to obey your vampire lord. Suddenly the events of the past few weeks began to make sense. “’As the counter revolution started milady?” he asked, and then began to reel off the necessary shibboleths.

The Vesper Tower, completely unknown to its defenders was falling level by level. From the ground floor upwards a large party of werewolves assisted by six extremely excited Americans and a handful of Szgany gypsies (plus Sandy and Carlotta) were progressing easily and competently. From the fairy-tale slate roofed spires of the pinnacles and turrets of the utmost level small parties of werewolves, led by experienced climbers, were lifting slates, removing lathes and entering forgotten lofts and attics, emerging unannounced through ceiling trap doors and roof void spaces, smothering and subduing all in their path. There was a plan to it all however, and very soon a ring of silent unexpected interlopers had penetrated and sealed off all but the State Rooms and the Imperial Suite. Sandy and Carlotta stood before the great gilded doors to the complex and took a deep breath.

“What next?”

“Well, we both know very well what the shape of the rooms are. A large ante-room for both the State Rooms, for the Kravitzen, and the Imperial Suite. This is meant to be the council chamber between the Monarch and the Empire, except in our time it’s always been the six Grand Dukes, and now its become just the Arch-Duke. We sill haven't encountered the Imperial Bodyguard, so-called, I'd expect to find them between us and the Arch-Duke. I don't expect the Kravitzen to be guarded, but we aren't too worried about them…"

"Oh yes we are! Those creatures are lethal at close range, human or revenant. If one of them goes berserk we'll have more losses than we can deal with, just a touch is all it takes for a werewolf. We need to keep them in our calculations."

"Alright. We've got enough captured crossbows now to put up a very effective defence. Will it come to that? Having to shoot them all down?"

"You want a vampires judgement on this? Shoot 'em down!"

"Weeeel, OK, you're in charge of keeping that side safe. I'm leading us into the Imperial Suite, join me as soon as you can. Look, if its possible, just lock them in? Eh?"

"Yees, alright, you win. I'm only going to tell our people to shoot them if they won't back off….but I've seen people die from a Kravitzen touch, Forsterite's not in it!"

In the great ante-room, the de facto Council Chamber of Transylvania, there was a feeling of lassitude. Nothing much had happened for a day or two. Staff were being withdrawn, softly and surreptitiously, and the remaining bodyguard were nervously counting how much they had stashed in their purses and looking at the increasingly aged and unwell Arch Duke with alarm. He seemed to be getting some sort of medical treatment, there were nurses in face masks, and injections and all sorts of odd, outlandish machines with tiny, intricate steam-powered devices running them. Everyday he looked more and more drained, less vampire than victim it appeared.

The current watch looked up to see a small group of servants entering. They'd given the password, so that was alright, and (wonders of wonders) they'd actually managed to round up some beer from the kitchens. It was in fact looking as if the day was going to improve.

Outside the ante-room Sandy was standing on a chair trying to wrestle an ornate piece of gold-leafed moulding away from the doorframe. It eventually yielded and he carefully pulled out a great tangle of fine metal wires, and then blew gently into the hole left behind in the plaster. Then, he applied an eye to the aperture, peering through into the ante-room. He was reliant upon relaying his thoughts to Carlotta, who in turn was instructing the group of werewolves clustered closely around her.

"Our people are in position, they haven't been noticed, they're ready to act when we do. Now, there's six men, in armour, swords but nothing else, to the left, that's in front of the Imperial Suite. The State Rooms have two similar guards, and the door behind them leading to the Kravitzen is…*its barred on the outside*! They're keeping them *in!* That's good. So, we need to take out eight guards. The ones on the left are the priority, they must have back-up within the Imperial Suite. If we can get them before they raise the alarm it'll help!"

Sandy stood down, cleared his mind and spoke softly to Carlotta.

"Ready? You know this is no longer a reconnaissance, I'm afraid we are about to lead a coup!"

CHAPTER 23

It was a mistake to have prioritised the six guards in front of the doors to the Imperial suite. Perhaps it would have been better to have given both sets equal attention.

The sudden werewolf invasion of the ante-room certainly over took the six soldiers on the left before they even had time to raise their voices to alert attention, but the other two guards, faced with such overwhelming a force panicked and promptly unbarred the doors behind them and attempted to escape through the State Apartments. It was not a well-conceived plan, since the Kravitzen had been held prisoners in their own palace for several months and had been subjected to short rations and routine abuse by their Chinese captors, who by virtue of their latex suits were not subject to the Kravitzen's lethal touch. The two guards had a fleeting vision of grey gaunt faces, mouths that were stained with a greenish saliva and clammy grasping hands reaching out to grasp their wrists and press home moist toxic-sweat laden palms . Nothing could have saved them, not even a compassionate 'bite' from a revenant, once the complex poisons entered their blood streams.

Fortunately the sudden bursting forth of the Kravitzen *was* countered, and Carlotta's squad of werewolf bowmen cut down the gristly wretches in an instant. So perished that threat, and also (though completely unplanned) the entire current Kravitzen dynasty (but that was something that would have its full impact a while later.

From this point onwards the Captain of the Guards passwords would not apply, so hoping that the thickness of the doors would have prevented the noises of the scuffle from alerting the rest of the Imperial Guard Sandy once again made use of his knowledge of the 'anti-psychic' wiring loom to find a peep-hole into the next room.

"Seem's they've completely re-organised the lay out." Sandy thought carefully for a moment or two and then managed to engage Carlotta's mind with his own vision through the peep-hole. He quickly felt her respond, her words coming clearly and easily into his mind.

"Oh! That's really odd. Used to be one huge room first off, and then a cluster of smaller bedchambers and the like….this is….bizarre!"

The old Imperial reception room, which had seemed the sort of thing you'd measure in acres rather than square yards, was now broken up into a maze of cubicles, all constructed from match-boarding, and finishing at about seven feet high. The balance of the current guard were seated around tables in front and to the left of this indoor shanty town, they looked an easy target. The great windows were tightly shuttered, and more than just shuttered, the wood-work had been reinforced with metal mesh of the sort used to construct poultry pens. Far more formidable than the guard was a complex of desks occupied by a mixture of Transylvanian's, of various kinds, black latex clad figures, presumably Chinese, and the occasional shadowy forms of the tired featured 'invisible' agents. There were so many of them, and they were so busy interacting with those around them that they became easier to see as Sandy concentrated. "Better get the Americans up, and any 'tizzy's that are still with us." He passed to Carlotta.

In a corner of the great chamber, seated on the floor and manacled with rather odd hand-cuffs and leg-iron were a small cluster of figures that Sandy had identified as recently 'made' vampires.

They were mostly wearing the distinctive *electif* uniforms , and as Sandy watched one of them was dragged onto his feet and roughly dragged to the block of desks. Some sort of paper-work was being completed, though not with the assistance of the manacled figure. A hypodermic syringe was produced and a tourniquet applied to the figures arm. After a moment or two the contents of the syringe were administered, the figure went limp, and the hand-cuffs and leg irons were removed. Two stretcher bearers appeared and the prone figure was hurried away into the maze of cubicles. Carlotta, who had been watching through Sandy's mind just made one comment "Vampiric Essence Extraction?"

…………………………….

To the citizens of Prague it was obvious that things were happening. The city was swarming with werewolves! The regular troops had decided to lock themselves inside their barracks and the Draculians and their *electifs* had started to disappear, initially because the strange werewolves from out-of-town had been capturing and imprisoning the ones who got in their way, and then because little parties of concerned citizens had carried on the good work, assisted by recently reconstituted vampire friends and undercover werewolves from the back streets. A rebellion was underway, but in a very restrained, polite and culturally diverse manner. The Arch-Duke could still be heard, by anyone who had the capacity to listen, but against the excitement and the thrill apparently emanating from whoever now seemed to be taking over the Vesper Tower it no longer seemed a real threat. The invading werewolves seemed to be bringing in re-enforcements, and the city gates had now been re-opened and their guards either locked in their own guard rooms, or (having shed their uniforms) now part of the very quietly rejoicing crowd. No one seemed to want to 'give the game away'. In whispered voices they spoke to newly awakened neighbours.

"The uprising!"

"What?"

"It's starting, have you got Schmit's dust?"

"Yes."

"Well, just give it a spot of blood, it's time to bring him back!"

Still not daring to believe that the danger was truly past New Prague was guiltily getting back on it's feet.

High in the Vesper Tower the Imperial suite was all that was left in enemy hands. With the aid of some commandeered latex suites the few remaining Kravitzen were being herded into secure rooms and offered sustenance. Until the whole sorry story unfolded no one was much inclined to give them very many privileges.

The administrative centre of the strange complex had been swamped by a saturation attack of werewolves. While the Imperial Guard had been happy to surrender to a superior force the desk workers had been much harder to subdue. Fortunately the crossbows that they had reached for, and the Forsterite and Silver daggers that they had had to hand never had a chance to be deployed, but nonetheless the fighting was intense if short lived. At Sandy's command the order of the day was to take prisoners rather than to kill, but even so some of the defenders had had to be rent asunder before it was all over. Right now a lot of calming down was taking place, a conscious regaining of control over the inner wolf (and if you think it's difficult for a werewolf, so called humans have a much harder job of it!)

At last it was possible for the Baron to report that all areas were under werewolf control, and for the American team to confidently state that no 'invisible' was hidden in either the building or remained concealed amongst the prisoners.

The forest of cubicles was beginning to yield up its secrets.

A mixture of store rooms, very Spartan accommodation and what resembled some kind of rudimentary hospital rooms. These were arranged in four lines of twenty, eighty stark square cells, each with a hole running through which allowed the movement of a leather belt communicating with a small steam engine housed in one of the old Imperial bedchambers at the far end of the great hall. Within each cubicle the belt communicated with a small flywheel that took the motive power of the belt off for local use. Oil lamps with sizeable reservoirs provided a crepuscular light in which the full extent of the cubicles horrors could be assessed.

Each cubicle held two folding beds, constructed of a pale green, heavy, stiffly woven canvas stretched across a rough pine wood frame. The bed's occupants were not restrained, and their physical condition and the levels of sedatives administered suggested they were incapable of even rousing from their beds, let alone escaping. Almost without exception they were *electifs*, and almost certainly they accounted for the large number of disappearances noted of late among the ranks of the would-be vampires. Each was somewhat clumsily catheterised and their blood supply being circulated through what Carlotta recognised as a kind of dialysis machine, Sandy had only seen such devices in text books and looked to Carlotta for an explanation.

"Uggh! I'd not have thought it possible. These things used to save people's lives, long ago before the accident, before….well. They used to run on electricity, that's not available anymore, so I guess someone found a way of having a mechanical pump. It would save your life, but that's not what the bastards have built it for. The blood of the victim is circulated through the filter, the pressure is increased, dissolved chemicals pass across this membrane, and then go back under lower pressure, leaving behind…well, it used to be waste substances, but I guess they've found a way to make sure the Vampiric Essence stays behind. Even when these devices were perfect, ideal conditions, they shortened people's lives, they were only ever a stop gap. This bloody thing is going to do so much slow, built up harm it'll kill the poor creature even if extracting it's essence doesn't do it! It's....it's...*inhuman,*...." Carlotta paused for a moment, looked a Sandy and said "Yes, you're right, Vampires *are* human too. This sort of thing proves it to me. Never, *never* ,even when I was delighting in being a vampire for the first time, *never even then* would I have considered something like this! What *are* we going to do?"

"I know what I'm going to do. I've got the Baron rounding up every vial of essence that they've extracted and we are going to put back what we can. Worse cases first, they won't recover, but at least they will be able to go to the 'other place' and in time they can come back, or whatever they want to do. Some of the recent ones look like they can recover, and with time who knows what will happen. If I've read Arthurs notes correctly that's what happens. This is part of what's been going on. They wanted a way to start manufacturing essence, and the poor silly *electifs* were the dupes. Eager to be bitten, to join in, but always seen as a little dangerous. If they disappeared, well it was to be expected, nobody was going to complain. I wonder just how many they 'processed'? If the record sheets are anything to go by each victim lasts for about eight weeks, and they've had a production line running, so if they started right away then, say twenty a week for about thirty weeks....it's an awful lot of people..."

The final set of cubicles were somewhat less stark, and also a great deal more roomy. On the standard folding beds they found two more victims.

"I recognise this one. It's Esterhazi, a Duke from down Vienna way. He's not in too much of a bad way, but from this chart it looks like they've been taking his essence bit by bit and then resting him….perhaps trying to force him into some kind of action…but this other one….*is it the Arch Duke?"*

"Looks like a very, very old man….not what you expect with a vampire, but who knows what they've done to him?"

Sandy lifted the coverlet of the bed, the withered arm of a very elderly man was revealed. Like all the other victims a crudely fastened catheter was fixed into the large vein of the arm, but in addition there was a metal cuff fastened with a screw fitting. It sat just above the wrist, a similar cuff was present on the other wrist, and after investigation further devices were found on the ankles and around the thin shrunken neck. Sandy started to fumble with the screw fittings.

"Stop! That's possibly the Arch Duke, undo his bounds and we are all lost!"

"No, not all! I'm not subject to him, and neither are you!"

"You don't understand!"

"Oh, but I do! You are a free vampire. I freed you, set you apart from any control, even mine. Here, take this dagger, if he gets stroppy stick it in for a count of six! Got it?"

Carlotta stood very still and silent, then seemed to come to a conclusion.

"Yes. Yes, of course. I don't have to worry. I can protect the others. But, what are we going to do?"

"We are going to find out!"

"Find out what?"

"Ah! That's the question. Just what will we find out?" Sandy speedily released the catches, unhinged the cuffs and the collar, and watched in fascination as the body on the bed began to change beneath his very gaze.

For those of you not used to the European way of doing things, of the 'usual-ness' of companions who transform, of seeing a werewolf in a hurry excusing themselves and rushing into a dress shop to use the changing cubicle, then watching a less than everyday transformation would probably be discomforting. Sandy and Carlotta were quite agog. This was not what you would expect. The body on the bed appeared to swell, to bulge, to exceed its boundaries, and then there just wasn't enough space, and an elegant but dissipated figure struggled up, leaving an emaciated, toothless, elderly person huddled on the bed.

"Goodbye Gunther! It has not been a pleasure, but perhaps you have been discomforted as well!" The Arch Duke stood up, taking a moment or two to become fully stable, and then turned to look at Carlotta and Sandy.

"Why do you not do yourselves the honour of showing deference to the Arch Duke?"

Carlotta quailed for a moment, and then rallied. "Sorry, I would have thought some degree of thanks from yourself would have been in order."

"What!"

"Yes," Sandy contributed "You have been allowed to return to the world in your right mind. I think you should show some gratitude."

The Arch Duke stood silent for a while, then "You do not perhaps realise just who I am!"

"The very fact you have needed to say that indicates that you are no longer who you think you are. Please, consider your position."

The Arch Dukes features registered first of all incomprehension, then anger, then fear.

"I am the protector of our people. I am the leader. I and only I make the rules!"

Sandy drew a deep breath, and Carlotta moved behind the Arch Duke and positioned herself to administer a half-nelson.

The Arch Dukes outline began to waver, to take on a new form, a great bat or perhaps a dragon. Sandy raised an eyebrow and held up a finger.

"I'm sorry. Times have changed. The people still need protecting, they always will, but nowadays we help them to protect themselves, won't you join us?"

The face contorted into a fearsome grimace.

"I was the first sacrifice! I took the responsibility. All the blame rests with me. I will answer for the sins of my people, no one else!"

"Perhaps" Sandy answered calmly, "perhaps the people have no sins, perhaps no one has. There are only fears , and those are our own, to be faced on our own. You cannot take the fears of the people on yourself, because each of them will have to face them on their own when the time comes. Let the people go, let them chose their own destiny."

The Arch Dukes voice rose a pitch or two, it took on a manic note. "I am responsible. I alone am answerable. You will not deny me my place. I *will* serve my people!"

"There are more there now than when you started. There are so many kinds as well, and being a vampire is not enough."

"But….I have done such things, let loose such evil. I must be allowed to bear it. It is my right!"

"There is no evil. There never was, only right and wrong. You did the right thing for your people, centuries ago, when you became the first vampire to protect them, the right thing to do now is to use that power to protect everybody. You are not evil, you never have been. You have nothing to fear."

But the comforting words did not have the effect upon the Arch Duke that Sandy had hoped. In the tiny group of people filling the cubicle all eyes were fixed upon the central tableau.

The Arch Duke seemed to be the focal point of a steady condensation of darkness, of a gloom that denied light rather than was caused by its absence. Sandy by contrast seemed to attract a sort of passive golden radiance as he sought to explain to the ancient Arch Duke that his whole *raison d'etre* was now obsolete.

"Oh dear!" thought Carlotta, "Sandy's far too kind and sensible for this sort of thing. It'll go on all night if I don't do something, and if it does go on all night who knows what'll happen?"

The Arch Duke had drawn himself up to full height and was resorting to a dramatic threat with raised arms and hands held claw-wise. Sandy was smiling gently and repeating that Dracula had nothing to fear. A desperate expression began to take hold of the Arch Dukes face, and his fingers fumbled deep within a breast pocket, he seemed to be trying to pull something out. Carlotta, standing behind and slightly to one side saw this new development, and in frustration at the dead-lock and in fear that the Arch Duke might have some device which would bring mischief to her man decided to strike. She grasped the upraised left arm of the Arch Duke and wrenched it down and behind his back, then with her own left hand placed across his face she twisted his head backwards and to the left, threw back her head and then lunged forwards biting sharply and deeply into the Arch Dukes neck!

The tension broke with an almost audible crack! The Arch Duke subsided gently onto the floor, Carlotta extending an arm to cradle him and prevent his too rapid collapse.

She looked up from her handiwork, spitting and retching.

"Ughh! It was like swallowing dust! Swallowing fly-dirt! I've never, never tasted……but, what's happening to him? You've got to be ready to say your bit!"

"You bit him! You inherit his power! *You* tell everyone to be free!"

"It's not quite like that. You bit me under the old rules, so whoever I 'take' is under *your* control! You must make the decision! If you don't like it change it! The next few seconds are critical. Go on…SPEAK!"

Sandy was silent for a moment, and then recalled the words he had spoken, spoken it seemed to long ago now that it was in another age, despite it only being earlier that year

"The first order is that I give you all is that you will, by force of your self will, easily and without pain or discomfort overcome the peril of daylight and all other difficulties experienced by Vampires. Secondly you will in future only obey instructions and commands of your own free will and shall never have to call anybody, any creature, or entity Master or Mistress.'"

There was a noise, and a physical feeling, like some enormous creature sighing, and normality returned.

Sandy looked down at Carlotta cradling the Archduke in her arms. The aged creature was holding something up before him like some kind of tiny shield. Sandy knelt down and looked into the frightened eyes.

The Arch Duke was in fact holding up a beautifully wrought crucifix made of bright yellow gold and encrusted with garnets. Long and painfully hidden, a relic from his pre-vampire past, and put by as a last resort should his powers be usurped. His hand shook and trembled, his fingers at once cramping and failing in their grip.

The wound on his neck had two small dark trails running from it and his lips worked feverishly silently mouthing some long forgotten litany.

"It is ended!" said Sandy" The people are free to make their own choices, there is no longer a place for an Arch Duke to command and direct them. Your task is over!"

But, again, the figure would have none of the attempts at reassurance, and supporting himself on one arm, whilst still holding out the crucifix before him, the Arch Duke railed on.

"You! You! I sensed you there in my madness, and now I see you! You have stolen my powers and you will, no doubt thrust me through the golden mists to the oblivion beyond! Back, back! If you have my powers you have my curse upon you as well!", and with that he hurled the crucifix at Sandy and then lurched face forwards onto the floor. Sandy picked up the crucifix, it was indeed a magnificent piece, but like all religious icons now bankrupt in a world where the afterlife was no longer a mystery. "Poor fellow! He must have feared something like this to have kept it by him all through the centuries!"

"Never mind him being a 'poor fellow'," said Carlotta. "He needs putting somewhere safe and then we need to get on. I doubt that the Draculians and their Chinese friends will give up this easily.

Decapitation strikes are all very well, but the body goes on twitching for a long time and the head can still bite!"

CHAPTER 23

TO BE CONTINUED!

This pre-view edition has been released so that readers can contribute to the creative process. Instead of a firm of publishers making the decisions, the author is inviting the public to read what is, in fact, a complete self-contained story and request what they would like to see in volume two! For example, should there be more explanations, more back story, an expansion of particular characters in book two, etc.. Eventually we hope to offer an omnibus 'second edition' which will feature an upgraded volume one and the thrilling second part where Sandy and Carlotta deal with the wastelands disaster and attempt the salvation of the Zombies (you just couldn't find it anywhere else…could you?)

Contact the author at

ponytailpoet@gmail.com for more details!

55476242R00160

Made in the USA
Charleston, SC
26 April 2016